A Persist to Show Him God's Way

STAND-ALONE NOVEL

A Christian Historical Romance Book

by

Chloe Carley

Table of Contents

Let's connect!

Impact my upcoming stories!

My passionate readers influenced the core soul of the book you are holding in your hands! The title, the cover, the essence of the book as a whole was affected by them!

Their support on my publishing journey is paramount! I devote this book to them!

If you are not a member yet, join now! As an added BONUS, you will receive a Personalized Novella!

WHAT IS A PERSONALIZED NOVELLA?

A personalized novella is a story that the Heroine is named after you! Yes that's possible and within an hour after your sign up, you'll get a Novella with your name inside! It's a Unique experience to read a HEA story with your name inside.

FREE EXCLUSIVE PERSONALIZED GIFT
(available only to my subscribers)

"Good day, miss. Are you Emily Parker?"

The man was roughly the same age as her and quite good-looking. Emily smiled and nodded. "Yes, I am."

"Good day, miss. Are you Judy Parker?"

The man was roughly the same age as her and quite good-looking. Judy smiled and nodded. "Yes, I am."

"Good day, miss. Are you Angela Parker?"

The man was roughly the same age as her and quite good-looking. Angela smiled and nodded. "Yes, I am."

Go to the link:

https://chloecarley.com/novella-personalized-amazon/

Letter from Chloe Carley

"Once upon a time..."

...my best childhood nights had started with this beautiful phrase!

Ever since I can remember, I loved a good story!

All started thanks to my beloved grandfather! He used to read to my sister and me, stories of mighty princes and horrifying dragons! Even now, sometimes I miss those cold winters in front of the fireplace in my hometown, Texas!

My best stories though were the ones from the Bible! Such is the spiritual connection that a sense of warmth pass through my body every time I hear a biblical story!

My childhood memories were not all roses, but I knew He would always be there for me, my most robust shelter!

Years passed by, and little-Chloe grown up reading all kind of stories! It was no surprise that I had this urge to write my own stories, and share them with the world!

If I have a God's purpose on Earth, I think it is to spread His love and wisdom, through my stories!

Now, it is your time to read my Best Seller Novel "A Feisty Gracious Bride For the Rancher"!

Brightest Blessings,

Chloe Carley,

Prologue

Springford Montana – 1878

Esther Larson glanced at her parents busy with customers in the small mercantile that they owned. She had helped Bernice, her mother, weigh out portions of beans and sugar, package them, and stack them on the shelves and had been given an apple as a reward. She wanted to take it outdoors and find a nice spot in the woods where she could watch the birds while nibbling on her apple.

Esther knew that her mother wouldn't be happy about her going off anywhere on her own, so she looked for an opportunity when she could slip away unnoticed. The moment came when her father, Arnold, called out to Bernice to look at some rolls of fabric that had just come in. Smiling to herself, Esther ran outside and headed for the woods. She felt a sense of freedom. Aware her parents' displeasure in her going off on her own was only because of their concern over her safety, she knew exactly what to do. She would indulge in her favorite pastime without their knowledge and hurry back before her absence stirred up too much anxiety.

Esther was an obedient child, and she strived hard to remain so. But neither her mother nor father appeared to share her love of the woods, so she felt she had no choice other than to take matters into her own hands. She had asked them on several occasions to take her to admire nature's beauty and pick wildflowers, but they had been less than enthusiastic. In fact, Esther felt, she was probably causing them less stress by wandering off to the woods without their knowledge than by constantly chivvying them to take her there.

She took a deep breath of the fragrant air as she walked, delighting in God's beautiful creation as she looked up at the sky and stopped to admire a goldfinch on a rock. Esther loved summer. Spring was a favorite too, especially when she spied the first blooms emerging through the snow. But summer was the time when she loved to stroll through the woods— only occasionally with her fingers interlaced with her mother's, but mostly alone.

It was safe there in the woods. Esther knew it because she felt it. From a very young age, she had been aware of God's protective presence in her life and all around her. That was why she was drawn to places where nature's beauty abounded, where she could experience creation in its purest form: in the wild undergrowth and the countless varieties of wildflowers that carpeted the forest floor. These she picked and filled her skirt with, sitting down to enjoy a bite of her apple while arranging the flowers into a colorful posy, which she imagined would beautify her sparsely furnished home. The words of Psalms 111:2 filled the air as she recited them aloud. *"Great are the works of the Lord, studied by all who delight in them.'"* Then she wandered out of the woods to reluctantly find her way back to her parents' store before her absence was discovered.

It was while she was returning, chewing on the last of her apple, that her attention was diverted by a goldfinch that hopped off a rock. Torn between the urgency to return to her parents' store and the urge to delay the moment for as long as she legitimately could, she decided to follow the bird and thus, in doing so, changed the course of her life.

So intent was Esther upon the pursuit of the bird that she was unaware some time had elapsed since she had slipped out of her parents' store and they were looking for her, calling out to each other anxiously as they wondered where she had gone.

The goldfinch had taken Esther into a lane she'd been told never to enter because the weaponry store was located there, but she was oblivious to everything save the bird hopping along before her.

The elusive goldfinch had flown onto the windowsill of the weaponry store, and Esther reached out to get to it, hoping that it would hop onto her fingers and allow her to take it home. Her thoughts were wholly on the bird, and all her attention was on it when a tiny ripple of sound assailed her ears. The ripple turned into a rumble, which grew in intensity so quickly that Esther found herself unable to run and instead stood rooted to the ground, trying desperately to reach the goldfinch. It almost seemed like the rumble had ceased, until Esther realized that it hadn't—instead, it had gathered momentum. When it tore into the atmosphere with an ear-splitting roar, Esther's eyes widened with terror. And even as the deafening explosion rent the air, her ears began to buzz and hum.

She saw people running helter-skelter. Their mouths opened and shut, but all she heard was a ringing in her ears. The weaponry store was wreathed in smoke, and Esther saw the goldfinch drop to the ground. Her own mouth opened in a scream, which fell soundlessly into her ears. She realized she was also enveloped in smoke, black and suffocating. *The goldfinch*, she thought. She needed to save the goldfinch. She reached out toward the bird, but the ground appeared to be convulsing, and the impact rolled the dead bird away from her.

Esther tried to rise, but she fell back, her hand going up to explore the sharp pain in the sides of her head. She turned over, attempting to lift herself off the ground once again, but then she saw blood drip from her head, and she passed out. Around her, the voices of the people merged in agonized cries for help, amongst them the screams of her parents when they found her lying inert in the street. But none of this penetrated Esther's consciousness. Her hearing had been forever eclipsed by silence.

Chapter One

Springford, Montana - 1888

Esther looked out of her bedroom window with an ache in her heart. Below her, she saw her parents—Bernice and Arnold—walking her aunt, uncle, and cousins into the house. She stepped back into the shadows when one of her cousins glanced up briefly and hoped she hadn't been noticed. To be seen was to incur her parents' wrath. She was an embarrassment to them, and therefore she was never to be seen by anyone who visited their home, especially their relatives.

Earlier that morning, Bernice had walked Esther to her room, speaking to her slowly and deliberately as she tried to explain that she desired her daughter keep out of sight, as they were about to have company. Esther had known instinctively what her mother tried to convey. For one thing, she was slowly becoming accustomed to reading lips, but mostly, she just knew from her parents' expressions what they wanted of her.

As she caught sight of herself in the dresser mirror, Esther paused and stared. She had turned eighteen a few days ago and was no longer the eight-year-old who had slipped out of her parents' store to take a walk in the woods a decade before. She was now a full-figured young woman of medium height, with hair the color of autumn leaves—burnished brown with flecks of gold where the dappled sunlight fell on it like raindrops—and eyes like honey fresh from the honeycomb and just as sweet, if only someone would take the time to notice. Her nose was tip-tilted, accentuated by the sheer arch of her eyebrows.

Her mother had insisted that Esther braid her hair, but now she shook out her luxurious locks, releasing her tresses from the tight plaits, and finger-combed her hair as it spilled over her shoulders. Yes, she was beautiful, but nobody could see it, because all they saw was a deaf, mute young woman who appeared to be mentally challenged. She had seen the doctor's report in which she had been termed "cognitively slow" and wondered why anyone, least of all her parents, would give credence to the opinion of a medic who was not esteemed very highly at all and whose very credentials had been called into question on more than one occasion. She particularly recalled the time her father had experienced pain in his chest. The doctor had said that Arnold had a heart condition for certain. Then their pastor had visited with some herbal tea that sorted out the pain, because it was caused by indigestion and flatulence rather than a problem with her father's heart.

Esther blinked her eyes as the tears, so long held in, flowed down her soft, flawless cheeks. She sat down on the edge of her bed, and as always, her thoughts went back to that day ten years ago.

She had been enjoying her few stolen moments of freedom, breaking out from the monotony of helping her parents mind the store, and was picking wildflowers and listening to the birdsong that filled the woods. That was when a goldfinch hopped off a rock, and Esther, mesmerized, pursued it.

Esther hadn't been paying any attention to anything barring the bird. All she'd been doing was following the goldfinch. She'd been trying to catch it and had thought it might be good to tame it, perhaps have it live on her windowsill where she could scatter crumbs for it each day. Esther was a lonely only child. Her mother, her womb never blessed again after Esther was born, had seemed more protective of her child than loving toward her. Her inability to have more children made her look upon Esther as something of a valuable commodity to be hovered over rather than a child to be cherished. Esther was barely ever allowed out of her parents' sight and even denied the joy of going to school, so she was unable to cultivate friendships with other children. Thus, she had followed the goldfinch, hoping to make a long-term companion of it.

Bernice was not very demonstrative, but she had cared enough to teach Esther how to read when Arnold was reluctant to send her to school. Esther's happiest moments were always the ones spent reading with Bernice. Her favorite stories were "The Nightingale" and "The Little Mermaid" by Hans Christian Andersen. She and Bernice would read in turns, and the stories would come alive in her ever-active and fertile imagination. During those moments, she had her mother all to herself, and they were special. She missed them now, because Bernice hadn't sat down even to look at a storybook with her since the day of the explosion. She was grateful to God her sight had been saved and her ability to read was still as strong as it ever was.

Esther dragged the back of her hand across her swollen eyes. Her attention drifted to the Bible that lay on her bedside table, and she reached for it. Her room had no adornments or accessories, just a bed, a bedside table, and a dresser. The only thing of value was her Bible, and she treasured it. In her moments of abject loneliness and rejection, this book contained the promise that God would never leave her nor forsake her, and the verse fell around her like a comforting blanket. She drew it closer, repeating the words from Deuteronomy 31:6. *"Be strong and courageous. Do not be afraid or terrified because of them, for the Lord your God goes with you. He will never leave you nor forsake you."*

She felt humbled by the promise. That the Lord would look upon a sinner like her and still assure her of His abiding presence! How grateful she was that she had stopped looking at herself as irredeemable and had stopped blaming herself for the situation she was in. She had gone through long periods of self-recrimination when she had berated herself for ever giving in to the temptation of playing hooky and running away to the woods to experience some fresh summer air.

She would never have done that if she had been in school. Helping at the store was often tedious. School sounded like a dream. She had wanted to go, before the accident, but her father had dismissed the idea immediately. They simply could not afford to put her through school. Oh no, she was required to help at their store.

Esther knew that the Larsons weren't wealthy in terms of having a lot of money or things. But she always felt rich because she had never thought of money as important. The flowers and birds made her feel like a queen. Well, now she had all the time in the world to explore her beloved woods and even wander around the town like a ghost of her former self and, like a ghost, invisible. People saw her but looked through her. Some even feared her. She was not considered normal because she was thought to be "cognitively slow."

One day, she prayed, they would perhaps see her as she truly was: a sensitive young woman with a love for the Lord and a great enjoyment of books. She read voraciously—fairy tales mostly, because they transported her far beyond her realm of unattractive reality. She also read the Bible with an almost desperate hunger.

That moment, as she asked herself how she could possibly be courageous even though she knew God was with her, she opened the Bible and read Matthew 19:26. "But Jesus beheld them and said unto them, 'With men this is impossible, but with God all things are possible."

Esther rose from her bed and stood by the window again, mentally repeating the verse and feeling the impact of it. All she had was this assurance, but it was enough for her. She had lost her ability to hear, and a careless diagnosis by an unfeeling doctor had cost her the love and regard of her parents. She could see they pitied her but were not compassionate. If they were, they would have realized the daughter they thought rendered stupid by an explosion was actually still able to read and write. She had tried to speak to them to explain, but they turned their faces away from her, and because she couldn't hear, she didn't know her speech often emerged as a series of incoherent sounds and mumbles.

Esther retrieved her journal from the dresser drawer where she hid it.

Dear diary,

I cannot tell you how sad I am today that I am not permitted to even say hello to my cousins Prudence and Katherine, whom I grew up with until that day of the explosion. I want to talk to someone my age, dear diary, and I just want someone to know the real me. Prudence and Katherine would know, I am certain, that I am not what they say I am. Even without being familiar with the term "cognitively slow," I can sense that I have been bracketed with those of mean intelligence.

Looking out across the horizon, Esther prayed that God would deliver her from her prison and set her amongst people who would understand her and believe in her abilities. In her parents' home, she was an outcast, banned from any task that involved the use of her agile brain and consigned to the ranks of, literally, a servant. This wasn't how she had anticipated her life would turn out, yet now that it was such, she was prepared to believe that things would change eventually. Her faith rested on the miracle Jesus performed in Mark 2:1-12, when four friends of a paralyzed man lowered him from the ceiling into a room where Jesus was laying hands on people and healing them.

She carefully copied the passage of scripture down in her diary and read it again. It was a beautiful story. She got up and began to act it out in silent eloquence, her expressive eyes bright with her burning faith in God.

"What are you up to now?" Bernice asked with a frown, storming in with a plate of food and seeing Esther waving her hands before the dresser mirror as she mimed the passage of Scripture.

Esther dropped her hands to her sides and turned her eyes downward the moment she felt the rush of cold air as her mother entered. Before she dropped her eyes, she glimpsed her mother's face with its forehead dragged into a deep scowl, nostrils flared, and lips contorted by a sneer.

She gave her mother an apologetic look and shrugged.

"Stop behaving—lunatic!" Bernice whispered, lest their guests overhear the conversation.

Esther's eyes filled with tears. She couldn't read lips very well, but she sensed that Bernice was calling her mad. She quickly told herself she had read her mother's lips wrong and she wasn't referring to her as a lunatic.

She shook her head, began to mime an apology, and protest, through actions, that she wasn't insane at all. Her hand was on the dresser when Bernice slammed the plate onto it, and the vibrations that Esther felt go through her sensitive fingers conveyed to her that her mother was displeased. Bernice turned rudely away, and Esther was left staring at her back as she rushed out of the room.

Esther picked up the plate and looked at it. She liked the pattern on it—red flowers on a white background. She traced the outline of the flowers delicately with the tip of her forefinger and imagined that she was in a sea of such flowers, drowning in their perfume. She turned her attention to the food and held the plate up to inhale the aromas of the steak and beans.

Steak was only served when they had company. The rest of the time they had potatoes and beans. Sometimes Bernice would make biscuits. Esther liked biscuits because when her mother made them, the whole house filled with their appetizing fragrance. This sumptuous scent had permeated the air that day, before her cousins arrived, but Esther didn't see any biscuits on her plate. She hoped there would be at least one left over after everyone had eaten and that Bernice would give it to her.

Bernice had not thought to give Esther a knife and fork to eat her meal with, so Esther picked the steak up with her hands and took a generous bite out of it. She chewed on it slowly, appreciatively, savoring the flavor of the meat and concentrating on it so she didn't notice that she was eating alone in her bedroom, perched on the edge of her bed. It was hard to eat the beans with her fingers. Esther picked up each bean individually and then drenched a piece of steak in the sauce.

Chapter Two

In another part of Springford, Montana, Paul Orton was on his way to the stables. Dawn was just breaking, and so was Paul's heart. It always felt this way at the beginning of every day ever since his dear wife had died and taken with her their newborn. Paul couldn't bring himself to even admire or appreciate the sun's first rays. He couldn't, in fact, look at nature at all, because it reminded him of his Creator and how angry he was at Him. What had he done to deserve his lot in life, he wondered. He had worked faithfully each day, attended church on Sunday, and always been on time with his tithes and offerings. Yet God appeared to have hidden His face from him.

Silently chastising himself that he must be grateful for what he had, Paul looked out across his ranch. After his parents' deaths, the responsibilities of the ranch had been thrust solely upon him despite the fact that he had a brother. It hadn't been easy taking charge of such a large cattle-breeding operation, but Paul had worked harder than ever because he felt he owed it to his parents to keep their legacy alive.

The ranch was spread over a sizeable acreage, with a homestead at one end, bunkhouses at the other, and enclosures for the cattle in between. To one side of the homestead were the stables, where Paul was headed as the first light filtered through the clouds and dispelled the darkness. Standing like sentinels in the half light were a variety of trees—ponderosa pine, weeping willow, quaking aspen, larch, spruce, and cedar. A weeping willow drooped over a stream, sheltering the banks on either side, and the stream itself ran along for a few miles, skirting the periphery of the ranch before it spilled into a lake bordered by fir trees.

Paul was aware he had been blessed with abundance, but that made him all the more aware of how much he lacked somebody to share it with. The beauty of the ranch overwhelmed him at times, causing him to remember the many occasions when he had strolled by the stream or the lake with his wife or gone horseback riding with her around their property or up the mountains. When the memories flooded back, Paul would firmly shut them out and swallow his emotions.

From his father, he had learned to be stoic even under great pressure, because to show how he felt would be unmanly. Paul was acutely aware he had to be strong—not just for himself, but for the others in his life. First it had been for his dear wife, and then it was for his brother. He would take the blows that life dealt out and allow the hurt to burn inside of him.

When it became difficult to cope with the anger that blazed within him, he would take his horse up the mountains, with the breeze against his face and in his hair. On each of these occasions, he would feel his anger against the Lord stir within him. When this happened, he would swiftly turn his attention to the beauty of the trees or the sheer magnificence of the wild horses he sometimes encountered. The burning rage would momentarily be quelled, and Paul would return to the ranch. Thus, he maintained his composure outwardly while never allowing anyone to pierce that stoic exterior.

Therefore, that morning, despite the ever-present ache in his heart, Paul had an inscrutable look on his face as he entered the stables, oblivious to the smell of horse dung. Paul let the horses into their paddock before returning to shovel the excrement into a wheelbarrow, which he tipped into a manure pit behind the stables. Hc swept the stables clean, saving one stall for the end. This was occupied by his trusty steed, Raider. Paul had found Raider in the mountains, a mustang with a will of his own. Paul had made a connection with the silver-gray horse and watched him over a period of time, visited him in the mountains and then ultimately brought him to the ranch and trained him. He now groomed him with care and then set a bale of hay before him. They understood each other, Raider and Paul, because they were so alike—wild spirits forced to submit to the will of their masters.

After the loss of his parents and then his wife and child, Paul had realized how powerless and frail humans were and how, ultimately, their fate was determined by the Lord. He had reluctantly submitted to God, acknowledging He alone was in control of his life, but he was also angry and bitter with his Master, just as Raider may have been with him for taking him away from the freedom of the mountains and confining him to the stables. He filled Raider's water trough and then went back indoors to wake his brother Luther.

Back in the two-story homestead, Paul sprinted up the two flights of wooden stairs to Luther's bedroom, knocked once before pushing the door open, and exclaimed in annoyance when he saw Luther's bed appeared not to have been slept in. The patchwork quilt that Paul's wife had made still lay on the bed, unruffled. Luther himself was nowhere in sight. Paul was not given to cursing or swearing, but at that moment he forgot his strict Christian upbringing and muttered an expletive under his breath. He sent up a silent prayer of repentance and exited Luther's room, tramping down the stairs to the kitchen.

As he passed the dining room, he tried not to look at the mahogany table with the painted china bowl placed at the very center. The bowl had once held the most beautiful blooms, picked every day by his dear late wife. Now it stood empty, bereft of beauty—a sad reminder of happier times. Paul preferred to eat his meals in the kitchen but had to pass through the dining room to get there. Each time he averted his eyes, as he did that morning, because he always imagined he saw his late wife seated at the table, pouring out coffee, carving meat, or just smiling up into his eyes as they exchanged the news of the day.

Once he was in the kitchen, he set a kettle of water on the stove and brewed his morning cup of coffee. As the aroma of coffee wafted up to his nostrils, Paul sniffed at the air appreciatively, momentarily forgetting Luther's absence and the anxiety related to it.

Paul was just raising his mug of coffee to his lips when, through the kitchen window, he spied the deputy sheriff riding up to his homestead. Paul set his mug down and hurried onto the porch.

"Howdy, Officer Gibson," Paul greeted him, with more bonhomie than he felt.

"Morning, Mr. Orton," the deputy sheriff responded.

"What brings you round at this early hour?" Paul inquired, though his gut told him what it must be.

Officer Gibson took his hat off and raked his stubby fingers through his hair, shifting his portly frame uncomfortably from one short leg to the other.

"It's that unruly brother of yours again, I'm afraid, Mr. Orton," he replied. "He's in a spot of trouble, and this time Sheriff Basley wants a word with you before he releases him."

Paul reined in his emotions with an effort.

"I'm real busy right now, Officer," he murmured. "And I need my brother here to help me with all the work on the ranch. What has he done this time?"

"You're going to have to come with me and find out," Officer Gibson replied.

"And who's going to take care of all the chores to be done around here?" Paul shot back.

"You should have thought about that before you let that brother of yours get out of hand," Officer Gibson replied wryly. "Now come along."

Paul took a deep breath and released it. Then he adjusted his hat on his head and followed the deputy sheriff.

"You'll have to give me a few minutes to saddle my horse," he said as he stepped off the porch.

"Just hurry," Officer Gibson growled. "I haven't eaten breakfast yet, and the missus always has a plate of bacon and eggs for me, which I sorely desire right now."

Paul shrugged and loped off to the stables to saddle his horse.

"I haven't eaten breakfast either," he threw over his shoulder.

As he saddled Raider, his mind wandered back to breakfasts in happier times—seated at the table with his wife, Angie, eating bacon, eggs, and biscuits.

"A rancher needs breakfast in his belly before he goes out to tackle the day," Angie would say.

"Are you coming or what?" Paul heard the deputy sheriff call out impatiently. "I can almost see my breakfast congeal on the table as it waits for me! Get a wiggle on, will you?"

"Don't let your breakfast get cold, Paul, my dear," Angie *said that last time. "Eat up now."*

"But you're going into labor, Angie," Paul *had protested.*

"And it will last a while, I'm told, as it's the first one." Angie *laughed. She winced and clenched her teeth all of a sudden.*

"What's that?" Paul *asked, jumping to his feet.*

"Birth pains," Angie *said. "The baby's coming."*

Paul shut his eyes against the onslaught of memories that came rushing back—Angie's inert body, the tiny infant who had scarce taken a breath before he was wrenched away, the finality of the words "ashes to ashes, dust to dust," and the crippling sorrow over losing his wife and son in a single strike of the Almighty's hand.

Paul's mouth was set in a thin, hard line as he adjusted the saddle on Raider's back and walked the horse out of the stable.

"What's going on?" the deputy sheriff asked as Paul came face to face with him.

"Nothing. I was saddling Raider," Paul replied.

"It doesn't take that long, does it?" the deputy sheriff asked. "Don't you want to plead your brother's case and have him released?"

Paul grimaced and shrugged.

"Look, I can't pretend that this is a welcome start to the day. I have things to get done, new foals to take care of. Those young 'uns need to be paid close attention to. I can't be off meeting Sheriff Basley every second day over my brother's shenanigans when I have a ranch to run and precious animals to take care of," he replied.

The deputy sheriff replied with a humorless laugh. "That's why you have a foreman," he remarked, pointing out to a thin, tall figure hurrying toward them, holding his hat down over his shoulder-length brown hair.

"What seems to be the matter, boss?" Sandy Kirk, Paul's foreman, asked.

"It's Luther again," Paul replied, not stopping his horse.

"Ah," Sandy said with a knowing nod.

Paul blanched. Sandy's reaction, in one single monosyllabic word, reflected the opinion of all the townsfolk. They knew exactly what a troublemaker Luther was.

"Take care of things while I'm gone, will you, Sandy?" Paul said as Sandy ran alongside Raider.

"You know you can rely on me, boss," Sandy replied.

Paul knew he could. Sandy was, in fact, his best friend and the only person he allowed close enough to see inside of him from time to time. But even Sandy didn't know of the roiling well of anger within him.

Taking Raider from a canter to a gallop, Paul followed the deputy sheriff to the station, his expression cold and hard.

"Look," Sheriff Basley said when Paul reached the station. "I feel your pain, Paul. You know you have the sympathy of the entire town. But you're going to have to do better with your brother."

He paused and studied the man before him. Paul knew what he saw: an impressive figure of a man, standing over six feet tall in height, with a muscular frame. But at that moment, his broad shoulders were slightly stooped beneath the weight of his problems.

Paul shook his head and squared his shoulders determinedly even as the sheriff studied his face. "What exactly happened, Sheriff Basley?" he asked, his gravelly voice well-modulated, his wide-set hazel-brown eyes fixed unblinkingly on the sheriff.

"He got himself into a mighty big brawl last night. Beat a fella up so one can scarcely recognize him and then fell over a table and banged his head so hard it bled all over the floor. If we hadn't gotten him patched up real quick, maybe you'd have been burying another of your loved ones." He stopped himself from going further and gave Paul an apologetic shrug. "Didn't mean to have that come out the way it did," he said.

Tears of anger stung Paul's eyes. *This is unfair,* he thought. And it made him furious. He stuck his chin out, his nostrils flaring as he battled for composure. His hand went up to his hair, pushing it back from his face, and he rubbed his beard as he swallowed the words he wanted to say and desperately looked for an appropriate response. Silently, he raged at Sheriff Basley for what he had just said. And he was angry at God for letting his life go the way that it had. He hadn't done anything to deserve such a raw deal.. In fact, he had done everything by the book, so to have suffered what he had and then to be saddled with a brother like Luther was more than he could endure.

"I'll make sure this doesn't happen again, Sheriff Basley," Paul said.

"Mr. Orton, you know and I know that it's going to happen again, because your brother is a major troublemaker," the sheriff replied. "So you're going to have to do a lot better from now on. Keep him by your side, and keep a strict eye on him, or next time I'll lock him up permanently."

Paul winced inwardly. Luther was his responsibility, and obviously he didn't know how to handle him. This was his fault. He would take a stronger stand from now on.

But when Luther came out, looking rebellious and unrepentant, Paul momentarily lost his composure.

"Hello, big brother," Luther said. "Come to spring me from here again?"

"This has got to stop!" Paul roared, and Luther looked taken aback.

"Ever since Ma and Pa died, you've been on a rampage and you've been acting out, like you're the only one who's lost something. Grow up, will you, Luther? I am sick and tired of this!"

"Who do you think you are, talking to me like that?" Luther spat. "You're not my pa!"

"No, I'm not. But as long as you keep behaving like a foolish child, I have to act like your pa. Believe me, it's not a role I enjoy, Luther, so do yourself—and me—a big favor and sort yourself out."

"Get this bag of trouble out of here," Sheriff Basley growled.

"I will, Sheriff," Paul said, tipping his hat respectfully. "And I apologize once again."

"I don't want to come home with you," Luther snarled when they were out of the station.

"Well, you're going to have to, or I will walk you back and have the sheriff put you behind bars once and for all," Paul shot back. "There's work on the ranch that needs doing, Luther, and you had better pull your weight or else!"

"Or else what?" Luther sneered through clenched teeth.

"Like I said, Luther, I won't hesitate to take you back to the station and have you locked up," Paul said. "You may think I'm not serious, but I am. The fact is, the sheriff let you out because I assured him you would turn over a new leaf, but if you show no inclination to stay out of trouble, then I can't help you stay out of jail."

Luther's lips curled resentfully as he slouched toward Raider and climbed on.

Paul mounted his horse and took the reins with more determination than he felt. But he knew he had to take Luther home and continue to do his duty by him as the older of the two. Not to do so would be to dishonor the responsibility that had been placed on his shoulders by the Lord and his upbringing to take his duties seriously.

He would not be like Cain, who said, "Am I my brother's keeper?"

His teeth came down hard on his lower lip, and he thrust his jaw out determinedly as he and Luther rode home together on Raider. He was his brother's keeper, and he would look out for him as best he could.

Chapter Three

Esther ran through the woods, the pure spring air filling her lungs, fragrant with the scent of woodland blooms. She sniffed at the bear grass and arrowleaf balsamroot and stroked the delicate petals of the yellow bells. She loved this season so much and was glad to be out in the open. It was still chilly; the landscape just emerging from a cold winter, but wrapped in her cloak, she was relatively warm. The cold still nipped the tip of her nose and turned her cheeks a rosy red.

Her calf-leather shoes were worn, but Bernice hadn't thought it necessary to buy Esther another pair. She didn't want to ask her either, because she was aware that Arnold was having a difficult time providing for them. She could feel the damp of the forest floor seep through the worn soles of her shoes, but it didn't detract from her enjoyment of God's creation. *Yes*, she thought, *with God, everything is possible!*

She ran from one cluster of wildflowers to the other, filling the skirt of her dress with the beautiful blooms, tears of both joy and sorrow running down her cheeks. There was so much beauty here, she wished she had someone to share it with. There seemed no such hope in sight, as everyone in Springford considered her to be mentally unsound. She hastily drew her attention away from that reality and immersed herself in the moment, thinking how like an illustration from one of her picture books the scene before her was. There was a page in the story of "The Nightingale," by Hans Christian Anderson, that featured the bird in the moonlight, surrounded by flowers such as the ones cradled in her skirt.

Spontaneously, Esther fell to her knees, her forehead on the ground, her hands still holding the flowers securely in the skirt of her dress.

"Dear Lord," she sobbed into the earth, "Thank you for this beauty. Thank you for the flowers. Thank you for my life. Please, Lord, if it be thy will, and if you think I need it, may I have a warmer cloak and new shoes so that I may walk in these woods and enjoy your creation without feeling the cold cut through my bones? Oh Lord, sorry if I sound ungrateful, because I am grateful—immensely grateful for these beautiful flowers. They make me so joyful. But Lord, I would like to share my life and enjoy all this beauty with someone. Right now, my life doesn't seem destined for happiness, but I beg you, Lord, if there be a way, please . . . ."

The prayer was fluent in her mind, but it poured from her lips in a series of muffled sounds. Her face remained firmly planted against the earth, and her body shook with the intensity of her sobs.

Almost instantly a verse from the Bible came to her, and she sat up and said it aloud. The occasions for such privacy were few and far between, and she tried once more to translate her coherent thoughts into flowing words. The words, however, were unformed, unintelligible, and incoherent. Yet she felt a sense of freedom in allowing these sounds to escape from the confines of her throat.

The verse she recalled was from Luke 12:27-28. "'Consider the lilies, how they grow: they neither toil nor spin, yet I tell you, even Solomon in all his glory was not arrayed like one of these. But if God so clothes the grass, which is alive in the field today and tomorrow is thrown into the oven, how much more will He clothe you, O you of little faith!'"

Getting to her feet, Esther held the flowers in her hand and gazed at them with renewed faith in God. She continued to wander through the woods, lost in the beauty of the morning, oblivious to the cold that seeped through her cloak and shoes, and warmed by the assurance of God's provision she had received through the scripture that came to her mind as she'd prayed.

So lost was she in the moment that Esther was surprised to look through the branches of the trees above her and see that the sun had shifted farther down in the sky. The light in the woods was now more diffused, and there was a sharper chill in the air so that she shivered. To her discerning eye, it was apparent it was late afternoon, and she would be in trouble with her father and mother for wandering away and staying out longer than usual.

Apprehensive, Esther quickened her pace and began to hurry out of the woods, her shoes squelching through patches of damp earth she hadn't noticed before. It became harder to walk faster, as her shoes stuck in the earth, and she began to panic.

At almost the same time that she emerged from the woods, she saw three young men strolling toward the thicket she had just come out of. At a glance, she observed they were all displaying their teeth in wide grins. One of them had a hat on, and he doffed it with his eyes on her, though his expression was more mocking and not at all gentlemanly.

Below his hat, Esther could see his dark-brown hair. He was walking ahead of the others and appeared to be coming toward her. His feet locked, and he stumbled, and Esther recoiled. She had seen men emerge from the local saloons, and it was apparent this man's better senses were veiled by a haze of grog.

Esther was about to drop her gaze when her eyes flitted to one of the two other men and noticed, in the movement of his lips, the word "laggard." His teeth were then bared in a sneer, and he lurched toward her. She didn't want to look up again to try to discern the rest of what the man was saying. She could generally interpret a lot from the way a person's facial features fell into different expressions. The way the man and his two friends were laughing and pointing at her conveyed their ridicule of her supposed and widely publicized condition. They must surely be talking about her being slow or insane.

Veiling her humiliation, Esther cast her eyes down and tried to quicken her pace, but one of her shoes stuck in the mud and came loose. She tried to retrieve it, but the young man who appeared to be the leader of his pack suddenly leapt forward. Esther sprang back, the flowers in her hands dropping to the ground. When she almost fell, the man's lips parted in a guffaw. Esther perceived his shoulders shake with mirth as he lunged at her. He was so close that she could smell the alcohol fumes on his breath. One of his friends put out a hand to steady him, but the man shook him off and made an attempt to grab Esther. She tried to change direction and run away from him, but he stuck his hand out and caught her arm.

Esther opened her mouth to scream, but the man fell upon her, his lips crushing hers and his greasy dark-brown hair falling on her face and making it impossible to see past him. Her eyes were wide open, terrified, staring into his face. She struggled, and the man pushed her down onto the ground. She could taste whiskey on his tongue and smell it on his breath, and she gagged. She thrashed about beneath him in an attempt to get free, pushing her hands up against his chest, but that seemed to make the man all the more determined to ravage her. Cold terror gripped her as she instinctively perceived the perils of her situation, and she tried once again to fight her assailant off.

Suddenly the man tore his lips off hers, and Esther gasped for air. She looked up, horrified, into the man's wild, dark eyes as his hands, like two evil creatures, crawled all over her body. She tried to prize them off, panic stricken because her voice seemed frozen inside her soundless throat, and she opened her mouth to scream. Aware he was doing something wrong, because of how distasteful it was to her, Esther fought bravely on. But each time she pushed one of his hands away, he threw back his head, and she saw his shoulders shake with glee. She recalled being able to laugh a long time ago, but now, in her silent world, she couldn't comprehend what reason he had found to amuse him so much.

When her assailant released her lips for a moment, Esther glanced behind him at his two companions. One of them took off the moment her eyes fell appealingly on his, dumbly pleading for help. The other was attempting to pull her assailant off her, but the latter turned around, and Esther saw his lips pulled back in a snarl. The man persisted, trying to drag her attacker off her weakening body, but her attacker kicked him in the teeth as he leaned over him. Esther's eyes widened. If her attacker, despite being inebriated, was strong enough to hold her down while kicking another man, then she stood no chance against him. It was clear that her attacker's friend thought so too, because he turned and ran away, wiping the blood from his mouth.

Meanwhile, her assailant's hands were crawling to the hem of her dress. Simultaneously, he kept pointing to her lips and then to his. Though momentarily incapable of coherent thought, Esther vaguely understood that he was instructing her to force her lips against his, the way he had done. She felt unclean, aware the man was trying to lure her into something sinful. Esther felt his fingers nudging her skirt up, and abject fear paralyzed her. She tried to scream again, but the sound caught in her throat, and the act of parting her lips to shout only provoked the man. He pressed his mouth down on hers again, cruelly crushing her lips and cutting off every breath of air. If he kept his mouth on hers that way, Esther thought, she would be suffocated.

Her flailing limbs grew still as mind-numbing terror gripped her entire body. In her silence, she was alone, unable to defend herself and even less able to call for someone else to help her. She tried to reach for even one comforting image or thought that would help her escape this moment, hoping that somehow if she were to mentally transport herself elsewhere, then what was taking place would cease to have any effect on her. But she was powerless even to transfer her thoughts away from the horror of her current situation.

Her mind searched desperately for an explanation of what was happening to her. Her instincts told her to fight the man off her, but any movement she made only served to incite him all the more.

Esther thought she was going to die. She cried out silently to God, repeating a verse four from Psalms 23. *"Yea, though I walk through the valley of the shadow of death, I will fear no evil. For thou art with me . . . ."*

She ceased struggling and thrashing about and lay still, her mind on the flowers, on God's beautiful creation, on the fresh spring air and on God's hand taking hers in this most dreaded hour. *Am I dead?* she wondered. If she was, it would be a sweet release from a world where she was not wanted. Perhaps this was the answer to her prayer.

Then, all of a sudden, Esther sensed a change in the atmosphere. She had her eyes tightly shut, but she opened them ever so slightly as she realized that the weight of her assailant's body was no longer pinning her down. Her eyelids fluttered open, and she saw, leaning over her, peering at her anxiously, another man. She noticed his eyes first. They were hazel brown. He had a beard and hair that was parted in the center and fell to the sides of his face. Esther closed her eyes again. Perhaps she had died and this . . . this was . . . Jesus!

Someone was gently nudging her, and she allowed her eyes to open again. The face above her was still there, only this time he was saying something.

"—Alright?" she could just about discern from the movement of his lips.

Then Esther realized, with a surprising sense of disappointment, that she was still in the land of the living.

She was lying on the ground just outside her beloved woods with a strange man hovering above her. Her eyes widened in alarm as the man tried to urge her to get up. He held out his hand, and Esther recoiled. She tried to get to her feet by herself, and the man reached out and helped her up. Esther looked at him uncertainly, wanting to trust him but still shaken from the sudden and unfathomable attack on her body she had just endured. She peered around this new man, looking for the one that had moments ago kept her pinned down and helpless, fearful he might emerge to assault her yet again.

"—Gone," the new man with the kind eyes said as her eyes searched his face for answers.

She looked down, and her eyes fell on her dress. It had been ripped almost up to her thigh. Esther's hand flew to her mouth, and she choked. A long-suppressed scream erupted from her mouth in a series of gasps and splutters, and the man patted her on the arm. He pointed toward a horse, and she understood, through a series of gestures he made, that he was going to take her back home on the horse.

"I know—you live—" She saw his lips form the words, and his fingers came together to form a roof. So he knew where she lived. From the way the man went on to shake his head and from the number of times his lips formed the word "sorry," Esther also knew he was deeply grieved at what had happened and that she was not to worry because he would take care of things from here on.

Had she been less traumatized and more in control, Esther may have admired the man's ability to communicate with her in such eloquent silence. But the mists of fear still swirled about her disturbed mind, and her body still trembled from the experience of being touched and fondled in a manner that she knew was terribly wrong.

She allowed the man to lead her to his horse and help her up, and she didn't protest when he climbed on in front of her and took the reins. She was too shaken to do anything at all except mutely obey what the man told her to do.

With mingled apprehension and relief, her eyes followed the route back to her home as they rode along. The sun was even lower in the sky than when she'd been preparing to leave the woods, and the air was chillier. She blinked several times as she hungrily fed her eyes on the familiar trees that lined the dirt road they were riding along. Here was a juniper tree, there a larch and a red cedar. Rows of Douglas fir trees and ponderosa pines followed. She had learned about them from her books when she was little and her mother used to read with her.

The well-known sights and environs brought momentary relief to her troubled soul. Inexplicably comforting too was her rescuer's back, stiff and straight in front of her, like a strong, safe wall. She wondered who he was and where he had come from to rescue her. Surely the Lord had sent him. Perhaps he was an angel dressed in the attire of cowboy. He had a gentle presence, but Esther also detected an aura of sorrow that seemed to emanate from deep within him.

Her thoughts swiftly sped away from the man who was conveying her to her destination and settled on the sight of her home before her. She wanted to run and hide her face in her mother's skirt the way she had sometimes done as a child, before her accident confined her to her world of shame and silence. The gate was open, swinging in the breeze, and a soft wisp of smoke rose from the chimney. Her mother would be cooking supper about now, and maybe there'd be some biscuits. She sniffed at the air, hoping to pick up the aroma, but she could only smell the smoke from the chimney and the smells of horses and the outdoors from the jacket her rescuer was wearing.

He rode all the way up to the porch and brought the horse to a halt. Then he slid off the horse and helped Esther down. She was home safe, she thought, and looked gratefully up at her rescuer, once again struck by his looks and resemblance to the pictures she had seen of Jesus. As she continued to stare, the man turned and walked up the porch steps and knocked on the door. Esther heaved a deep sigh. Now she could just run into her mother's arms, and all the confusion of the day would melt away. She stopped the thought even as it came to her mind. She so wanted the comfort of their arms, but she was aware her mother and father had changed their attitude toward her after she lost her ability to hear. She had been reminded, time and again, that they regarded her as deficient and an embarrassment to them. So she told herself she must not be disappointed if they failed to behave in the manner she desperately hoped they would.

Thus, when the door opened and Arnold and Bernice appeared on the porch, and when Esther ran up the steps and fell into her mother's arms and failed to receive the warmth and comfort she had hoped for, she moved away from her mother and swallowed her tears.

As Bernice pushed her roughly away, Esther was violently brought back to reality and found that nothing had changed. On the ride back, she had allowed herself to imagine that her parents would be glad to have her back safe. But now she knew nothing she had suffered would soften their attitude toward her. She would always be perceived as a burden. She fell back, tearful, and looked from her rescuer to her parents and back again. She tried hard to follow their lips, but they were talking too fast.

In her world of silence, she tried to comprehend the situation by observing each tiny nuance of their features as they talked. From the way her mother's features pulled into a teeth-baring grimace and from the bright hue of her face and her flashing eyes, Esther gauged that she was livid. From the way her father's chin quivered and the frequency with which he hit the door post with his fist, Esther saw, with growing alarm, that he was so furious he could scarce contain his wrath.

"Where? How? Why?" were the words she read off the movements of her parents' lips. They spoke together, and the man who had brought her home was explaining something to them. It appeared he was taking the blame for her assailant's wrongdoing. Her eyes grew wide. *This is what a true Christian would do*, she thought, reminded of Jesus taking the sins of the whole world upon Himself when He died on the cross. Surely her rescuer was a true follower of the Lord and must therefore strive to do as He did.

Esther's brow was furrowed as she looked from the man's lips to her parents' lips and tried to piece together a picture of what was happening. She detected the word "brother." Could the man with the greasy dark-brown hair be this man's brother? They didn't appear to be related. There was nothing similar about them. Esther shook her head in confusion.

She pinned her eyes down on her rescuer's lips, trying so hard to interpret the words he was saying, that her face turned red with the effort. "Send him away," she thought she read. Esther dared hope the man was going to send her assailant away from the vicinity. She loved visiting the woods and knew she would never be able to go there again unless her assailant was sent away.

Esther observed that her mother wasn't paying attention to what her rescuer was saying. She was ranting at her. She shook her fists at her now, and Esther's spirits plummeted further as her mother pointed to her torn dress and shook her head contemptuously. Her father raised his hand and wagged it at her as if threatening to use it.

She hung her head in shame until Bernice charged forward and jerked her chin up so that she was staring directly at her. Her lips trembled. She wanted to cry. Bernice was motioning to her to pay attention. Esther could just about discern her mother was accusing her of encouraging her assailant's attentions. She implied she had asked for it and had done nothing to stop it. Her rescuer stepped forward and began to wave away her mother's accusations. He appeared to be trying to give her parents an explanation of his own, but Arnold motioned for him to step back, and Bernice ranted on.

The tirade continued. "You are a sinner, and you will pay!" Bernice's lips shrieked into Esther's face. The words fell into her silence and cut into her heart, and Esther dropped her head again. Her chin hurt where her mother's fingers had bitten into her skin, but her heart hurt more from the pain of the false accusations.

Bernice rushed forward and shook her as tears of humiliation poured from Esther's eyes. She tried to convey she had merely gone to the woods to pick flowers to decorate their house with.

"You liar!" Bernice's lips said, and Esther cringed as her mother's hand came down toward the side of her face.

Before the expected impact, however, her rescuer jumped forward, planting himself firmly between Esther and her parents, his face turning from Esther to Arnold and Bernice as he spoke words Esther garnered must be in her defense.

"Not her fault," she discerned the man said as he turned to look toward her and then away again.

Esther could see Bernice's and Arnold's lips working so furiously that she couldn't read a word they said. Her eyes fell on her rescuer's lips instead, puzzled by what she was reading. She was still not fluent and couldn't be sure she was deciphering the words accurately.

It was only when he turned to her and went down on one knee that Esther stared at his lips intently, uncomprehendingly. She read the words, "Right thing." She looked at her mother and father. Bernice's mouth had fallen open, and Arnold's eyes were round with surprise.

Her own eyes widened as she returned her gaze her rescuer, still on one knee and looking up at her as if he was apologizing for what had happened to her that afternoon. She swallowed, unable to tear her eyes away from his because they were such kind eyes, beseeching her at that moment. She wanted to tell him it wasn't his fault but hers. She shouldn't have wandered off into the woods alone.

His lips formed the words "Will you?"

Esther gaped at him in confusion, but a sudden movement from her father made her glance at him.

"Take her, Paul Orton," Arnold shouted, but Esther misread the words as, "Take her, all okay."

Her head went to one side as she struggled to make sense of the situation even as her rescuer got to his feet and nodded to her parents.

This kind man just begged my forgiveness, kneeling down before me, Esther thought, *and then, for some reason, Father said the words, "Take her."* Esther didn't know what to make of that. All she knew was she felt ashamed and unworthy of her rescuer's gesture. To kneel before her in contrition was not right, she reasoned. Maybe it was because he took the blame upon himself for the incident.

How easily, it seemed, her father had said, "Take her." There had barely been a moment's hesitation. Esther had always suspected she was a burden, but now it became even more eminently clear of how little worth she was to her parents. The realization made her pain even more acute, and though Esther had always felt isolated, she had never felt more alone than now.

There was some further interchange between her rescuer and her parents. From stray words picked up by reading their lips, Esther suspected she was being banished from her home and that her rescuer was going to take her somewhere else, perhaps to his home. As if in answer to her questions, Bernice nudged her toward Paul, as if pushing her out of their lives.

I'm going to be sent away, Esther thought. She was paying for a sin she had committed a decade ago. All this was taking place because she had skipped out of her parents' store one day when she was a little girl to wander in the woods. And now she was being taken away from her parents for something that had happened right in the vicinity of those same woods because of her own sinfulness.

She felt a surge of grief. She didn't want to leave her home. No matter how she was treated there, it was the only world she knew. *Perhaps God is relieving my parents of me because I've been a burden to them*, she thought tearfully. They deserved better, a child they could be proud of, someone they could introduce to their relatives instead of hiding her away. She had always wished she could somehow work and earn to make their lives comfortable and thus give them a reason to be proud of her, but she knew that any job would be impossible to get when the whole village held her in such low esteem.

She was no good to them and never would be. And though the thought tore through her like so many knives, Esther wanted her parents to be happy, even if it meant her being sent away in order for them to feel some measure of joy.

She went up to her room, walking awkwardly with one shoe. Once she was safely by her bed, she knelt down and thanked God for saving her that day. Then she prayed for her rescuer. The door opened, and Bernice came in. Esther quickly got to her feet, looking at her mother expectantly. But she merely saw the dresser shake as her mother slammed a plate of food on it. Some of the sauce from the beans splattered surface of the dresser, and the bread fell onto the floor. After Bernice left, Esther picked it up, dusted it off, and began to eat, aware she had displeased her parents so much that she wasn't allowed to eat with them at the table.

She had barely finished eating when the door flew open again, and Bernice entered. She opened a dresser drawer and threw an old potato sack onto the floor, motioning for Esther to put her things into it.

Esther obediently began to pack, still wondering where she was going. Maybe she was being sent away to a place for lunatics. A Bible verse came to her from Joshua 1:9. "Be strong and courageous. Do not be frightened, and do not be dismayed, for the Lord your God is with you wherever you go."

Chapter Four

Paul rode back to his ranch with a sense of incredulity. Luther had not just gone too far—he had done the unthinkable. The strange thing was that Paul felt responsible. He was the older brother, and it was up to him to keep Luther in check. That he had resorted to drinking even during the day was bad enough, but that he had assaulted an innocent young woman—one who, by all accounts, was not altogether normal—was unconscionable.

He took a deep breath. Despite his anger at God, he had to admit that He moved in mysterious ways. After the morning he had been summoned by Sheriff Basley, Paul had instructed one of the ranch hands shadow Luther at all times. It was some days after Luther had been apprehended by the sheriff when the ranch hand, Tom, had come running back to the barn to report that Luther was in a saloon, the one near the woods, and had been in there for some time.

Paul had rushed there as quickly as he could only to find that Luther and his two cronies had disappeared.

As Paul had ridden through the town, searching for Luther, one of his brother's drinking companions lurched into his path, wiping blood from his teeth and gesturing wildly for him to stop. If he hadn't found him in the middle of the street, there would have been no telling what might have happened, but he knew he would have missed saving an innocent girl's life. The thought made his blood run cold.

"Mr. Paul!" Luther's friend Jed had shouted. "Come quickly! It's Luther!"

"Is he in some kind of danger?" Paul had called back, spurring Raider forward.

"I can't say what—what it is," Jed stuttered, his eyes wild with fear. "Just come with me!"

As Paul had burst into the clearing by the woods, he saw Luther on top of a girl, and the bile rose in his throat. Luther's lips and body pinned the hapless victim down, and she was thrashing about under him as he sought to violate her modesty. Paul saw the girl's skirts, petticoats and all, were ripped, displaying one of her thighs, and strange, muffled cries escaped the girl's throat as she struggled.

"I tried to stop him," Jed cried, "but when he kicked me away, I came to find you."

She had gone limp when Paul pounced on Luther and threw him off the girl. His eyes widened in alarm when he saw she was the one everybody said was cognitively slow.

"Take Luther back to the ranch," Paul told Jed. "I'll be along shortly to deal with him. I need to get this poor girl back to her home first."

Jed had been trembling with fear, but he dragged Luther away, protesting and cursing.

"Want her for yourself, do you?" Luther leered at Paul as Jed tugged at his arm. "We can share the spoils, brother. I won't say I found her first and keep the whole meal to myself!"

Paul flushed. Luther was a monster, he'd realized, horrified, but one that he had created simply by not being vigilant enough.

"Douse his head in a trough of water, will you, Jed?" he instructed, and then turned to Luther. "Mind how you talk about a woman, Luther. Have some respect." Even as he spoke, he made a silent vow to ensure that Luther didn't go further along the path he was o0n. He would have to do whatever it took to help him change.

When Jed and Luther had gone, Paul leaned over the girl. He remembered her name now. It was Esther. He had seen her a few times, wandering through the town with her arms full of flowers.

"Esther," he said, leaning over her, and then remembered that she was known to be deaf and mute. She also seemed to be unconscious or had passed out from the shock of the assault. Paul looked anxiously at her and hesitantly patted her cheek to wake her up. Her eyes fluttered open, and she stared at him wide-eyed, as if she was looking through him. She had beautiful honey-brown eyes and light-brown hair. Her lashes were long and curled up to her eyebrows, which arched above her small snub nose. Paul flushed in embarrassment, tearing his eyes away from hers because he felt remorse for what Luther had done and shame for noticing each beautiful feature of the face he had stared at. In that moment, he wondered if he was no better than his brother. He was almost relieved when Esther's eyelashes fell against her ivory skin once again and he didn't have to look into her eyes.

Paul didn't know how long it actually took to stir Esther to consciousness, but during the time he helped her up and onto his horse, he berated himself for Luther's latest misconduct. He needed to do something about his brother, but first he had to get this poor girl home.

Her appearance tore at his heart. The ripped dress and worn-out shoes—or shoe, for she only had one on—and disheveled hair stirred up a host of emotions within him. He was reminded of an injured mustang he had encountered up in the mountains, how he had won the animal's confidence enough to bind up its broken leg. Something about the sadness, pain, and confusion he saw in Esther's eyes reminded him of that poor, wounded horse. He had subsequently brought it down to the ranch and there ministered to it night and day. It galloped again, perhaps not at its original speed, but he loved it because it had reminded him that even the broken can be mended.

On the ride to her house, he had been acutely aware of Esther seated behind him. She didn't hold on to him, so he rode slowly, keeping Raider at a trot. He wished he could converse with her, mostly to apologize, but as he couldn't, he began to prepare a speech for her parents. This he went over and over until Esther's house came into view.

He had taken Raider all the way to the front porch and then dismounted and helped the girl off. Nothing could have prepared him for what happened next. After he knocked on the door and Esther's parents came out onto the porch, Paul could scarcely believe what he was hearing and seeing. When Esther ran into her mother's arms for comfort, she was thrust aside roughly. And when he began to explain what had happened, neither the girl's father nor her mother wanted to believe their daughter was an unfortunate, innocent victim of a drunken assault.

"Get out of my sight!" Bernice had screamed at her daughter. "You shameless hussy!"

"With all due respect, ma'am," Paul intervened, "this was not your daughter's fault. She was thrown to the ground and overpowered by my inebriated brother."

"Oh, she could have fought him off if she wanted to, but it's quite obvious that she didn't. How are you so sure she didn't have something to do with him in the first place?" Bernice had retorted, her voice rising several decibels higher.

Paul glanced at Esther. She was looking from him to her parents in confusion.

"Your daughter did not have anything to do with my brother," he said.

"Then why didn't she stop him?" Arnold shouted.

"She tried," Paul replied. "But he had her pinned down."

"How do you know she didn't encourage him?" Bernice shrieked. "You harlot!" she spat at Esther. Esther's forehead was furrowed. She didn't appear to have grasped the trend of the conversation, which was just as well, Paul thought.

"I know, because I arrived at the scene just in time," Paul said. "Your daughter was innocently walking by the woods. She didn't anticipate that this would happen."

He felt powerless as he spoke, because Esther's parents were clearly not willing to listen to anything barring their own impression of what had taken place. They wanted to believe their daughter was at fault, and so they would. No argument he made in her defense would have any effect at all. He glanced at Esther again and badly wanted to shield her from any further onslaught from her parents. He couldn't comprehend how any mother would treat her child—especially one like Esther—with such a lack of tenderness or compassion.

Esther's mother was hurling invectives and false accusations at her daughter. Esther had her head bowed when her mother roughly took her chin and jerked her head up so she could look into her face as she continued to scream at her. Paul recoiled at the sight, feeling a desperate need to intervene. The moment came when Esther's mother raised her hand to strike her daughter across the face.

Paul felt not a whisper of hesitation as he sprang forward to plant himself firmly between Esther and her parents. He was acutely conscious of the fact that Esther had just been through a grueling experience at the hands of his brother and was now being subjected to unfair judgement and hurt inflicted insensitively by her mother and father. His heart ached to rescue her, to bind up her wounds as he had done for the mustang and take her under his wing.

He had stared at Esther's parents dumbfounded, and then he reacted in a way he hadn't ever imagined he would and certainly in a manner that took him by surprise.

"I would like to marry her," he said, raising his voice slightly in order to be heard above Bernice's shrill tirade.

"What!" Arnold exclaimed, his mouth falling open in surprise.

"You heard me," Paul said. "I would like to marry your daughter."

He noticed Esther staring at him, her eyes on his lips, and he flushed slightly. Her warm honey-brown eyes then shifted to his, and for a fleeing moment they looked at each other, and he felt like he was looking into Esther's soul. There was something else he felt, but he dismissed it. Yes, she was very lovely to look at, he reasoned, but he couldn't be attracted to her. That would be impossible, since he was still mourning the loss of his wife and child.

"You want to marry Esther?" Bernice queried.

Esther had looked from her parents to Paul and back again, her eyes darting back and forth rapidly like a frightened animal waiting for its fate to be decided. He wondered if she understood what was happening, as it appeared, from her demeanor, that she couldn't follow the dialogue between him and her parents.

"It's the right thing to do to protect the reputations of both our families," Paul said to Esther's father. "But first, I need to get back home and deal with my brother." He turned to

Esther, and once again taking himself by surprise, he went down on one knee. Gazing up into her face, seeing her disheveled appearance, pierced his heart. He saw dry leaves still clinging to her partially undone braids, a reminder of what she had just suffered. And when he looked down, he saw, poking through the ripped hem of her dress, the one remaining shoe and the one bare, unshod foot that spoke volumes about the neglect she faced in her own home.

Paul felt tears prick his eyes. He blinked rapidly and kept his eyes on Esther's. She was staring at his lips, looking puzzled. He began to make a speech, but it was evident that Esther didn't quite follow what he was saying.

"Will you?" he asked her, after proposing marriage.

"Take her, Paul Orton!" her father said, making a sudden movement that drew Esther's attention to him. She stared at her father now with that same bewildered look on her face.

And then, when Paul stood up, Esther's mother had pushed her daughter roughly toward him. The girl's eyes had widened slightly, her head cocked to one side as if in an effort to better comprehend the situation.

Esther had looked up at Paul, and he'd given her a reassuring nod.

"I'm so sorry," he had apologized again.

"It is my brother who is at fault, and I will deal with him in a suitable manner. I will send him away so he can get his life together," Paul had said to Esther's parents. "And the marriage will take place without too much delay."

Riding back to his ranch, Paul was overcome by a wave of apprehension. *What have I done?* he asked himself, driving his spurs into Raider's side, intent on getting home quickly to confront his brother. He was going to marry a woman who was reputed to be cognitively slow—beautiful though she was. No doubt he was paying for his sin of not taking better care of his brother and watching him more closely.

What has gotten into me? he wondered. This was uncharacteristic, to make a commitment based on nothing more than pity and a sense of duty. But was it pity he felt for Esther? Or was it something else? He flushed as he remembered her eyes as they looked up at him after he had dragged Luther off her. He remembered the details of her eyes. Brown with flecks of gold. He had felt something for her at that moment. It was compassion. But would mere compassion cause his pulse to quicken when her eyes inexplicably fell on his lips and remained there? When he was proposing marriage to her? he mused.

It was late evening when he got back to the ranch. The hired help had already retired to their bunkhouses, so Paul rode Raider up to the stables and then walked him to his stall. He took the horse's saddle and bridle off and left him with a bale of hay. *Animals are so uncomplicated to deal with,* Paul thought as he hung up the saddle and bridle and checked to see that the water trough was full. *If only humans could be as simple to deal with.* He sighed as he reluctantly mounted the porch steps to the ranch house and let himself in.

Luther had fallen into a drunken stupor on the couch, and Sandy was sitting by him.

"I stayed here to keep an eye on him, boss," Sandy said.

"Thanks, Sandy," Paul replied, grateful Sandy was more friend than foreman.

He stared at his younger brother, and his first instinct was to pull him off the couch and give him a hiding. It was what his father would have done had he been alive. But then the more he looked at Luther, the more he saw the result of a great lack in his life. Luther had always been in Paul's shadow. And he had rebelled. He hadn't picked up the slack on the ranch, and he had spent more hours in the local saloons drinking and gambling than tending the livestock. Most noticeably, he had stopped going to church and appeared to have no faith in God. He once said he had lost all trust in the Almighty after their parents had passed. But also, he resented Paul.

"The future is in horses, big brother," Luther had once said. "And I can run that end of our operations if you would set me up."

"We have a cattle ranch, Luther," Paul had replied. "And if you can't pull your weight here, how are you going to head an entire operation? Do you think breeding horses is easy, Luther? It's not. A stud farm takes hard work."

"I'll only work at something I'm interested in," Luther had retorted. "And I'm not interested in cattle."

Perhaps I should have let Luther have his way, Paul thought. Maybe then this wouldn't have happened.

"Shall I wake him up?" Sandy asked, gesturing to Luther.

"In a minute," Paul replied.

"What happened?" Sandy asked. "Jed wouldn't say a word."

"I need to send Luther away, Sandy. His behavior has gotten out of hand," Paul said. He took his hat off and raked his fingers through his hair as he recounted the events of the day to his foreman and friend.

"You're going to marry this girl?" Sandy queried, aghast. "Boss, are you sure you need to do this?"

"I have to do this, Sandy, to preserve and protect the reputations of both the families. I should never have let Luther out of my sight, and yet I did. I have been so preoccupied with the ranch and have selfishly tried to bury my sorrows in work when I ought to have been looking out for my brother. It's a duty that was given to me by God, and I didn't do it well enough. But I have to try and make things right now."

"By marrying a girl you don't even know, one who's, um . . . slow, no less?" Sandy asked.

"It's my responsibility," Paul said, his chin thrust forward determinedly.

He went over to Luther and shook him. "Get up, Luther," he said, his voice cold and menacing.

"What do you want?" Luther asked, springing up suddenly and clutching his temples. "My head feels like it's on fire."

"That would be because you were at the saloon this morning when you should have been helping out on the ranch. Do you know I had to go looking for you?" Paul said.

"I saw that little rat you've had on my tail these past weeks," Luther sneered. "What's his name? Tom, isn't it? Yes, Tom the ranch hand. Sneaky fellow, but not smart at all. He thought he was keeping a low profile, but I knew exactly what he was up to. And you know what, big brother? That stunt you pulled actually spurred me on to drink a few extra glasses of whiskey."

"So that's your excuse, Luther?" Paul shot back. "That you had more to drink than you could handle because I asked Tom to keep an eye on you?"

"I'm not going to answer that question," Luther snarled. "You always think you need to control me. Well, you know what? You can't!"

He shook back his greasy hair and glared at Paul, his dark eyes gleaming rebelliously.

Paul held back a fitting retort and bit down on his lip.

"Luther," he said, "do you remember what happened today after you got drunk and went for a walk with those so-called friends of yours?"

Luther blinked and rubbed his eyes, and then his lips parted in a grin.

"Oh, the girl. The slow one. Aren't you going to thank me for leaving her for you?" He laughed.

Paul flushed.

"You violated her modesty," he replied. "And I won't have you talk of her in that tone. She is a woman, and you need to respect all women."

Luther guffawed. "Paul, Paul," he slurred. "She's slow. She probably didn't even realize what was happening to her." He guffawed again. "Or maybe she did . . . and didn't want me to stop."

It was Sandy who caught Luther by the collar, pulled him up to his feet, and shook him hard.

"Hold your tongue, Luther!" Sandy roared in his face. "Have some respect! Do you know what you've done? You've consigned your brother to a lifetime of being married to this poor girl in order to protect the reputation of her family—and yours. Don't you know how far your brother will go to protect you? And this is how you talk to him? Sober up, man, or your life is going to be an even bigger mess than it already is."

"You're marrying the slow girl?" Luther asked, squinting at Paul.

"Don't call her that," Paul ground out through clenched teeth. "And yes, I'm marrying her."

Luther threw back his head and laughed all the more. "Well, I see that despite her mental state, she's quite a looker and all," he said. "But Paul, you could enjoy the goods without having to purchase them. You know that, don't you?"

Paul raked his fingers through his hair. Luther was behaving despicably, and his attitude was abhorrent. He wondered if he would ever be able to repair the damage done.

"I am marrying her to make things right," Paul replied, as Sandy pushed Luther back onto the couch and held him down.

"Whatever you say, brother," Luther sneered. "You always were one of those 'holier than thou' types, worrying what the pastor would say or the church folk."

Paul shook his head. Luther was baiting him and wanted to see how far he could go before he, Paul, snapped.

"Maybe if you'd paid a little more attention in church, you'd have turned out a bit less like this," Paul replied. But even as he spoke, he saw the merest flicker of pain in his brother's eyes and felt a stab of compassion for him.

"Look," Paul said, "I know it was bad the way Ma and Pa died, leaving us alone in the world, but things could have been a lot worse. Who knows, maybe if I'd have spent more time with you instead of being so obsessed with working the ranch, you'd have been alright."

"Don't patronize me," Luther growled. "And don't go implying that you would have been a good influence on me if you had spent more time with me as you said. The fact is, Paul, I don't give a damn about you, this ranch, or our parents. I'm my own person, and that's all there is to it."

Paul looked more closely at his brother. That last statement told him all he needed to know. Luther was obviously missing his parents more than he cared to let on. He knew that because Luther's nature was to continually dismiss the idea he could feel hurt or pain. This was false bravado, Paul realized. He recalled an instance when they were boys and Luther's pet dog had died. He had gone on a rampage that day, breaking a window and getting into a fight with a friend, and when their ma had asked if he was missing his dog, he'd shaken his head violently. "I don't care about that mangy old dog dying," he had said. *Yes*, Paul thought, *Luther is obviously hurting, and maybe some time away from Springford will do him good.*

"I'm sending you to stay with Uncle Mack and Aunt Tillie," Paul said, ignoring Luther's remarks. "Because I am marrying Esther Larson, and she will not feel safe with you here."

"You're sending me to South Dakota? Well, I'm not going," Luther retorted mutinously. "Besides, I'm your brother, and that woman is just a simple half-wit and nobody to you. I have more right to be here than she does."

"Whether she's a half-wit or not, she's going to be my wife. You will leave Springford and stay away from this ranch. Get your life on track, or you'll be behind bars," Paul shot back.

"Behind bars? What for?" Luther shouted.

"For trying to molest an innocent woman and taking advantage of her condition," Paul replied evenly. "So make your choice, Luther. I would say that some time spent with Uncle Mack and Aunt Tillie would do you a world of good. And if I were you, I would take the opportunity to take a good hard look at my life and take steps to turn it around."

"Well, I'm not you," Luther ranted. "And I'm glad I'm not. I'll run away, I will. Just try and send me there!"

"You're not a kid anymore," Paul said. "And you can't keep drifting through life in a whiskey haze. You need to sober up and do your duty. I'm sending a telegram to Uncle Mack and Aunt Tillie right away."

"Who do you think you are? My keeper?" Luther roared.

Paul nodded. "Yes, I am. I am my brother's keeper. And I am trying to do what's best for you," he replied.

He was taking on more than he felt confident of handling, Paul realized. On one hand, there was Esther, and on the other, there was Luther. He was sending one away in order to tend and care for the other.

What stood out clearly to Paul was an alarming revelation. Esther and Luther were both victims of circumstance, and both were damaged in different ways. They both needed to be ministered to, day and night, as he had done with the injured mustang.

But he needed help with Luther, and he was willing to seek that from his uncle and aunt. He hoped he was making the right decision and that sending Luther away would not have a deleterious effect instead of a beneficial one.

Chapter Five

Esther woke up and went to the window. Kneeling down, she greeted the first streaks of dawn with a prayer. It had been fourteen days since she had been rescued by the good man with the kind eyes. Her mother had made her pack her things that very night, and each day of those two weeks had reminded her she would no longer be living with them once her attacker had been sent far away from Springford. Esther had wept and prayed. She couldn't understand why she was going away or what kind of life she would be going to. But that morning, kneeling by the window, she remembered Psalms 30:5. "Weeping may tarry for the night, but joy comes with the morning."

Her mother hadn't told her when she would be leaving, so each day she would get prepared and wait. The uncertainty of her situation tormented her so acutely that she trembled whenever one of her parents came into her room to summon her for a meal or to help with the household chores.

Esther's prayers were interrupted when she felt the windowpane before her vibrate in a way that indicated her bedroom door had been opened. She jumped to her feet, looking bewildered, as she perceived her mother standing there holding a box. Instinctively her eyes went to her mother's lips as she began to speak.

"Wear this," Esther read, and her eyes went to the box.

Bernice jerked her head backward and continued to speak. "He sent," Esther was just about able to decipher, when her mother dropped the box on her bed and exited hastily.

As Esther opened the box, her fingers shook. Obviously this had something to do with her going away, she realized. She lifted the lid off and gasped. Inside was a dress prettier than any she had ever seen. And it was made of delicate white lace. Esther looked at her hands as if to make sure they were clean before she touched the dress. Unsatisfied, she went to the washstand that stood by the window and used the ewer to pour icy cold water onto her hands. She dried them on the towel that hung on a peg next to the stand and then slowly walked back to the box, lifting the dress out carefully. It was only when she held it up that she realized what could possibly be happening. This was a wedding dress, and her mother had just asked her to put it on. Did that mean she was getting married? If so, to whom? She drew in her breath. She hadn't noticed the box also contained a lace veil and a pair of white shoes.

Esther sat down on the edge of her bed, still holding the wedding dress, her mind going back to that day two weeks ago when, after rescuing her, the kind man had dropped to one knee and said words to her she didn't comprehend in their entirety. Two words stood out: "Will you?" In the story of Cinderella by the Brothers Grimm, which was another favorite tale Esther loved to read, she had seen a picture of Prince Charming kneeling before Cinderella and asking for her hand in marriage. She saw a connection now.

Esther's hand went flying to her heart as if to still its rapid pounding. Could this be happening? She had prayed for someone she could share her life with, but she didn't know how to react to marrying a stranger—if that was indeed what she was about to do.

The door was once again thrust open, and Bernice stood in the doorway with her hands on her hips. She was clearly displeased.

"Hurry!" her lips shouted.

Esther set the dress back in the box and stood up. "What would you like me to do?" she asked, miming the question.

Bernice rolled her eyes heavenward and grabbed her daughter's arm. She pulled her up to just within arm's length and stared into her face. Pointing to Esther's eyes and her own lips, she conveyed she wanted Esther to pay close attention to what she was saying.

Esther's forehead creased, and her eyes narrowed as she tried hard to comprehend the words formed by her mother's very thin, hard lips.

"Wash yourself. Wear the dress. Brush your hair." Three clear instructions emerged.

"Why?" Esther mimed. She just needed to know for sure.

Bernice shook her head in exasperation and began to speak very rapidly as she usually did when she was angry and flustered, and Esther couldn't quite understand what she was trying to convey.

"Married!" Her mother's lips formed the word, and her face came closer to Esther's as she repeated the word a few times.

Esther stepped back and nodded. She dared not ask who her groom was. It must be the kind man who had knelt before her. Obviously he had made the same gesture as Prince Charming had in her picture book about Cinderella, perhaps by way of apology for what his brother had done. That was the only explanation she could think of. But she couldn't be certain of anything. If only she knew his name . . . . She sighed.

"Bathe!" her mother said, once again standing right in front of her and shouting the word into her face.

Esther nodded vigorously and hurried out of her room and down the stairs to the kitchen. She found a tub of hot water waiting behind a screen.

When she was back in her room after her bath, she was shivering. She was also quaking within at the prospect of what was to come, because of the strangeness of it all. After putting on her undergarments, she slipped the dress over her head and watched it fall to the floor. She couldn't tell exactly how she looked in it because her room lacked a full-length mirror, so she climbed onto the bed in order to see as much of her reflection as she could in the small mirror on her dresser.

Having had a less than satisfactory view of herself in the inadequate looking glass, Esther leapt lightly off the bed, holding the dress up to protect the hem, and then took the white shoes out of the box and slid them onto her feet. She now felt unlike herself, and it bothered her. She brushed her hair and began to braid it like her mother always insisted she did, but this time she coiled the braids over her head and pinned them down. She didn't quite know what to do with the veil, but as she hesitated, the door swung open once again, and her mother appeared.

Bernice snatched the veil from Esther's hands and threw it over her head. She then stuck two pins through the fine lace and into her coiled braids. The pins hurt, and Esther's eyes filled with tears, but she resolutely blinked them back.

"Your things," Esther read off her mother's lips, and she hastily picked up the bag containing her two everyday dresses, two nightgowns, and one church dress. She reached down to lift the box that had her books and then turned to take one last look at her room. It hadn't been bad to her. In fact, it had been her only haven. She would miss it. A lump formed in her throat, and she reached up to sweep the tears off her cheeks. Then she felt her mother give her a nudge and stumbled forward, leaving the room behind and walking down the stairs, carrying her few worldly possessions.

Her father was by their pony cart and signaled to Esther to put her things into it. She wanted to stand before her house for a while so the image would be forever imprinted in her memory, but her mother nudged her again, and she had to tear her eyes away from the home she had spent all her life in and get into the pony cart.

Esther hoped every detail of the route from her house to wherever it was they were going would be etched into her memory so she could write about it in her diary when she had the time to do so. She looked at the passing landscape with a sense of loss, holding her hands out as if to embrace the firs and pines they passed. *Where are we bound for?* she wondered. *Who will be at the other end?* She was still uncertain. But she kept going over and over the different elements that had led up to that moment and tried to connect them.

She was wearing a wedding dress, and two weeks ago her kind rescuer had knelt before her and asked a question she hadn't been able to answer because she didn't know what it was. But it was apparent that the question that was asked had led to this moment. She could only hope they were going to church. It would make her feel better to be close to God, in His house, when she was making a transition into a situation she wasn't even sure of.

Before she had any time to ponder the matter further, the church came into view, and Esther felt a small ripple of relief.

When her father stopped the pony cart, Esther reached for her bag and the box of books she had brought with her, but her mother slapped her hands away from them, indicating she should leave them where they were until later. Esther looked anxiously up at the sky, willing it not to rain. She didn't want her beloved books to be destroyed.

She was still thinking of her books as she walked up the aisle with her mother and father on either side of her. But when she came to stand before the man with the kind eyes who had rescued her from a situation worse than death, she began to panic. As if he sensed her anxiety, the man gave her a gentle smile.

She stood looking up into his eyes, drawing comfort from the unspoken words of reassurance he conveyed to her. A rosy flush crept up her cheeks as she felt her pulse begin to race. She still wasn't sure of his name, but at that moment all she could think of was how handsome he was in his dark-blue tuxedo and his wide-brimmed hat covering no more than half the length of his brown hair, which gleamed in the diffused light from the lamps in the church.

He had made an effort to dress for the occasion and had made sure she had the appropriate attire too, and the townsfolk had turned up in church to witness the event. *If only he was marrying me for love,* Esther thought wistfully, but quickly chastised herself for her ingratitude. She was thankful indeed that God had heard her prayers for a companion who would accept her as she was and sent her rescuer to her. It was only the fact that he was marrying her to somehow pay for what his brother had done that made Esther a little sad. She would have preferred it if the man standing in front of her was marrying her because he genuinely wanted her in his life.

Esther glanced to the side, seeing her father and mother seated in the front row. They looked as displeased with her as they ever did, and Esther felt a stab of pain. She returned her gaze to her husband-to-be and fixed her eyes on his lips as he took her hands. It was a strange and not unpleasant sensation to have her hands nestled in the strong hands of the tall, broad-shouldered man before her.

She looked down at their hands so intimately placed one within the other and knew she would never forget either the image or the emotions it stirred up within her. She tried to analyze what she was feeling. It was a sense of being accepted by this man in a way nobody else had unconditionally accepted her. She blinked up at him and then once again looked at her hands engulfed by his, and she felt protected.

There was something about this man that conveyed to Esther he would defend her and keep her safe.

She glanced uncertainly at the pastor, who spoke to each of them in turn. His lips formed the word "vows." He kept glancing sympathetically at her, and Esther tangibly felt his pity. From his demeanor, it was clear he couldn't understand why the kind man was marrying her.

Esther turned to her rescuer once again. She couldn't decipher many of the words he said, but it didn't seem to matter either to him or to the pastor. She wished there was some way of knowing what he was saying, and she dearly desired to respond, but she resided in a bubble of silence through which no words penetrated and no words escaped. She eased her hands away from those of her rescuer and began to mime. But when she saw him look anxiously at the pastor and then at the few people who had curiously gathered for the event, she stopped. The assembled witnesses leaned forward in their seats and gaped at her, and Esther sensed some of them perhaps hoped for her to do something dramatic. She turned back to the man in whose eyes she saw no judgement, pity, or malice. But he didn't take her hands in his again and continued to speak with his folded in front of him.

Esther stared at his lips, noticing that the moment her eyes settled on his mouth, he turned red and looked down at his feet. Then he looked at her again and continued to speak. It might have made her smile, but the gravity of the situation far outweighed the lighter aspects of it, and so she remained unsmiling and somber.

The pastor was saying something. Esther knew, because her rescuer had turned to face him. She did too, her eyes desperately trying to read the words he was saying.

"I now—husband—wife!" Esther deciphered from the movement of the pastor's lips, and at that same moment her rescuer turned back to her with a smile and a nod.

As they exited the church, her mother and father came toward her and her new husband. Esther looked straight at her mother, wishing she would be happy for her. But Bernice merely seemed sad. Esther began to mime an apology, folding her hands and bowing her head, but her mother moved closer, nudged her chin up, and stared into her eyes. She was about to say something but appeared to change her mind. Esther was surprised to see her mother's eyes glisten with unshed tears. Then Esther's husband doffed his hat to her parents before he took her arm and led her to the buckboard standing by the church.

Esther looked desperately at the pony cart she had arrived in. She didn't want to forget her bag and her box of books. She ran toward the cart and dragged the box off it. Suddenly she felt the burden taken from her hands. Looking up, she saw that her husband had taken the box and picked up the old potato sack as well. She cocked her head to one side, gazing up into his eyes, and he gave her a brief, reassuring smile.

Arnold and Bernice were getting into the pony cart, preparing to leave, when Esther ran to them to bid them farewell. Arnold quickly looked away, appearing overly preoccupied with the horse's reins, while Bernice nodded, tight lipped, blinking rapidly all the while. Then they rode away without so much as a backward glance.

Esther walked slowly back to the buckboard and climbed on, not looking at her husband because she suddenly felt so alone. Her rescuer seemed to be a very kind and just man, and getting married to him seemed like one of the fairy tales she loved to read. But the image of her mother's eyes, glistening with unshed tears, returned to tug at her heartstrings. By now it was noon, and though the sun was high in the sky, it was obscured by gray clouds, and there was just the merest threat of rain. Her dress was too beautiful to diminish with her old cloak, so Esther chose to endure the cold breeze and hoped they would reach their destination before she caught a chill.

The buckboard had started moving, and she glanced at her husband. He was looking straight ahead with a grave expression on his face. The wind filled Esther's veil and lifted it up so that it billowed behind her, and she planted one hand firmly on her head to keep it from blowing away completely. There was something carefree about her veil, tossed playfully this way and that, teased by the breeze, and Esther wished she could feel that way even for just a moment.

The landscape drifted past, and Esther viewed the passing scenery through unseeing eyes as she played over and over the ceremony. Though she knew it was a marriage to preserve the honor of both the families, she allowed herself a brief moment to pretend it was something with more depth.

They were passing the woods where she had so recently been accosted, and as the image of her assailant rose up to torment her, she began to tremble. That man was evil, and she hoped she would never again encounter him. She took a deep breath as another powerful declaration from the Bible came to her mind from Genesis 50:20. "As for you, you meant evil against me, but God meant it for good." Looking at the man beside her, she realized how true that verse was. If she hadn't been attacked, she would never have met the man who had chosen to marry her.

It was perhaps three quarters of an hour later when the buckboard slowed down, and Esther's eyes widened as they drove through a very large iron gate with the name "Orton's Cattle Ranch" cut into the arch. Esther turned to her husband, and he looked at her simultaneously. Their eyes met, and he smiled and nodded. She pointed to the name on the arch and then at him, and her eyes questioned if that was his name there. He nodded.

Esther sat back and sighed. His name was Orton. She frowned. No, it couldn't be. Orton sounded more like a surname. Well, at least she had solved part of the puzzle.

She turned her attention to the vast tract of land they were driving through. There were fenced-off areas with cattle grazing and paddocks with horses. Above them, as they rode along, the trees on either side formed an avenue, their branches meeting in an arch above them. Through the avenue, in the distance, she saw a large house, and Esther leaned forward eagerly.

This was more than she even dreamed of. This was the bounty of the Lord! She allowed herself a little moment of excitement when she rocked back and forth on the seat. She could see wildflowers in the meadow they passed by. Never having lived on a ranch, she realized this could be the adventurous, exciting life she had dreamed of.

The house loomed large in front of them as they moved closer toward it. And when they stopped by the porch, a tall, thin man with long, sun-bleached hair came running to the buckboard, and Esther could tell he was exchanging greetings with her husband. *Husband,* she mused. It had a nice ring to it.

Her husband had turned to her and was trying to tell her the name of the man. It was clear he was an employee by his deferential attitude. The man glanced at her curiously, and Esther wondered if he was trying to figure out why his master had married "the laggard." But she tossed the thought aside as she leapt off the buckboard, holding up the skirt of her wedding dress, and hurried toward the man as he picked up her box of books. She held out her arms for the box, but the man nodded to convey that he would carry it for her. Esther quickly mimed that what the box contained was very precious and she would rather carry it herself. The man's eyes briefly narrowed as avid curiosity replaced a passing interest. He handed Esther the box and picked up the old potato sack containing her meager possessions.

Esther wrapped her arms possessively around the box of books. They were not just fairy tales and stories to her but memories of a time when her mother had talked to her and read with her . . . before her world was plunged into lonely silence. Still holding this receptacle, she looked up at the two-story ranch house. It had a wide porch with two rocking chairs and a swing seat. Though pretty enough, it desperately begged for a woman's touch. *Hanging pots filled with pretty flowers, perhaps,* Esther mused.

Her husband stood aside to let her precede him up the porch steps, and she gave him an uncertain look before she walked up, her gait awkward, owing to the weight of the box. The thin, tall man had run up ahead of them and was holding the door open.

Esther stepped into the ranch house living room hesitantly and almost reverently looked around her. An old wooden chest and sofas with floral upholstery captured her attention, and she drew in her breath. *This place is special,* she thought, looking at her husband, who was awkwardly trying to convey some kind of explanation about the layout of the house.

He threw open the door between the living room and the dining room and turned left, leading her into the kitchen. Esther looked around her, enrapt. She could scarcely believe she would be living in such unprecedented comfort.

She nodded at her husband as he continued to show her around the kitchen and set her box of books down on the floor. Then she mimed a request to be shown to a room where she might change out of her dress. Her husband stared at her uncomprehendingly, but the tall, thin man seemed to get the gist of what she was trying to communicate, and he pointed Esther up the staircase and to the left. Her husband then stepped forward hurriedly and gestured for her to follow him, so she picked up her things once again and began to walk up the steps. Her husband stopped, turned around, and took both the box and the sack from her, and once again Esther felt she had been relieved of a burden.

Chapter Six

When Paul took the box of books from Esther's hands, he realized, once again, just how heavy it was. He also saw that it was heavier than her bag of clothes. This said something significant about his new bride. Esther obviously treasured her books above everything else. Or maybe her parents weren't so bad after all and had indulged her passion for looking at books. He had been given to understand that Esther couldn't read. She had once been able to, he had been told, but since the accident, she had lost that ability because of some damage to her brain.

He preceded her up the stairs and showed her to the room across from his, watching his wife as she first went to the window and looked out. She appeared to like what she saw, because she heaved a deep sigh, and Paul saw her shoulders relax.

"I'll just set these over here," he said, and then realized she possibly couldn't understand what he was saying.

"Esther," he said, walking over to her and tapping her on the shoulder. She turned to him and searched his face, her eyes finally settling on his lips. Paul flushed. It was disturbing when she did that.

"This is your room," he said, pointing to the bed and indicating the spot where he had placed her bag and books. Then he gestured to the chest of drawers, bookshelf, and closet and drew aside a curtain at the side of the room to reveal a washstand.

Paul held up two fingers and pointed outside the window, his lips forming the word "outhouse." Esther's eyes never left his lips as she nodded slowly and then looked out the window.

"There . . . are . . . two . . . outhouses," Paul repeated, emphasizing each word.

Esther nodded again, and he hoped she understood. His heart went out to her, standing there still clad in the lace wedding dress and veil he had bought for her. He had guessed the size of her feet and was glad the shoes appeared to fit. His eyes fell on the inadequate-looking bag of her belongings, and he felt stirred by compassion. He would get her more things should she need them, he decided.

"You can come down and eat something when you're ready," he said, but Esther didn't seem to understand.

"Eat . . .food," Paul said, but Esther was distracted, so he left her in the room and went downstairs again.

He felt more than a little overwhelmed at the swift change in his marital status. *In a way, it's good Esther is the way she is,* he thought. Because at this point in his life, he didn't have room for love or romance.

"Sandy," Paul said, as he saw his foreman still in the living room where he had left him. "Thank you for hurrying back after the wedding ceremony to welcome us home."

Sandy looked like he wanted to say something, but he shook his head. "Don't say it," he said to his foreman. "Don't you go telling me I have made a mistake, because I don't need to hear that." He threw himself into a deep chair and leaned back. "You know," Paul said, "I had to do this. It's a marriage of convenience and a matter of honor, but to be honest, I don't know how things will work out. My new bride can't seem to communicate at all."

"I hear she has an elaborate way of playacting to communicate when she has to," Sandy replied. "So maybe, when she has settled in, she'll begin to use that method to your mutual benefit."

"Maybe," Paul said. "But right now, I have to find a way to make myself understood. For instance, how do I tell her she needs to come downstairs to eat? I can't knock on the door because she wouldn't hear, and I just can't barge into her room."

Sandy stood up and shrugged his shoulders. "I wish I had a solution to the problem, Paul. Perhaps you should have thought this through before taking such an extreme step as marrying the poor girl."

"I couldn't bear the way her parents spoke to her," Paul replied. "And I will find a way to communicate. I'm sure that I will."

After Sandy left, however, Paul dropped his head into his hands. His foreman was right. He should have thought this through before marrying Esther. But being a man of his word, he had to fulfill the commitment he had made when he proposed to her. True, he had been hasty when he went down on one knee, and the two weeks that followed had seen him several times on the verge of calling off the wedding. But each time, he'd recalled the look in Esther's eyes when her parents berated her, telling her it was all her fault she had been attacked, and he'd felt the need to rescue her from her situation.

He looked up at the clock on the wall and saw that it was almost five o'clock in the evening. He could scarce believe how quickly time had flown. Reluctantly he pulled himself out of his chair, seeing that he would have to summon Esther for supper. He began to walk soundlessly up the stairs, only realizing when he was halfway up that he could make all the noise in the world and his wife wouldn't hear.

When he got to the top of the stairs, Paul saw that the door to Esther's room was ajar. He glanced surreptitiously in and saw his wife on the bed, fast asleep. She looked so peaceful he didn't dare wake her and instead allowed himself a brief moment to admire her undeniable beauty. If only she could communicate with him, he silently lamented. He pulled the door shut and went down the stairs.

Sometime later, he went up the steps again and paused outside Esther's door, wondering if she was awake and hungry. Not hearing any sounds, he went back to the kitchen and put food on a plate for her: roast beef, beans, and biscuits. He carefully placed the plate on a tray with a knife and fork and a glass of water and took it up to Esther's room. This time he knocked, though he was aware she wouldn't hear. Then he gently opened the door just a crack and slid his hand through and waved. When there was not even the sound of a footfall, Paul opened the door and peeped in. Esther was still asleep, only now he saw she had slid under the heavy quilt and was peacefully curled up under it. He laid the tray on the dresser and slid out the door, shutting it behind him.

Back in the kitchen, Paul sat down alone at the table and carved into some roast beef. *I must look odd,* he thought, *seated at the rough wooden table in the lamplight, dressed in my wedding suit.* He had taken his hat off, and his brown hair fell on either side of his face, with the lamplight dancing off it. His countenance was sorrowful. Try as he might, he couldn't prevent memories of his previous wedding from flooding back. The feel of Angie's slender finger as he slipped the wedding band onto it. The whisper of rose petals raining down on them, tossed joyfully by their family and friends. In particular, the sound of Angie's laughter as he carried her over the threshold would ring in his ears forever. But he fought for composure, determinedly filling his mouth with a heaped forkful of roast meat and beans. He almost choked, grief causing his throat to constrict, making it difficult to swallow.

Paul quickly shifted his thoughts to other things, other preoccupations. It was necessary to shift focus each time the past threatened to overwhelm him. He swallowed slowly, deliberately, and took a sip from the glass of water by his plate. He hoped the young girl in the room upstairs would wake and eat something, because he felt guilty eating by himself. It struck him then that once again he had someone in the house to take care of and feel responsible for. He meant the vows he'd taken that morning.

It had been a strange day, to be sure, and one he would never have anticipated. Nothing could have prepared him for something like this, and as always, Paul silently stormed the heavens for answers. God was obviously putting him to the test, and it was a severe one. *Is Esther coming into my life God's way of punishing me for not taking better care of my brother?* he wondered.

As he bit into a biscuit, Paul thought guiltily of Luther. Their uncle Mack and Aunt Tillie had received his telegram and arrived immediately to take Luther away. They feared that if he had been left to travel alone to them, he would have taken off and run away.

I have failed my brother, Paul chastised himself. It was his duty to take care of him, and now he had sent him away and chosen to bring home a strange mute girl instead. He raked his fingers through his hair as despair seized him. Had he made the wrong choice? And would this prove irreversibly damaging to his brother? He knew his brother with all his faults and failings, and yet he had chosen a stranger over him. Would he be taken to task for this shortcoming on his part?

He leaned over his plate, focusing his attention on the food he himself had cooked that morning before he left for the church. He had hoped he might partake of the meal with the girl he'd married so precipitously and perhaps get to know her a little better. But now he wondered if he would ever get to know the girl who lay fast asleep in the room upstairs or if she would remain an enigma to him. He forced another forkful of meat and beans into his mouth, and another wave of guilt submerged him. Was Luther alright? Was he eating? Or was he, like the prodigal son, sitting amongst the pigs—hungry and alone, longing for his father's house?

Paul pushed his chair back and rose to his feet. He was being unduly fanciful. Luther was with their Uncle Mack and Aunt Tillie, where he would be well fed, sleep in a warm bed, and visit the local pastor every other day to receive advice and counseling. The time away would do him good and make a man out of him.

Paul washed his plate and put the lids on the dishes containing the leftover food. Then he went outside, deeply inhaling the clear night air. He went to the stables to check on the horses, filling their water troughs, shoveling up the dung, and throwing down some hay—repeating tasks that had already been carried out by the ranch hands before they had left for the day. He could see smoke rising up from their bunkhouses and wondered what their lives were like after their workday.

Beyond his property, he could see the outlines of the mountains. They always brought him comfort. Despite his anger at God and all the unanswered questions he had been relentlessly throwing at the heavens, he remembered a verse from the Bible. It was from Psalms 121:1-2. "I lift up my eyes to the hills, from where does my help come? My help comes from the Lord, who made heaven and earth."

Yes, the sight of the mountains was comforting, but the words of the Psalm made him think bitterly that God had abandoned him to a lifetime of sorrow and disappointment. King David in the Bible must have felt as he did alone in the wilderness while tending his sheep, alone facing Goliath, and alone running from Saul.

Paul had often found solace in reading about David and in reciting the Psalms. But after losing his wife and child, he had shunned the Word, and his Bible had gathered dust, though he held it devoutly in his hands at church every Sunday. Was he a hypocrite? Perhaps he was, but with good reason. He hadn't deserved what life had dealt out to him. *But then, who can tell what one deserves or doesn't deserve?* a still, small voice spoke gently to him. Did Jesus deserve to be mocked, lashed, and nailed to the cross? Would his suffering, like Jesus's, be someone else's salvation?

Paul shook his head as he looked up at the heavens. There seemed to be no answers to his questions and no relief from the pain. His uncertainty had, in fact, been compounded that day as he debated over and over the issue of how he was to communicate with his mute wife.

He went back inside, bolting the door shut, and went upstairs to his room. He paused outside Esther's room for a moment. This used to be Luther's room, and now his brother had been banished from the ranch. Paul once again felt the weight of his responsibilities press his shoulders down. Maybe Luther had acted out because he was too controlling. Or maybe he knew how vulnerable Paul was under that façade of immovable strength.

Paul sighed and moved on to his room, closing the door behind him. Tonight he would sleep. Tomorrow he would shoulder his burden again.

***

The next morning, he woke early, washed and dressed, and then went into the kitchen to prepare breakfast. This had become his routine since his wife had died, and he didn't think it was going to change. He hadn't showed Esther around the kitchen in detail, and he had to admit to not being at all confident of her ability to prepare a meal. Once again, he wondered just how he would summon Esther to share the meal with him. While scrambling eggs and frying bacon, he debated whether he should go up and wave through her half-open door. He didn't want Esther to feel awkward and was eager to convey that his home was now also hers. He was so deep in thought he startled in surprise when he turned away from the stove to set a dish of eggs on the table and came face-to-face with the object of his contemplations.

"Good morning!" Paul greeted her nervously, a now-familiar flush creeping up his cheeks as he saw that Esther's eyes were studying his lips.

She looked fresh and lovely in a simple tan linen dress, with her hair in a single braid that fell over her left shoulder.

She gave him a half smile in response and began to mime. Paul observed her intently but couldn't comprehend what she was attempting to communicate. Then he realized Esther was holding an empty plate in her hands and that it was the one he had filled with food and placed on a tray in her room the night before. She nodded to him and showed him the plate. It was clean. She placed her right hand on her belly, and Paul realized she was conveying to him that she had eaten the food he had left on the dresser for her. She set the plate down, folded her hands, and bowed her head. *This must be her way of saying thank you,* he mused.

He found himself staring at her lips, noticing the shape of her mouth and the warmth of her eyes, and the color crept up his neck again. She was so fresh and untouched, and he couldn't help noticing that even the drab linen dress she was wearing didn't diminish her beauty.

When he was embarrassed, Paul tended to speak quite rapidly, and this he did, quite forgetting that Esther couldn't hear.

"Did you sleep well? Are you hungry? Was the bed comfortable? Did you enjoy the food?" The questions poured out one after the other. Then he saw Esther regarding him with a puzzled look on her face, her head tilted slightly to one side and her eyes on his lips.

Paul hurriedly masked his discomfiture by pulling a chair out and inviting Esther to sit down and eat. She obliged him and then motioned for him to sit down too. Paul was busy brewing coffee, so he pointed to the kettle and turned away from her with a sense of relief. When her eyes were on his lips, it made him feel as shy as a schoolboy. This was going to be harder than he'd thought it would, he realized.

The aroma of freshly brewed coffee permeated the air. Paul carried the kettle to the table and saw that Esther had her eyes half-closed and was inhaling the fragrance appreciatively. He also saw that she hadn't touched the food and was instead looking up at him expectantly.

He motioned to the dish of eggs.

"Do eat, please, Esther," he said. "Before everything gets cold."

In reply, Esther pointed to him and then to his plate. He knew she wanted him to eat with her, and he wondered how he would hold up, sitting opposite this very attractive woman who kept staring at his lips.

He passed her the dish of scrambled eggs, but she stood up and reached across for his plate. Then she served him some bacon and eggs. Paul looked at her as she glanced around the kitchen, miming. His forehead was creased as he tried to understand what exactly she wanted, but before he could interpret the gestures she was making, Esther's face broke into a smile. She darted across to the stove and picked up a loaf of bread, which Paul had purchased at the mercantile along with some butter.

He watched, intrigued, as Esther proceeded to butter slices of bread for both of them. Then she helped herself to some of the scrambled eggs. Paul nudged the dish of bacon toward her, but Esther didn't seem to know what it was. He was getting used to her cocking her head to one side inquiringly, and she did that now as she looked from the bacon to him. With a stab of sympathy, he realized she had perhaps never eaten bacon. He had heard of the Larsons' straitened circumstances, and his heart once again went out to the girl who was now his wife.

He picked up a rasher of bacon and proceeded to eat it with relish, licking his lips as he did so. "Ba-con," he said slowly.

He observed Esther's expression as she watched him for a moment before she also reached for a rasher of bacon. Holding it gingerly between her thumb and forefinger, she took the tiniest nibble.

The flavor obviously appealed to her, because she took another nibble and then a large bite. She began to mime her approval, making expansive gestures with her hands and smiling, and Paul felt a sense of satisfaction.

"It's tasty, isn't it?" he replied.

Esther looked at him and blinked. It was obvious she hadn't understood what he had just said.

He nudged the dish of bacon toward her again. "More?" he asked as he gestured to her to help herself, but she shook her head. Then, with a hand to her tummy and a blissful smile, she indicated that she had eaten enough and greatly appreciated the meal.

She is an unusual girl indeed, Paul thought. He could stay there all morning trying to figure out how best to communicate with her, but he had to get to work.

From his position at the table, he could see Sandy and the ranch hands waiting for him to come out and issue the instructions for the day. But how would he leave Esther alone? Was she capable of taking care of herself? Paul sighed and rose from the table. She would have to cope, he decided. There was much to be done, and spring was one of the busiest times of the year.

As he reached for their plates, intending to take them to the sink to wash them, Esther shook her head. She gently eased the plates out of his hands and, carrying them over to the sink, began to wash them. Paul dried the plates and stacked them on the shelf above the sink. Esther was gesturing frantically to him all the while. "I can do all this," her actions seemed to say.

"It's just your first day here," Paul said, immediately sensing Esther's eyes on his lips. "Plenty of time for you to get down to doing housework."

He hung up the cloth he had used to dry the plates and looked into Esther's eyes.

"I have to go to work now," he said. "Will you be alright here by yourself?"

Esther cocked her head to one side and blinked up at him. Paul looked at her and nodded. Then he took his hat from the hook by the door and left the house.

Outside, Sandy and the ranch hands eyed him curiously. Perhaps they had been conjecturing about the nature of his wedding night. He didn't owe them any explanations. He knew they thought he had made a big mistake, and he didn't know yet how he would prove them wrong.

Chapter Seven

After her husband had left, Esther went up to her room, onc hand on the bannister, feeling the vibrations of her footsteps on each stair as she ascended. She paused in the corridor, looking at the door to the room opposite hers. *Who is this man I'm now married to, and how did I come to be in his life so suddenly?* she wondered as she pushed open the door to her room and went inside. All she had for the moment was the name Orton. That was his name. Or one of his names.

She went to the window first and looked out, feeling a sense of comfort in being able to observe some of the activity around the ranch. There were men amongst the horses in the corral and some repairing a barn roof. She liked the view from her window. She could see past the barn and corral to a part of the fence and beyond to the mountains. She hoped she could soon take a walk and pick the wildflowers she had seen on the way to the house. She could just make out the yellow bells, and there were Indian paintbrush and arrowleaf balsamroot.

Esther dragged herself reluctantly away from the window and looked at her things lying in a corner of her room. She had opened the sack in the morning to take out one of her dresses, and now took the other day dress and the one church dress out and hung them in the closet. Then she turned to the box of books, taking each one out carefully and setting it neatly on the bookshelf. She had nine storybooks in all, and after she had arranged them, she sat back on her heels and admired how fine they looked in her new living space. *Grimm's Fairy Tales* was right next to the stories of Hans Christian Anderson and *Aesop's Fables*. There was one book left in the box, and this she removed with special care. It was the *Encyclopedia Britannica*, which had been given to her by the church pastor. He had lent it to her before the accident and never returned to reclaim it after that. She carried it to the bed and sat down, opening it carefully to reveal her journal concealed in a box within the pages.

Within the box were also three pencils and a blade to sharpen them—some of Esther's most prized possessions—and she used these judiciously. The pastor's wife had once taken her under her wing before she lost her hearing. She and two other children used to sit with that good woman twice a week to learn how to write. In her enthusiasm, she had bought each of them some writing materials, and Esther had preserved hers, hiding them away to use for her journal entries. She took them out and looked around for a surface to write on. Seeing there was only the chest of drawers, she set her journal and pencil down on it and began to write while standing up.

Dear diary,

Something miraculous has happened. I am now married to a very kind man. I know nothing about him, except that his name, or surname, is Orton.

Esther set her pencil aside as her hands began to tremble. This was something that happened each time she recalled the events preceding her wedding. She hadn't been able to write about it and in fact had found it difficult to make any entries since her ordeal in the woods. But now she picked up her pencil and resolutely continued to write.

Something bad happened before my wedding, dear diary, when I went to pick flowers in the woods. I cannot write about it, because even thinking about it makes me afraid. The Lord delivered me from the hands of the evil one, and that's why I am here now at Orton's ranch in a very nice bedroom.

I don't want to record what happened to me before the wedding, though I am quite sure I will never forget it. Well, I just think it's better that I don't write about it, because I will only relive that fearful day. Instead, I would rather remind myself of the Lord's promise in Jeremiah 29:11: "'For I know the plans I have for you,' declares the Lord, 'plans to prosper you and not to harm you, plans to give you hope and a future.'"

I would like to tell you about my wedding, which came as a surprise to me. I didn't know that when Mr. Orton (as I will now call him) went down on one knee, he was quite possibly asking for my hand in marriage rather than asking my forgiveness for what took place before that. But then, on the morning of my wedding, Mama brought me a box with a white wedding dress and shoes. I understood that Mr. Orton had sent them over.

The dress is the most beautiful flowing lace dress I have ever seen, feather light and so delicate, like the petals of a wildflower. I wore a veil too, and I felt so blessed to own such exquisite garments. Even the shoes are perfect: made from calf leather and so warm and comfortable. I am wearing them now, as I write, because they are the only pair I own. I hope I don't spoil them, as I will have to wear them to church as well.

There were a few people present at the ceremony, and I do believe that they were the ones who were most curious about why this handsome man was marrying "the laggard." Yes, I am aware they call me that. I've mentioned it before to you, dear diary. It hurts each time, but the more I see it, the more it reminds me that I am indeed not normal at all, nor will I ever be. I am beginning to suspect that there was something the matter with me even before the accident, which is why Mama and Papa never accorded me the kind of care that other parents give to their children. Perhaps I was never deserving of it, being the way that I am.

A part of me felt like it was dying when Mama and Papa rode away in the pony cart after the wedding. I suppose they were quite relieved to be free of having to care for me. I am aware that, being a girl, I must have been quite a burden to them from the time of my birth and most especially after the accident relegated me to the ranks of the cognitively slow. But they are my parents, and I have memories of happy times before the accident. Mama might have felt some regret at having to literally abandon me like that, because I thought I saw tears in her eyes, which she blinked back quickly.

Oh, I had so hoped I would do something to make them proud of me, but I suppose nothing I do will ever change their opinions of me. They will always think—and rightly so—that it is all my fault I was rendered the way I am through that accident ten years ago.

Esther proceeded to describe the house thereafter, her pencil making a scratching sound she didn't hear but that she imagined she did. She read over her entry, then closed the journal and slid it back inside the *Encyclopedia Britannica,* which she placed at the back of her closet.

Drawn by the view from her bedroom window, she decided to go outside and explore her immediate environs. It was a fine day, and Esther was grateful for some sunlight as she walked out into the fresh air. She looked up at the yew trees and Douglas firs that stood by the two sheds at the back of the house. She thought of them as washing sheds, because one had a bathtub and the other had a washboard and basin to wash clothes. Obviously Mister Orton didn't fancy washing clothes or taking a bath outdoors.

She walked around to the side and saw a chicken coop there, perhaps solely to serve the needs of the house. She stepped inside, and the chickens scattered. By the movements of their beaks, she knew they were squawking, and she hoped the sound wouldn't alarm her husband. The kitchen door opened onto the side of the house too. That was where her husband had exited that morning when he'd left for work. A few feet to the right of the house, she saw the entrance to what she presumed must be the root cellar built into a mound and hesitated outside, wondering whether her husband would mind if she took a look at it. The door gave quite easily, and she went inside, marveling at the variety of vegetables and fruits stored in that confined space. She left the root cellar, and her attention was soon diverted to the barn some distance from where she stood, where men were working on the roof. She stood very still, not wishing to draw attention to herself, and then quickly went back indoors when she felt panic set in at being all alone with not one familiar face in sight.

Inside the house once again, Esther explored the living room in greater depth. The previous day, she had merely glanced around, but now she had the time to look for clues that would help her know her husband better. There was a bookshelf in the living room, but apart from a family Bible and a hymn book, there was nothing.

Esther continued to search for clues, and her natural instinct brought her back to the Bible. She hesitantly drew it off the shelf and opened it. It was large and heavy, and she had to seat herself and support its weight on her lap. She ran her finger over the smooth surface of the page she'd turned to at random. It was gilt edged and crisp, as if it was seldom opened and read. She then flipped to the front pages, pausing first at the flyleaf, where she had hoped to see one name—her husband's—but instead, she stared down at an entire genealogy. There were many names, most of them ending with Orton, so Esther knew it was her husband's surname as she had suspected all along. She dragged her forefinger down the column of names and signatures, wondering which of the Ortons at the bottom of the column was her husband. There was a Paul Orton and Luther Orton. Which one of them was she married to? She traced the indentations made by the neatly written letters with the tip of her forefinger as if she hoped that in doing so, she would get some indication of her husband's name.

The next page consisted of marriages in the family. Once again, Esther hurried down the columns to the end and saw that on a date two years ago, someone had married a certain Angela Mary Stowe. Esther's forehead wrinkled as she tried to see which of them it was, but the names were smudged, perhaps with water—or tears. Esther sighed. Try as she did, she couldn't decipher which Orton was—or had been—married.

She turned the page to see a record of deaths in the Orton family. There seemed to be so many, and Esther eagerly began to read through them one by one. But suddenly her eyes, out of habit, flew to the clock, and she realized, with a start, that it would soon be lunchtime and she had done nothing except potter around the house all day.

Esther closed the Bible, leaving the column of deceased Ortons for another day. It was more than a little depressing to be sitting in the living room amongst so much history of a family she had married into but didn't know at all.

Esther looked at the clock again. *It would be nice to give Mr. Orton a surprise by preparing him a meal,* she thought, finding her way to the kitchen. She would make him beans and potatoes, she decided, both of which she found easily. There were cans of beans on a shelf by the stove and potatoes in a wicker basket on the side.

Esther had never actually used a stove, because her mother had never allowed her too close. One time she had tried to get close to stir some vegetables that were about to burn, as her mother had stepped out of the kitchen for a minute to fetch a pan holder. When she returned, Esther had seen her lips trembling and her hands shaking as she pushed her away and indicated she must never again get that close. Thus, Esther had developed a strange outlook on cooking—aware it was supposed to be the woman's job, yet also aware she was never allowed to perform this task if it involved a stove.

Esther sighed. At least it was relatively simple to heat up canned beans—once she got the stove started, of course. She had opened cans before, and this was not too difficult either once she found the can opener in the sideboard drawer. She had noticed the sideboard that morning as she sat down to breakfast with her husband and admired the patterns on the china plates displayed on it.

She pulled open the drawers and saw they contained silverware, paring knives, and steak knives. She took out knives, forks, and spoons and laid the table with two plates from the sideboard, aware that time was slipping away from her and she needed to get started on the meal.

She quickly tipped the beans into a saucepan and looked doubtfully at the stove with the wood and kindling next to it. The stove itself looked sparkling clean and was obviously one of the best available. She could tell from its streamlined design and enamel finish. Someone, perhaps Mr. Orton himself, had taken pains to scrub the enamel backsplash clean. She could see her reflection in it when she bent down to check if there were any embers left from stoking the stove for their morning meal. Seeing that there were none, she cleared out the ash removal tray, and then she straightened up and stared at the burners. There were four in all, so she could put the beans on one and the potatoes on another. She wished she had more to cook so she could use the other two burners as well. They might look desolate without something bubbling away on top of them.

Esther felt a surge of hope as she washed and peeled the potatoes and set them in a pan of water on the front burner. She also felt a surge of apprehension at lighting the stove, but she so desperately wanted to show her appreciation of her husband's kindness in rescuing her and giving her a new life that she was willing to take a risk and do something she had no prior experience of.

She stared at the wood for a while, trying to gauge how much to put into the firebox, and decided more was better than less, so she packed the wood in firmly, almost to the top. She needed to speed up the process, because another glance at the clock showed her that her husband would be back anytime. So she struck a match and lit the wood. When the wood didn't catch fire immediately, she piled on some more kindling. Then she tried again. This time she managed to start a small flame. She fanned it and watched it spread, then shut the firebox.

Esther smiled to herself as she imagined how happy her husband, Mr. Orton, would be to find a hot meal waiting for him when he returned tired from work. She would sit him down and serve it to him, and he would look up at her and give her one of those smiles that made her heart beat faster. All she desired at that moment was for someone to think she was worth the trouble. She had been a disappointment to her parents, and she wanted to work as hard as she could not to be a disappointment to this man who had been courageous enough to take a chance on her.

So caught up in her thoughts was she that Esther didn't notice the wood was burning with greater ferocity than was either normal or necessary. The roar of the flames couldn't penetrate her wall of silence, and her attention was wholly on the potatoes, which she had put on the stove to boil using the last of the water from the kettle. So, when the kitchen began to fill with smoke, and the glass door of the firebox—perhaps because it had not been closed securely enough—burst open, Esther was caught unawares. For one thing, the sound of the firebox as it burst open was lost to her. For another, she was so engrossed in her thoughts that she only noticed the fire in the stove was out of control when she saw a flare from the corner of her eye. She couldn't understand how she had missed that pungent smell of smoke. Or maybe she had smelled the smoke and just assumed it was as normal as all the other times she smelled smoke when a cookstove was on.

Panic-stricken, Esther ran this way and that, realizing too late she had used all the water in the kettle, and there was no water to douse the flames unless she went outside and pumped it. She frantically looked for a bucket, and finding none, ran out the kitchen door to search for the water pump. The breeze blew through the open door and fanned the flames, and soon they were licking the lip of the firebox and rising higher.

Meanwhile, Esther was outside, running hither and thither, looking for the water pump, which she then found right by the kitchen door. There was a bucket under it, and she set about filling it with water, all the while casting her eyes in dismay at the smoke-filled kitchen.

Smoke billowed out of the windows as Esther ran back into the kitchen, shielding her eyes with the sleeve of her dress, and fought the fire. It seemed to have spilled out of the firebox and was curling up around the stove. Her eyes burned, and the smoke caught in her throat and filled her lungs, and still she threw water on the stove, running out again to fill the bucket. She failed to see that each time she opened the kitchen door, the breeze blew in and fanned the flames, and when she returned with the water, she had to begin her task of reducing the flames all over again. And so it was that the blaze was now out of hand, and there was little she could do to control it.

Chapter Eight

Paul looked up at Sandy and the ranch hands branding their newly acquired heads of cattle. They had worked steadily all morning, and there was still a ways to go.

"What's up boss?" Sandy asked. "You look a little concerned."

"Just wondering when we'll get finished with this task, Sandy," Paul replied. "We have only two men working on the fence repairs, and we will soon need to relieve some of you from this task so you can join in securing the fence. We don't want coyotes breaking in and going for our new calves . . . or the lambs in the corral over yonder, for that matter."

"True," Sandy said, nodding in agreement. "You sure there's nothing else bothering you?"

Paul shook his head, not willing to admit his thoughts kept returning to Esther alone in the homestead. He wondered if she was safe. Somehow the remark he'd made about the coyote and the calves and lambs made him think of her all the more, and a restlessness came over him. Over the years, Paul had developed very sharp instincts, and now they were telling him that something wasn't right. He needed to go home and check on Esther.

He ignored his hunch for all of a minute before he dropped the branding iron he was holding and called out to Sandy.

"I think I'll just go check on home," he said. "Take care of things here, will you?"

"Sure thing, boss," Sandy replied, not looking up as he worked.

Raider was tethered to a tree just outside the fenced-off area where they kept the cattle. Paul sprang up on him and drove his spurs into his side. He could feel it in his gut even stronger now. Something was very wrong.

He galloped toward the homestead and was still at least a few hundred yards away when he saw the smoke pouring out from the kitchen. "Giddyap!" he cried, spurring Raider on to a flying gallop, feeling a sharp stab of fear pierce his heart. He shouted Esther's name as he brought Raider to a quick and sudden halt, leapt off, and threw the reins over his back. Sprinting the last few feet toward the house, he saw some of his men already there, standing helplessly by and staring at the smoke.

"What happened?" Paul shouted to the men.

"We were working on the barn roof when we saw the smoke and came over as quickly as we could," one of them shouted, stopping to gasp for air. "But we can't find a bucket!"

"Where's my wife?" Paul cried, momentarily frozen with fear. Seeing the bewilderment on the men's faces, Paul rolled up his sleeves and plunged into the kitchen, feeling a wall of heat rise up to meet him. One thought was at the forefront of his mind: God was angry with him, and like he'd taken his first wife, he was going to take Esther. *There is no winning with my Maker,* he thought, feeling the urge to cry out, "What did I do wrong, God?"

Instead, he pulled his shirt over his head to shield his eyes, lowering it every little while as he searched the thick mist of smoke for Esther.

"Esther!" he shouted, realizing with a sense of hopelessness that she wouldn't hear him, locked as she was in some world of her own.

And then he saw her lying on the floor, clutching the handle of a bucket. She had fallen near the kitchen table, but mercifully the flames from the stove were surging upward and not toward her.

"Esther!" Paul cried again. "Oh, Esther!" He picked her up and ran outside.

"Watch her while I go back inside!" he shouted. "One of you come with me and grab the bucket that's on the floor. Fill it with water and get back here quick!"

The men found the bucket Esther had been using when she passed out. They filled it with water and raced back inside to throw the contents onto the fire. As the fire seethed and hissed, they went back and forth, filling the bucket and tossing water onto the blaze.

Paul saw that his men had the situation under control and sped back outside to Esther. She was sitting up now, coughing and spluttering, and Paul rushed to her side, alarmed. Her beautiful skin was marred by soot through which her tears were making tracks. Her hair had come loose from her braid and clung to her cheeks, glued there by tears, perspiration, and flecks of ash. It was evident she had labored long and hard. Her reddened eyes were filled with fear, and her body trembled. As Paul picked her up and carried her to the tap, he gazed down into her face, whispering words of reassurance. He knew she couldn't hear him, but he hoped she would feel the words of comfort he was speaking to her.

Cupping his hand under the faucet as he worked the pump, he got Esther to drink some water and then bathed her face. Touching her cheeks, he was disturbed by how hot they were. She was weeping in distress, the tears mingling with the water he gently drizzled onto her skin. He held her close in his arms, wiping her tears and washing away the soot. At that moment, he felt more protective toward her than he had to any living creature, human or otherwise. As she clung to him weeping, he stroked her hair.

The men were emerging from the kitchen, and Paul reluctantly moved away from Esther. He wanted to keep holding her, but he had to go and acknowledge the men's efforts at putting out the fire. After they left, he went back into the kitchen, but first he laid his hand on Esther's shoulder. "I'll be back in a minute," he said, looking her full in the face and only leaving after he got a nod of assent from her.

Gauging the circumstances that must have led up to the fire, Paul realized that Esther must have been trying to cook a meal. There were potatoes in one pan and beans in another, now burned by the sheer heat of the stove. But the miracle was that the walls hadn't caught the flames. Even the furniture remained untouched. The smoke had been more profuse than the fire. Or Esther must have fought the flames from the first moment she found that they had gotten out of hand.

"You are one brave, brave girl, Esther," Paul whispered to himself.

He returned to the spot by the tap where Esther still sat on the ground, her head in her hands.

"Esther," he began, "you don't need to do any of the cooking around here. I'll do it all. I just want you to be safe."

He was waiting for her to respond, when, through the mists of confusion, he realized he was waiting in vain. He gave himself a mental slap on the cheek. Obviously Esther wouldn't understand a word he'd said, so he moved closer until she sensed his presence and raised her head to look at him. Then, through a series of gestures, pointing to his mouth, miming the stirring of a pot and carving of meat, he conveyed to his wife that she needn't bother with trying to prepare meals. He was used to it, and he would cook for both of them.

As he continued to mime while speaking, Paul noticed Esther's eyes on his lips. While this made his heart race as it always did, he also wondered if he had conveyed some message other than the one he intended. *Have I confused her?* he wondered. But then he looked into Esther's eyes and saw the light of understanding in them. She nodded slowly and pointed to herself and then to her head. "I understand," the gesture seemed to say, or at least Paul hoped that was what Esther meant. If she had indeed understood, this might be a significant breakthrough for them, and he wouldn't have to wonder how to communicate with her. He would just have to get better at it.

Paul saw Esther start and look straight ahead, and he turned to follow the direction of her gaze to see Sandy riding up.

"I smelled smoke!" Sandy exclaimed. "What happened?"

"Nothing much. Just a little cooking accident, but everything is fine now," Paul replied, not wishing to acknowledge the gravity of the situation lest Esther somehow discern what he was saying and be alarmed or mortified.

"A cooking accident?" Sandy queried, looking at Esther curiously.

"Don't worry about it, Sandy," Paul said firmly. Then, changing his mind about not going further into the subject, he stepped away from Esther and took Sandy aside.

"This is all my fault," Paul declared miserably, raking his fingers through his hair.

"You're covered in soot, Paul. What's going on?" Sandy asked.

"Esther must have been trying to cook a meal and may have misjudged the amount of kindling to be loaded into the firebox," Paul answered. He put his hand on Sandy's arm and lowered his voice.

"Look, I should never have left Esther alone so soon. And I should never have expected her to figure things out in my absence. It's far too much of a burden to lay on such delicate shoulders." He began to pace. "I honestly feared I may have lost her," he said with a gasp.

"I'm confused. What really happened here,?" Sandy asked.

"She could have died in that fire," Paul said, his voice ragged. "That's what really happened. Esther—she is trembling, frightened— shattered. She had passed out on the kitchen floor, Sandy, and when I saw her, I thought—I thought . . . ."

"So it was as serious as I feared," Sandy murmured.

"It is serious," Paul said. "I'm trying not to think about what could have happened, and I'm trying to acknowledge what did happen, which is that Esther is safe and the damage to the kitchen is minimal. But I can't do this to her. It's not fair. I can't risk her going through another ordeal of this nature, because it could cause her immense harm. I need to look out for her—more closely, if you know what I mean."

"What are you trying to say?" Sandy asked.

"I'm going to have to leave you to handle things for a while. Maybe for the next week or two, while I stay close to the house. I'll take care of the stables and oversee the corrals and everything that doesn't require me to move farther than a few feet away from the house," Paul replied. "It's important I ensure that Esther is safe whilst on her own, and that can only happen if I teach her how." He raked his fingers through his hair again. "For instance, all this would never have happened if I had taken the trouble to either teach Esther how to use the stove or warn her against using it when she was alone. There are so many things that can go wrong, Sandy. I'm afraid even to think of them, much less talk of them."

"Of course, Paul," Sandy said. "Do whatever you feel you need to. The men and I are here to get the jobs done around the ranch."

Paul gave Sandy a grateful smile as the latter mounted his horse, tipped his hat to Esther, and rode away.

"Would you like to take a bath?" Paul asked Esther, pointing to the tap and miming the act of pouring water on himself.

Esther nodded and stood up, but Paul motioned for her to sit down on the step again while he got a bath ready for her. He would heat water over a wood fire outdoors and fill the wooden bathtub in the bathing shed. That might be relaxing for her after her ordeal. But he had also noticed that her dress was ruined. He'd observed her staring at it in dismay. The ripped hem she must have stumbled and tripped on, the soot that had permeated the very pores of the fabric in a way that might make it impossible for the dress to ever be restored to a wearable condition.

Paul began an internal battle. There was a closet full of dresses that would very likely fit Esther, and he had noticed that the potato sack of clothes she had brought were few and inadequate. He couldn't bear to look at Angie's clothes, but perhaps now was as good a time as any to give at least a couple of her dresses away. With a sigh of relief, he also realized that Esther couldn't ask questions about where the dresses had come from.

It took a while for him to fetch the kindling and pile it up, set a match to it and then fan the flames. He did it behind the house, lest the sight of the fire bring back to Esther the horrors of her recent ordeal. When the tub was full, Paul returned to the steps, where Esther still sat, staring into the distance. He signaled to her that he would be back, and then, thrusting his chin forward determinedly, he ran up the stairs to his room. There were two closets there: one his and one Angie's. He pulled open the one that had belonged to his late wife and took out a simple blue linen dress with a white collar and frills on the cuffs. *This will do,* he thought, quelling the ache he always felt when he thought of his wife. He was grateful there were a few dresses in the closet she had never worn. This was one of them.

"I have a clean dress for you to wear," Paul said to Esther, handing her the dress and pointing to the bathing shed. "There are towels there, as you must have noticed," he added. Esther looked at his hands and his face as he mimed, but mostly she kept going back to his lips as if she was trying to glean something from them.

"For me?" Esther's seemed to ask, pointing to the dress and then to herself and cocking her head to one side.

"Yes," Paul said, nodding vigorously. "For you. Put it on after your bath." He mimed the act of wearing something by pulling it over his head, and he was gratified to see the hint of a smile through Esther's teary, sooty face.

He went back indoors to give her some privacy. While she bathed, he washed the kitchen and wiped down the walls, once again marveling at the fact that the damage wasn't worse. He tossed out the charred food and emptied the burned wood and ash from the firebox. It took a while to clean the stove because his men had poured so much water on it to cool it down. He was glad they had, but he had quite a job on his hands to dry it out. He brought in some more kindling from the pile of wood outside the kitchen and stacked the firebox once the stove was no longer waterlogged. Then he set about cooking a fresh batch of beans and set it on the table with some bread.

Anxious at why Esther was taking so long, Paul went to the kitchen window and looked out. He could just about see the bathing shed from where he was standing and watched as Esther emerged, clad in the blue dress from Angie's closet. Paul swallowed the lump in his throat as he saw not Angie's dress on Esther but Esther in a dress that sat so well on her it could have been made especially for her.

She was drying her wet hair. Paul observed how her movements were perfectly coordinated as she finger-combed her long tresses flowing down to below her waist. She looked up at the sky as she did so, perhaps with the hope that the sun would be strong enough to dry her hair. She turned just then, and Paul stepped away from the window, but he couldn't help glancing at her one more time. She looked so beautiful and ethereal—like an angel caught in a shaft of sunlight. He caught his breath as his eyes caressed her from a distance, and his heart softened and unfolded just a little bit more.

Was Esther really as slow as people made her out to be? She seemed capable of bathing and dressing and taking care of herself. Then he looked at the stove, still fresh with the memory of how close Esther had come to suffering grave harm. *No*, Paul thought. *Esther is not entirely capable of taking care of herself.* The sight of her lying helpless on the floor, clutching the handle of the pail, returned to him with startling and poignant clarity, and Paul felt choked with emotion. He hoped she hadn't suffered any lingering damage from the smoke. On an impulse, he picked up the dish of beans and bread and set them on a tray along with two plates and forks.

Stepping outside the kitchen, Paul walked over to Esther.

"We could eat outside under the trees," he said, pointing to the tray he balanced on his left hand, the trees farther away, and his mouth.

"Like a picnic," he added, but Esther appeared not to understand him.

"Come," he said, holding the tray aloft and beckoning to her.

Still shaking out the water from her locks, she followed.

When they reached a shady yew tree, Paul stopped and set the tray down on the grass. And that was when Esther smiled up at him. It was not just a polite smile but one of complete delight in that simple activity.

She spread her dress out around her and sat down, eagerly reaching for a plate. She served him first, then helped herself. And then she did something he had all but forgotten to do since all the tragedy he had suffered. She folded her hands and looked up at the sky, and Paul knew Esther was saying grace. She didn't make a sound, but her eyes were filled with the most serene light.

At that moment, he wished he could feel what she was feeling. Her face reflected such love for and trust in the Lord above. Perhaps she was thanking Him for more than the food. Perhaps she was grateful to be alive after her ordeal in the kitchen.

Esther closed her eyes briefly, then opened them and looked straight at him, and Paul nodded to her. They shared a smile, and Paul felt his heart melt within him. Esther pointed to his plate and, in mime, urged him to eat. He ate a forkful of beans and paused, savoring the flavor as if for the first time, relishing the sweetness and saltiness of the sauce and the softness of the beans as he bit into them. How long it had been since he had actually sat out under the trees voluntarily and done something as carefree as have a picnic, he mused.

Chapter Nine

Esther woke up. Dawn was just breaking, and she lingered in bed for a while, thinking back to her ordeal with the kitchen stove. A week had gone by, and the memory of that day brought back so many mixed emotions. She felt great remorse at not having been able to cook her husband a meal and even greater shame at failing him by almost setting the whole kitchen on fire. When she thought about the smoke and the fire leaping out of the firebox, she went cold with fear at what could have happened.

Her thoughts settled on that surprise meal under the yew tree, the way her husband had held her as she wept, and when he'd found her on the kitchen floor and carried her outside. She could still taste his skin as he gave her water to drink from his cupped hand and still feel his gentleness as he stroked her hair to comfort her. Her thoughts then drifted to the blue dress he had given her to wear. It didn't seem to have been previously worn, so could he have bought her some new clothes that he was going to give her eventually? Or had the dress belonged to someone else who once lived here? It fit her almost perfectly, Esther mused.

Mr. Orton had been more attentive to her since that day. He had been spending time teaching her new things around the ranch, like how to milk cows. He had even laughed with her when she splashed milk all over herself the very first time. She hadn't revealed to him that she was afraid of the cows and hoped she would conquer her fear before he noticed how nervous she was around them. But the thing Esther wanted him to teach her, he didn't—or hadn't yet, anyway. She so badly wanted to learn how to cook so she could finally feel like she was taking care of him just as he was taking care of her. But

Instead, he had conveyed to her that she mustn't go near the stove and that he would do all the cooking.

What grown woman doesn't cook? Esther asked herself. It was quite obvious from his instructions to her that he didn't think of her as responsible. In fact, she had noticed he wasn't going any farther than the corrals and would ride back several times a day to check on her. She had tried to show him just how capable she was, rising earlier than he did so as to pack more chores into her day.

She got out of bed, washed, changed out of her nightgown, and made her bed. Then she knelt down by the window and thanked God for the day. Getting to her feet, she brushed and braided her hair and then went downstairs. Her first chore was to gather the eggs from the chicken coop, clean it up, and scatter the feed. Once that was done, she went to the dairy shed by the barn. She hadn't known it was there until her husband had showed it to her after the fire. She entered the shed with her shoulders squared and a determined look on her face. She would not be afraid of the cows. She had to prove to Mr. Orton that he had not taken a chance on her in vain. As it was, she felt like she had let him down by not being knowledgeable enough about using a woodstove.

She leaned in and began to milk the cow, relieved as the milk splashed into the pail. She was getting better at this, but her fingers still felt sore, and her back ached a little from the strain. She milked the second cow and then the third and eyed the full pails with a sense of pride and accomplishment.

She took the milk indoors and set the covered pails in the kitchen. She would wait for the cream to form and then churn butter, but for now, there were other things to do.

She glanced at the clock. It was just after half past five in the morning. She knew Mr. Orton would be coming down the stairs any time now, and she waited by the staircase with her hand on the bannister so she would feel the vibrations. The moment he began to descend the stairs, Esther smoothed her hair down, returned to the kitchen, and prepared to greet him. He always nodded politely to her and then went straight out to the stables. She couldn't touch the stove, but she could pour him a glass of milk, and this she did using a dipper. He gave her an indulgent smile, and Esther watched him as he quaffed the milk and set the glass down by the sink. She hoped he hadn't drunk it only to please her. She hoped that by giving it to him, she was pleasing him. All she wanted was to make her husband think well of her.

She watched as he set his hat on his head and nodded to her, and she responded. This was his time to go clean the stables and groom the horses. Esther wished he would take her with him. He had told her the stables were cleaned twice a day and suggested he clean them in the morning and she later in the day.

He had been there the first time, when he showed her how to go about the job, and she had trembled when she was near the horses because she had never been that close to them before. But Mr. Orton had patiently coaxed her not to be afraid. She'd prayed continuously in her mind as she'd gone about this task. She had so wished they could do this chore together, but Mr. Orton seemed keen that she learn to be alone in the stables.

With a sigh, she fetched the broom and dustpan from the broom closet under the stairs and began to sweep the house.

It seemed to have been a while since the house was thoroughly cleaned. There were cobwebs in the rafters and dust lodged in stray corners. Esther attached a broom to a long pole she'd found outdoors, tying them together with some twine from a kitchen drawer, and cleared the cobwebs off the rafters. Then she set about dusting every item of furniture, once again struck by the empty bookshelves, devoid of books. She had hoped Mr. Orton would have some books she could read, but it was apparent he didn't value them as much as she did.

Esther lingered by the family Bible, dusting it carefully. Then, irresistibly drawn to probe for more details about her husband, she read through the genealogy on the flyleaf again and turned the page to the list of deaths. A shadow came over her as she went down the column, because she felt as if she was entering forbidden territory. If her husband wanted her to know about his family, he would have shown her the Bible. But then, he was also aware of her reputation for being cognitively slow, so that might have prevented him from doing so, she reasoned.

She was looking down the list of deaths when suddenly a name jumped out at her: Angela Mary Orton née Stowe. She quickly turned back to the list of marriages, sighing in exasperation as she beheld the smudged names yet again, and realized she would never know which Orton had suffered such a tragedy. And was one of the two names at the end of the list given in the genealogy her husband's?

Sighing, she put the Bible back and continued with her chores for the day. She still had to clean the rooms upstairs. She tramped up the stairs, mentally going over all the chores she had yet to get through, and found herself between her room and her husband's. She hadn't had the courage to go inside Mr. Orton's room to clean, but she wanted to do something to make him happy, so she resolutely pushed open the door.

Pausing on the threshold, Esther looked around her husband's room with a sense of regret. It wasn't familiar territory to her, and she felt like an interloper. She first noticed the very large four-poster bed and blushed as she visualized Mr. Orton lying asleep in the very center of it. She also observed that his bed was neatly made, but as she hadn't seen his sheets in the washtub since she'd arrived, she intended to strip his bed and lay on some fresh bed linens. Her eyes next went to the two closets in the room. *Mr. Orton must have a lot of things to store in such large closets*, Esther thought. She turned away, feeling guilty at the fact that she was in a place where she perhaps ought not to be. She walked over to the dresser and looked down to see a lady's comb and brush. Perhaps Mr. Orton's mother had once lived in the house, Esther mused, and maybe this used to be her room. Maybe Mr. Orton used to sleep in the room opposite, which was now hers. It made sense, since her room was smaller than this one.

Esther sighed and shrugged. There was so much she didn't know, and she wondered how and when she would be able to learn more about her husband. Right now, however, there was work to be done, so she picked up her cleaning implements.

The cobwebs came down first, and then Esther decided to change the bedsheets. She stripped the bed, tossed the sheets onto a chair, and began to sweep out the room. *I will do the most thorough job I can,* she told herself. She was down on her knees, sweeping under the bed, when her broom made contact with something. Closer inspection revealed a wooden chest. It was smaller than the one in the living room, but she found it quite heavy when she moved it aside to reach the accumulated dust with her broom.

Eventually Esther ceased trying to nudge the wooden chest this way and that in order to get what looked like months of dust out from under the bed. Instead, she drew it out. It wasn't locked, she realized, so she lifted the lid and looked inside. The contents made her smile with delight, and she sat back on her heels and inspected each object one by one. They were toys, handcrafted from wood and uniquely beautiful. She began to dust them, completely absorbed in her task until she felt the floor vibrate. She could tell it was a footfall, and she turned around, a smile on her face, happy her husband would see she was getting his room in order. But Mr. Orton looked far from happy. In fact, it appeared he was barely able to conceal his displeasure.

Esther was holding a delicately carved horse, lovingly cradled in her hand, when her husband strode forward. She found herself rooted to the spot as she observed Mr. Orton's features: his eyebrows drawn together in a furious scowl; his lips pursed and trembling with ostensive suppressed rage; his nostrils flared, tense and white; his head shaking from side to side; and his hands pointing to her, to the toy in her hand, and to the box as he tried to convey what he wanted her to do.

Esther's eyes filled with tears, and she choked back a sob as she quickly put the toy horse back into the wooden chest. She felt the floor vibrate again and looked up at her husband. He had moved quickly to the door and was holding it open, gesturing for her to leave. Esther jumped to her feet, hastily picking up the broom and dustpan. She mimed that she wished to finish cleaning and to at least make his bed and sweep the fallen cobwebs off the floor, but Mr. Orton was adamant. He wanted her out immediately.

As Esther exited the room, she tried to mime an apology, but the door was shut so firmly in her face that she jumped back even as the floor vibrated. The closed door and the expression on Mr. Orton's face caused Esther more pain than she thought she could ever feel. She ran into her room, shutting the door behind her and crumpling up into a heap on the floor, sobbing uncontrollably. First she had almost set the house on fire, and now she had obviously trespassed on some forbidden territory that had incurred her husband's extreme wrath. *I am foolish*, she thought. She was definitely cognitively slow, because any normal person would never make the dreadful mistakes she had. How could she ever have thought she'd be able to make a man like Mr. Orton happy? She was only here because he was making good for what his brother had done to her. And he was probably already regretting his gesture after all the blunders she had made.

She got off the floor and went to her closet, reaching for her journal concealed in the *Encyclopedia Britannica*. She needed to talk to somebody who would help her figure out where she was going wrong, but the only confidante she had just then was her diary. She carried it over to the chest of drawers along with her pencil, and standing up, began to write in her clear, rounded hand. But her hand trembled as her body shook with her sobs, and the letters were not rounded but going in different directions. *Almost like my life is at this moment,* Esther thought.

Dear diary,

I feel so foolish. I wanted so badly to please Mr. Orton that I took a risk and went where I was not supposed to be. I should have been more respectful. It is obvious that even though we are married, I am never meant to cross an unspoken, unwritten line. Only the Lord knows my heart and how all that I wanted to do was to please him by cleaning his room. I should never have opened that box I found under his bed. I acted more out of curiosity and less out of a desire to dust the beautifully carved wooden animals resting in the box. There was a pony cart too, but I didn't get to admire it in greater detail. The animals were so realistically formed and so obviously crafted with a loving hand. But as I held them, I wondered why they were there, under Mr. Orton's bed, and whom they belong to. I was trying to solve a mystery I had no right to. So I was rightfully punished and banished from my husband's room, where I had never been before, even to clean. I thought the time was right, but I was wrong. I should never have been so presumptuous as to think that someone like me could ever belong to the world of someone like him. I am, and always will be, cognitively slow. I accept that now. If I were normal, I wouldn't make the mistakes that I continue to make. But was it a mistake to dust the toys? Whose toys were they? Did they belong to Mr. Orton, perhaps, when he was a child? But they looked new and unused.

How I wish there was more that I knew about the man I am married to. Everything seems like a mystery I have to unravel, and sometimes it makes me feel like I am in a strange world where I cannot make any choices for myself but must go along with whatever is decided for me.

I will never forget how furious Mr. Orton was. His anger was tangible. It made me afraid. When he asked me to leave the room, I felt like I always did when Mama and Papa shut me away because people came to visit our home—like an outcast, someone not wanted because they are displeasing to the eye or in some way terribly flawed. I feel regretful at this turn of events and the change in Mr. Orton's attitude toward me. From the day he rescued me, I have always looked upon him as my hero and one who can do no wrong. He has been so kind to me. I can never forget the touch of his hand on my hair after the fire or the way he looked into my eyes when we ate together under the trees. I hoped that he might feel for me what the prince in "Cinderella" felt for her. I know my heart beats faster when he walks into a room, but today I wish my heart would stop because I cannot take the pain of his rejection.

I have chores to complete, so perhaps I had better get back to them or I will fail in yet another thing. I will wait long enough for Mr. Orton to return to his work, and then I will go *downstairs and carry on with cleaning the house. I don't think I can face him again. What should I do? I can't hide in my room forever.*

Setting down her pencil, Esther folded her hands and prayed for strength, and through the silence came the words from Isaiah 41:10. "Fear not, for I am with you; fear not, for I am your God; I will strengthen you, I will help you, I will uphold you with my righteous right hand."

As Esther put her journal away, she felt comforted by the words of Scripture that had come to her mind. Even if she couldn't hear people speak, at least she could hear the voice of God. *And that is all that matters,* she thought.

She picked up the broom and dustpan lying on the floor and cleaned her own room. Then she made her bed and took her clothes downstairs to wash.

She had noticed that Mr. Orton would leave his clothes in a pail by the washing shed and get to them whenever he could. Esther hoped he wouldn't be angry with her for laundering them for him. She just wanted to be useful. In the shed was a large wooden tub and a washboard, with a cake of lye soap next to it. Esther filled a bucket of water from the pump by the kitchen and carried it to the tub. The water was cold. Shivering slightly, she scrubbed the clothes and put them back in the bucket. She then carried them to the washing line she had seen suspended between two yew trees toward the back of the house.

The previous day's washing was still hanging there, and Esther took down the dry clothes and hung up the newly washed ones. While folding her husband's clothes, she felt a sudden surge of tenderness toward him. There were stitches coming apart near a collar and a rip in his trousers. Esther was good at sewing and darning clothes, having helped her mother with the task on numerous occasions. But with no needle, thread, or scissors, she didn't know how she would be able to mend her husband's clothes.

She knew she would have to look for these items and that the search for them might cause her husband to once again suspect her of snooping. Her hands trembled. She never wanted to incur his wrath again. Even now, the memory of that door closing in her face made her weep.

Esther carried the dried clothes inside, entering the house through the kitchen door, casting a regretful look at the stove. She reminded herself of how an out-of-control fire was the reason why she had felt the comfort of her husband's arms for the first and only time. There was a movement behind her, and she turned around, startled, and found herself face-to-face with the object of her thoughts. She dropped her gaze, but he laid a hand on her arm, and she was forced to look up into his face. Before he could speak, though, she stalled him by holding up the clothes that needed mending. She mimed the act of sewing and then looked all around as if searching for something.

Her husband nodded. Then he went to the sideboard and pointed to the top shelf, above the display of china plates. Esther looked up. A sewing basket was there. He took it off the shelf and placed it in her hands, and Esther set it on the kitchen table along with the clothes. Then she folded her hands in contrition, attempting to ask pardon for her mistakes. "I wasn't thinking," her actions said, as she pointed to herself and then to her head and mimed the act of dusting the toys.

Her husband's eyes glistened, as if with tears, and he looked desperately sad. Then he took her hands in both of his and said something. Esther looked from his eyes to his eyebrows—now raised, now coming together—to his mouth working furiously in an attempt to communicate with her. Then he said one word she hoped she wasn't misreading. It was "sorry."

Chapter Ten

The day after he had found Esther in his room, Paul watched her sit down at the kitchen table with the sewing basket and his clothes. Bowed over her work, so intent on placing delicate stitches in the fabric of his shirt and trousers, she didn't seem even close to what people made her out to be. He sighed. She was an enigma to him.

He walked out of the house, returning to the corral where he and his men were gauging the market readiness of some cattle. It was close to the homestead, so he felt more comfortable leaving Esther on her own. He still felt mortified at his behavior the previous day and wondered how he could communicate to Esther that he hadn't meant to be so unfeeling toward her.

"What's up, Paul?" Sandy asked. "You have the look of a man who is struggling under the weight he is carrying."

Paul shrugged as he stroked the flank of the heifer he was inspecting. "I am feeling the weight of great guilt, Sandy," he replied.

"Why? Is this something to do with Esther?" Sandy queried. "I don't mean to pry, so you don't have to reply to that question," he added hurriedly.

"It is," Paul answered. "I was insensitive to Esther yesterday. And it was uncalled for." He heaved a deep sigh. "But she was there in my room, crouched on the floor with a broom and a dustpan. She had been cleaning, and I didn't even acknowledge that act of kindness. Instead, I just showed her how angry I was at her being in my room."

"I'm confused," Sandy remarked. "You can talk to me, Paul. We've been friends for so long."

"And you've been a good friend, Sandy." Paul nodded, leaning over to run his hand over the heifer's head. "You remember those toys I had made for . . . my, um . . . child?" Paul began.

"Yes," Sandy replied. "I most certainly do. They were so beautifully made."

"Well, I had hidden the box containing them under my bed. Esther was there yesterday morning—obviously doing a thorough job of cleaning the room— but she had opened the box and was dusting the toys," Paul said.

Paul saw that Sandy was giving him a look of mingled pity and confusion.

"I shouldn't have subjected her to my disapproval when she was acting in all innocence," Paul murmured.

"But you did?" Sandy asked.

Paul nodded. "I did. And then the next thing I heard was the sound of her weeping in her bedroom. It broke my heart. But I was steeped in self-pity too. Thinking of how unfair life has been for me these past years. And now this—a precipitous marriage to a young girl with the reputation of being cognitively slow."

"Except that I suspect Esther is not slow at all, Paul," Sandy said.

"I see what you mean," Paul replied. "I have been observing her, and she is so good at what she knows how to do. Like mending my clothes, for instance, or milking the cows after I taught her how."

"Well, what I observed goes back to the day you brought Esther home. That box with her books . . . remember that?" Sandy replied.

Paul frowned, as if trying to make a connection with what Sandy was trying to convey. "I remember it," he replied.

"When I tried to get it off the buckboard, Esther wouldn't let me. She wanted to carry the box herself. It's apparent she values them."

"They obviously mean something to her," Paul remarked.

Sandy shrugged. "It's not just that they mean something to her as objects. She obviously reads, and that's why she values them."

"I have thought about that, Sandy, but discounted the possibility of her being able to read . . . because of her reputation for being . . . well . . . cognitively slow, I suppose," Paul replied.

"Paul, I am sure you too have your doubts about that," Sandy declared. "Esther doesn't act like she is slow. If you ask me, she is brighter than most. But there is some disability she may have that prevents her from understanding what we are saying when we speak. She struggles to

127

comprehend speech, but when she mimes, she does so with intelligence and thought. A slow person wouldn't be able to do that."

Paul sighed. "I see your point, Sandy," he said. "I just wish I knew more about the woman I am married to."

He felt his friend's hand on his shoulder. "You have been preoccupied with adjusting to this new situation in your life, so I don't fault you, Paul," Sandy replied. "But maybe you should've done what I've been doing. I've been making some enquiries about Esther in town. I heard she used to be quite normal at one time. A loner, but normal. Until she was caught in a blast at the armory store. She happened to be in the lane, but nobody knows why. A mere little girl of perhaps ten years old, all by herself in the most dangerous part of the town. And that's when she changed. That's also when everyone changed in their attitude toward her."

Paul was incredulous. "You found all that out? From whom?"

"I met the pastor after church on Sunday. He asked where you were and why your wife wasn't attending services."

Paul felt a stab of guilt. "I should have made sure that Esther went—even if it was without me," he said.

"Really? And risk her having barbed remarks thrown at her when she's all alone and without any way to defend herself?" Sandy asked, aghast.

Paul knew what Sandy was saying was right. "I'll go to church with her. Just give me some time to get right with God," he murmured.

"Go to church and get right with God there, my friend," Sandy said.

"You were talking about meeting the pastor after church. Did he tell you about Esther's past?"

"Yes, he did," Sandy replied. "I'm surprised you never thought to ask him about her."

"I honestly thought I knew all there was to know about her," Paul replied, overcome by guilt at the realization that Sandy appeared to care more about Esther's welfare than he did. "Though I have actually been learning a lot about her abilities since we got married. She takes care of so many chores around the house, but I never questioned how somebody who is called slow could actually accomplish all that she manages to in a day."

"If you want my advice," Sandy said, "find out what Esther's disability really is. In my opinion, it is not what people say it is."

Paul went through the rest of his time in the corral deep in thought. Even as he inspected cattle and conversed with the ranch hands, he turned over in his mind the conversation that he had had with Sandy. More than anything, he felt a deep sense of regret that he hadn't shown more sensitivity toward his wife. Rescuing her was one thing. But to bring her to his home and not be more attentive or vigilant to her needs was enough evidence that he had fallen short. First Luther, and now Esther. He was responsible for both and hadn't been able to take care of either of them. It was because of his negligence that Esther had suffered the fire, and Luther had taken so many wrong turns that he had to be sent away. Paul bit down on his lower lip so hard it all but bled. He was a failure and had let down all the people who depended on him. He needed to be more vigilant with Esther than he had been with Luther.

That evening, he returned to the homestead, stopping on the way to check the dairy shed and the stables. He found that Esther had already been in, cleaned the stalls, and filled the horses' water troughs.

He stood in silence now, surveying her handwork, realizing it must have taken tremendous courage on his wife's part to even enter the stables because she was still quite nervous of the horses and hadn't yet established a connection with any of them. He saw in this gesture a great desire on her part to prove she wasn't afraid to go out of her way to do something she deemed pleasing to him. And this made him feel even more repentant about the manner he had adopted toward her the previous morning. He recalled how she had trembled when he had taken her into the stables and shown her how to clean them. But she had courageously done what was required of her. Now he needed to do what was required of him and take better care of her.

He wanted to do something special for her this time. And then it struck him. Maybe the most special thing he could do for Esther wasn't a material gift but something more valuable—like his time and attention. So he went into the house and looked for her. She was seated on the porch, reading her Bible. He watched her for a while, thinking how fine she looked in the new blue dress he had given her to wear. His heart beat just a little faster as he watched her. It was only after he sat down on one of the chairs that she turned toward him enquiringly. He observed her eyes. They were so keen and had such depth. He felt humbled beneath her gaze, repentant and eager to please her.

"What are you reading?" Paul mimed, curious to see if Esther really could read.

"David and Abigail." Esther pointed out their names in the Bible.

"Tell me the story," Paul asked, pointing to the Bible, himself, and then to Esther's lips.

Her eyes shone. She set the Bible down and stood up. And then, most eloquently, Esther enacted the story for Paul entirely in mime. Paul was transfixed. Even if he hadn't been familiar with the story, he would have learned it just from the way Esther related it through actions and movements. How clearly he could see Abigail going to meet David and his men with food and other provisions her own husband had denied them. How beautifully Esther mimed how Abigail's husband, Nabal, died after a night of revelry and how David took her as his wife. How fluid and graceful were Esther's movements, Paul mused, looking at her in amazement. This girl couldn't be slow. Oh no, she was intelligent. And she could definitely read.

"Tell me more," Paul asked when Esther came to the end of David and Abigail's story.

So she enacted for him the story of Esther in the Bible. She communicated to Paul through actions that she was inspired by her namesake, that Esther was a woman, yet she was courageous, and God used her for a great purpose.

Paul watched Esther convey her thoughts action by action and felt overcome by admiration for her profound faith in a God he had come to only feel anger toward. He wished so desperately to have even a fraction of that simple faith Esther had. He yearned for that peace he'd once had before Angie and his firstborn had died. He wanted what Esther had, that serenity and love for God. He was almost convinced now that she was reading the stories in the Bible. She was pointing to them and relating them. Maybe she had marked them out somehow, he mused. But whether she was actually reading them or not, two things were certain. Each story had made an impact on her, and she was passionate about her faith.

Paul was staring so hard at Esther as he tried to understand this dimension of her personality he almost missed that she was trying to ask him a question. She had opened the Bible to the book of Esther. She was pointing to the name and then to herself. Her eyes were eager as she pointed to him and then held her right hand palm upward, drawing her ring finger and little finger toward the center of her palm. He realized she was asking him what his name was. He took the Bible from her and turned to the New Testament and found the book of Acts. Then he pointed out his name there.

Esther's eyes widened, and she smiled. She pointed to Paul's name in the Bible and then to him. He nodded and managed a half smile. But even as his eyes returned to the story of his namesake, he felt like God was putting him on the spot as he'd done when Saul the persecutor was thrown off his horse and confronted with a blinding light through which the voice of Jesus asked why he was persecuting him.

Saul was blinded by a light, Paul mused. He looked at his wife and blinked. Sandy had told him she had been caught in a blast near the armory store. He knew what happened when explosives were ignited. Was there a blinding flash when the blast took place? Or was there a deafening sound? Paul stared at Esther, the word "deafening" resounding in his mind. Could the deafening sound have rendered his wife hearing-impaired? Suddenly it didn't matter whether she couldn't hear or couldn't speak. She was stirring up feelings in him that had been dormant for so long. On an impulse, he reached out and touched her hair, then ran his forefinger gently down her cheek.

Esther looked at him, her eyes soft and dewy and her cheeks stained pink. He apologized for staring at her the way he had been, though he knew she couldn't understand what he was saying. Or maybe she could . . . if she could hear?

"I'll go and get supper ready, shall I?" Paul said. Esther's eyes wandered to his lips, and he felt his pulse quicken. *She is so innocent and her beauty so fresh,* he thought. But when she looked at him like that, he became aware of her as a woman. He became acutely aware of her proximity and the fact that she was his wife. And even as she looked at his lips, he looked at hers, noticing how full they were and how they trembled ever so slightly with some hidden emotion.

Esther closed her Bible and stood up. It seemed like she was trying to convey something to him. He got to his feet too, and they walked to the kitchen together. She set the table while he cooked. Occasionally his eyes would stray to her as she helped peel potatoes or stir a pot on the stove—when he gave her permission to—and he was struck by her quiet intensity. She made each task she performed seem like an act of worship because of the way she approached it. He almost wondered if she was praying as she stood there by the stove, because of the look of serenity on her face.

They ate supper in companionable silence, and then Esther picked up their plates and the dishes and proceeded to wash up. Paul watched her, wishing he could render a more fitting and complete apology for his behavior. Somehow all the words he had tried to say fell short. He needed a better way to show Esther how sorry he was. He had denied her the simple act of enjoying the toys he had caught her so lovingly dusting. He would give them to her to show her that she was more important than the toys. So he went up to his room and fetched them.

Esther was drying the dishes, and he feared she might drop the one in her hand when she saw him walk into the kitchen with the wooden chest that had caused so much heartache the previous day. He set it on the table and motioned for her to sit down. When she did, he tried to tell her his story, but she couldn't seem to follow. Instead, she became uncomfortable, perhaps misunderstanding his gesture and thinking he was chastising her. Her lips began to tremble, and Paul feared Esther was about to burst into tears. When she stood up and tried to leave the room, he jumped up and drew her back to her chair once again.

"I made these toys," he said eventually, and her brow cleared. She gazed intently at him as he pointed to himself and to the toys and mimed the act of chiseling. He held out the horse she had been holding in her hand that morning.

"This is for you," he said. "One day I will teach you how to ride one of these."

He saw Esther's head lean to one side as she looked questioningly up at him. Paul repeated what he was trying to convey.

"For me?" Esther mimed, pointing to the toy horse and then to herself.

Paul nodded.

But she shook her head, not taking the toy from his hand, and Paul realized whatever had happened the day before had left a scar and that the toy horse might possibly open up the wound. He returned it to the box and then placed the box at the very center of the table. He wanted to remind himself that at some point he would have to tell Esther about his wife who had passed away.

Chapter Eleven

Esther came inside from her morning chores, and her gaze was drawn to the wooden box of toys in the middle of the dining table. She wasn't sure what Paul Orton was trying to convey by setting the box down there. Paul . . . She had turned his name over and over in her mind. Finally, she knew what her husband was called. It made her feel like she was a step closer to learning about the man she had married. So far he was a mystery to her. She didn't know where he had come from so suddenly that morning in the woods, and she didn't know why he had chosen to marry her.

She was tempted to open the box and look at the carved wooden horse. It was so perfect, she thought. She bit her lip and silently chastised herself for refusing to take it from him when he had offered it to her. But she thought he was only giving it to her because of that morning when he had been so upset she was holding it. She knew it was ungracious of her to refuse such a lovely gift, but she wanted to be absolutely certain he really wanted her to have it. She also felt undeserving of it.

Her gaze went to the stove. There were now two reminders in the kitchen that she had fallen short as a wife. Esther heaved a deep sigh, tearing her eyes away from both the stove and the wooden box in the center of the table. All she wanted was to be a good wife to him. She so longed to have him hold her again the way he had after the fire. Within his arms she had felt protected and safe in a way she never had before. She had also felt a warmth and comfort she couldn't describe.

She went up to her room and knelt down to pray. She thanked God for delivering her through many snares and trials and prayed that Paul might one day truly look upon her as his wife and not just regard her with pity. Then she reached for her Bible and opened it to the passage that had been speaking to her heart. It was the story of David and Abigail in 1 Samuel 25. She began to relate to Abigail, so suddenly bound to David in marriage because of her husband's inexplicable death. How good David was to marry her just to save her from the ignominy of widowhood. And how courageous was Abigail to bring food and drink to David's men when her husband had denied them hospitality.

Esther looked at David as an exemplary man. He was brave and strong. He had fought and killed Goliath to protect the people of Israel. He had battled wild animals with his bare hands to protect his flocks. He had entered into a marriage to protect Abigail. Esther looked up from her Bible and thought of her own husband. He was like David. He'd married her to protect her from shame and humiliation. She wished she could reciprocate his kindness one day.

Esther put her Bible away and went downstairs to resume her household chores. Paul was already in the kitchen, preparing breakfast, and Esther felt embarrassed she wasn't standing at the hob instead of him. She wished she could ask him to give her another chance.

Paul greeted her. Esther smiled at him. Though she couldn't interpret what he had just said, from the way he had smiled and nodded, she guessed he must have wished her a good morning.

"You've done a wonderful job cleaning out the stables," Paul continued. Esther gazed intently at his lips. She wanted to get better at understanding him. It was the least she could do. Paul turned fully toward her, and she fixed her eyes on his lips. She could make out the word "stable."

On an impulse, she reached for the wooden box and opened it. Taking out the figure of the horse, she mimed the act of grooming it. She pointed to Paul and then to herself and requested he teach her how to groom a horse. He had conveyed to her his wish that she learn to ride one. He had also urged her not to be afraid of going alone into the stables. After the way he had stroked her cheek and her hair the previous night, she wanted to please him so he might repeat that gesture. It had made her feel cherished, and she wanted so badly to feel that way again.

She met his gaze unblinkingly. This was important. She would be courageous, like Abigail. He was her David, and she wanted to do whatever she could for him.

Paul smiled, pausing in the act of stirring a pot of oatmeal, and nodded. He pointed to himself, then to her, and then to the horse and mimed the act of brushing down a horse.

"After breakfast?" Esther mimed, and put the toy horse back into its box.

Paul nodded as he placed the pan of porridge on the table.

Esther sprang forward and ladled some of the porridge into a bowl and set it down on the table, motioning for Paul to sit down and eat. Then she served herself and sat down opposite him. They ate in silence. The porridge was good and healthy, and Esther appreciated how her husband always made sure he fed her with nutritious food. She stole a glance at him. He appeared to be wrapped up in his own thoughts, perhaps preoccupied with ranch business, Esther thought. If only she could take on more of the work, she could truly be a helpmate to him.

When they finished eating, Esther washed the bowls and put them away, then looked expectantly at her husband. Paul put his hat on and gestured to her to follow him, and her heart leapt. She was nervous of horses, but she would conquer her fear today for him.

As they entered the stables, Paul turned to Esther.

"It's never—spotlessly—in here," he said. "And it's—thanks—you."

Esther didn't understand every word Paul had said, but by the way he was looking around, his eyebrows raised and a smile of appreciation on his face, she could gather she had pleased him with her efforts at cleaning out the stables. She was so blessed to have such a handsome husband. She sometimes wished she could touch his hair the way he had touched hers. She liked how it fell on either side of his face and how it blew away from his face when teased by a breeze. How gentle were his eyes, how strong his hands.

Paul went into the first stall and drew the horse out. Esther quickly fetched the grooming brushes and handed them to Paul, but he shook his head.

"No. You need to make friends with the horse first," he said, pointing to her, then to the horse and clasping his hands together. Esther had never had a friend, so she was excited to make one. But she wasn't so certain how she would go about becoming friends with a horse. Still, if Paul said she needed to be friends with the horse, then she would make every possible effort just to see him smile at her.

She quaked inside but smiled outwardly.

Paul signaled for her to come closer. He stroked the horse's muzzle and then invited Esther to do the same.

Esther knew how large a horse's teeth were, but she swallowed her fear of being attacked and went closer to the animal. This was a chestnut mare, and Esther vaguely remembered it had pulled the buckboard on the day of her wedding to Paul.

"She's gentle," Paul reassured her, miming as he spoke. She didn't understand what he was saying at first, but when he had repeated the words a few times, she did.

Esther extended her hand hesitantly and was surprised when Paul took it in his. Laying his hand over hers, he guided her toward the mare. Esther felt the blood creep into her cheeks at Paul's touch and proximity. She held her breath so long she thought she might pass out. So afraid was she to even breathe and thus shatter the moment.

Paul moved her hand onto the mare's muzzle. And ever so tenderly, he guided her hand to stroke the mare. Esther didn't want her husband to take his hand off hers, yet she wanted to prove to him she could do this on her own. He was so close to her that she could feel his breath on her cheek, and she remembered how he had stroked her hair as he held her when she wept after the fire and touched her cheek out on the porch.

Paul said something. Esther felt his breath in her hair as he spoke and turned to face him, her eyes on his lips. She saw his face redden, and his hand, on hers, shook ever so slightly.

"Honeycomb," he enunciated carefully, and Esther watched his lips move. She nodded and turned back to the mare. Paul took his hand off hers, and she continued to stroke the mare—Honeycomb—though missing the warmth of his hand on hers.

Esther had read about people feeding horses with carrots and sugar, and she resolved to go down to the root cellar to see what she could find there for Honeycomb. She picked up a brush and looked enquiringly at Paul.

"This is how you do it," he said, taking the brush from her. Esther watched him closely, gauging how much pressure he used and which direction he drew the brush in.

When he held out the brush to her, she took it, more confident now, and began to brush down the horse. It was harder than it looked, and Esther realized just how much effort it would take to groom even one of these splendid animals.

"You—to groom—all," Paul said, pointing to all the stalls.

Esther nodded, understanding that Paul was telling her she could groom all the horses.

"I'll just—and—out—the corral," Paul said. Esther could make out "corral" from the shape Paul's lips took when he said the word, but she knew he was riding Raider out there because Paul drew the horse out of his stall and went off with him.

Esther finished grooming Honeycomb and then moved to the next stall, little realizing it held the mustang Paul had rescued from the mountains. This was the only stall that had a name on the door. Written on a sliver of tree bark pinned to the stall was the name Typhoon. *Obviously this is a special horse,* Esther thought.

She approached it with some caution because it was bigger than Honeycomb, but she wanted to impress Paul with her skills at grooming. Before she could make friendly overtures to the horse, however, it surprised her by coming forward and nuzzling her shoulder. Esther stood absolutely still, petrified, and backed away. She looked up at the horse hesitantly, afraid to meet its eyes, but forced herself to while praying for courage. Taking a deep breath, she then reached up and stroked his muzzle. The horse nuzzled her once more, and again Esther felt a surge of fear, which she quickly suppressed. She backed away, but the horse nuzzled her again. *Maybe Typhoon is hungry,* Esther thought as she fetched the grooming brush and began to brush him down. She would fetch him some carrots later perhaps.

She was standing just inside the horse's stall when she felt a gust of breeze and turned around, sensing that somebody had entered. It was Sandy.

"Oh my!" he exclaimed. Esther was staring straight at him, so she caught both the words formed by his pale lips. She also observed that Sandy had turned white at the sight of her with the horse and there was something akin to terror on his face.

"Step away, Esther," he said. Esther looked at him, and her brows came together in confusion. She didn't understand. She saw him waving to her to come away, but his actions were restrained, like someone who was making a desperate attempt not to upset the atmosphere.

Esther shrugged, turned back to the horse, and continued to brush it but was aware of Sandy's anxious presence. *Why is he even here?* she wondered. Had Paul sent him to check up on her because he had gotten held up with work at the corral?

Just then she felt the wooden floor vibrate. She recognized her husband's footsteps, and she turned away from the horse to look at him. Paul had gone white, and his hand was raised in warning.

"Come away, Esther," he said, repeating Sandy's words.

Esther's eyebrows went up inquiringly when she saw the two men looking at each other, panic-stricken. She wasn't sure why they wanted her to leave the horse alone—if that was what they wanted her to do—when Paul had only a short while ago told her to groom all the horses. Was she doing something wrong? This was confusing. But she was not one to leave a job half-done. She wanted to please Paul at all costs, so she turned back and continued to groom Typhoon.

She felt a hand on her shoulder and turned around to see Paul right behind her. Taking her shoulder, he eased her out of the horse's stall and shut the door. He had broken into a sweat, and he dragged the back of his hand over his brow.

"What's wrong?" Esther mimed.

"He's a mountain mustang," Paul replied, but Esther didn't follow what he was saying.

She began to mime another question when Paul took her hands and looked her directly in the eye.

"That horse isn't fully tame. He can be dangerous," he said. And then he repeated the words.

Esther saw Sandy leaning against the wall, looking as if he had just dodged a bullet.

"I'm okay," Esther mimed, looking at Paul. "I like this horse. And I'm not afraid of him."

Paul took Esther by the arm and led her out of the stables. Something about his demeanor reminded her of the day he had found her holding the box of toys. her spirits plummeted. She may have displeased her husband again through no fault of her own.

"You're very brave, Esther," Paul said, looking her full in the face so that she was able to follow every curve and movement of his lips. "But that horse is still considered wild. He's not a normal horse."

Esther shrugged. "Like me?" she mimed, pointing to herself.

She saw a flicker of surprise in Paul's eyes. He was obviously taken aback by her question. But even as she asked it, she wondered how her husband perceived her. Did he think of her also as not being normal? Had he always considered her different?

"Let me take care of that horse, please," she mimed, but Paul took her by the shoulders and stared intently into her eyes.

"It's too soon," he said. "You need to get used to the horses before you can take care of them."

But something about that wild horse had touched Esther. And the horse clearly felt some connection with her; that had to be why he'd kept nuzzling her. She felt a connection too, because Typhoon had helped her overcome her fear of horses by being so kind to her. She had one friend on the ranch now—an animal who saw her as a kindred spirit—and she wasn't about to let that go.

But Paul was adamant, so Esther bowed her head and left the stables.

Back in the house, she fixed a broom onto the end of a long pole and set to work removing the cobwebs in the rooms upstairs. She cleaned the corridor ceiling and the rafters in her bedroom but avoided going into Paul's room. She was in the corridor when she spied some cobwebs she must have missed on the ceiling and was probing the corners to get all the dust and dirt off when the ceiling appeared to give way.

Esther clapped her hand over her mouth, afraid of what fresh problem she had caused. But the anxiety gave way to curiosity when she saw that her broom was pushing against a trapdoor of some sort. It blended into the ceiling so seamlessly that she hadn't noticed it before. And it was giving way now because this was the first time she was cleaning the cobwebs off that section of the ceiling. She pushed it farther upward and a rope ladder detached itself from the trapdoor and fell invitingly down before her.

Esther stared at it, reminded of the ladder that came down from heaven to the stone where Jacob had once slept. He had encountered God at that time. What was she going to encounter? Intrigued, Esther tested the step ladder to see if it would hold her weight, and then, without a second thought, she climbed up.

Emerging at the top through the trapdoor, Esther found herself in an attic with a single closed window, which let some light through. Her eyes grew wide with wonder as she looked about her. There were mysterious-looking chests and unused furniture. But everything faded into the background when Esther saw, right in the middle of the attic, a heap of books.

She leapt on these like someone who had been on a long quest for treasure and just discovered a pile of gold. To her, there was no bigger treasure than books. She picked them up, one by one, dusting them off and looking inside of them. There were the plays of William Shakespeare, the works of Oliver Goldsmith and Jonathan Swift, and the poetry of John Milton, amongst others. A whole new world of reading pleasure was opening up to her, and she felt a surge of unbridled joy. She brushed the accumulated dust off with the palm of her hand and lovingly turned the pages of each book.

So the Orton family did read. But why were these books hidden away?

Chapter Twelve

Paul took his hat off as he emerged from the stables and pushed his hair back, taking a deep breath as he did so. After Esther had left the stables, he couldn't help replaying a fearful scenario where Typhoon hadn't been as tolerant of her ministrations and thrown her life into peril, as he had one of the ranch hands. Paul's blood ran cold at the thought. Typhoon was still regarded as unpredictable, since he had reared up and almost thrown over that unfortunate young boy who had made an attempt to mount him. He hadn't realized just how protective he had become of his wife until that moment and shook his head in disbelief when he recalled how she had asked to take care of Typhoon.

"Whew," Sandy said, following Paul, "that was one of the most frightening moments we've had recently!"

"Yes," Paul agreed. "Unless you count the kitchen fire as far more dangerous."

He began to rake hay as if his life depended on it.

"I wish I knew what to make of her," he said, his eyes on the tines of the rake working through the hay. *If only it was as simple to work through life's problems,* he thought as he spoke.

"What do you mean?" Sandy asked.

"You know . . . Esther," Paul replied. "There was something about her expression when she was interacting with

Typhoon. I introduced her to Honeycomb just a while before that and didn't see that expression as when she was ministering to Typhoon."

"I didn't see fear, that's for sure," Sandy remarked, baling the hay as Paul raked it up into tidy piles to be taken into the horses' stalls later.

"Exactly," Paul declared. "In fact, what I saw was empathy . . . or understanding." He paused. "True, I was only observing her profile, but even then, I could see that she did have a bond with that horse."

"Like you did," Sandy said matter-of-factly.

"I guess you could say that," Paul murmured. "I just don't know what to do. I'm afraid to let Esther take any risks. But I can tell she's eager to cook by that expression of longing that comes over her face when she's watching me prepare a meal. And she made it clear just now that she wants to take care of Typhoon."

"So why are you stopping her?" Sandy asked.

"You know why. It's dangerous," Paul replied. "The stove—and Typhoon—could both cause her harm . . . and I couldn't live with that."

"Pardon me, boss," Sandy said. "I may be speaking out of turn here, but I trust a person's instincts. Especially in relation to a horse the likes of Typhoon. Sure, I also reacted as you did. I was petrified. But maybe it's time to trust your instincts rather than react out of fear. I think it may be worth your while to let your wife have her way with this one. And with the cooking too. Perhaps if you show her how to stack the firebox, she won't start a fire the next time."

"I know, Sandy," Paul replied. "We've talked about this before. Now all that remains is for me to let go of the fear. I sure would like to see Esther happy. I just hope she's not insisting on caring for Typhoon out of a desire to please me . . . like with that attempt at cooking."

"There's no harm in a wife trying to please her husband—or the other way around, Paul," Sandy remarked sagely. "I see you trying to please Esther, so why not allow her some opportunities to please you?" He paused and appeared to be deep in thought. "Though in the case of Typhoon, I don't think it's to please you. It's something more than that."

"She asked me, using actions, if I thought Typhoon was different . . . like she was," Paul commented. "Well, actually I said Typhoon was different, and then she pointed to herself and her eyes asked the question. Now I understand that Esther has always been made to feel different from everybody else, and I haven't helped matters by being so protective of her . . . . So maybe she just feels like they are kindred spirits."

"Well, I hope you figure that out soon," Sandy said, beginning to walk away. "I can see that your wife has you quite distracted."

"I think she has me more amazed than distracted, to be honest," Paul remarked, looking up at the sky, his eyes misty as he thought of Esther. He turned to Sandy. "You know, she is so capable and hardworking. She has been taking on more than her share of chores and doing a remarkable job. She seems tireless and keeps going all day. And if she isn't doing chores, then she is reading her Bible as if her life depended on it."

He stopped talking as he saw Sandy staring at him with a strange look in his eye.

"I'm sorry," he said. "I've been talking on and on, and there's work to get done."

Sandy gave him an understanding smile and doffed his hat. "You're right, boss, there's work to get done. I'd better get back to the cattle corral now."

After Sandy rode away, Paul returned to the stable and stood by Typhoon's stall, reaching out to stroke the mustang's muzzle. He had broken him in and had ensured he was not a danger to anyone. And he wasn't—just as long as Paul was the only one handling him. Recently he had even become accustomed to Sandy grooming and riding him but had also thrown a ranch hand who had attempted to mount him. As Paul gazed up into the horse's expressive eyes, the image of Esther looking up at Typhoon returned. She had seemed captivated, mesmerized. And there was something else he beheld in her. It was peace. He couldn't very well deny Esther everything she wanted. She could end up feeling like a prisoner, and that was the last thing he wanted. He would offer to teach her how to ride, he decided—perhaps on Honeycomb, and then she could help take care of Typhoon.

Paul felt more at peace as he exited the stable and walked over to the tree where he had left Raider. As he rode back to the homestead, he wondered what Esther was doing. She had looked so injured when he had denied her request to care for

Typhoon and had walked away soon after. He hoped she wasn't crying and that he hadn't appeared unduly harsh. Even as he began to worry about Esther's feelings, he felt resentment creep into his musings. Had God really punished him for not being more vigilant of Luther? Was his punishment to live the rest of his life with someone like Esther whom he couldn't even trust around a simple woodstove?

Paul was riding Raider at a trot, unconsciously delaying the moment he had to face Esther again and see that look of hurt and bewilderment in her eyes. He was beginning to feel things for her he hadn't thought possible, but he still felt the need to hold on to his pain over losing Angie and their child. It was as if he didn't feel worthy enough to ever be happy again. He cried out to God silently, but there seemed to be a wall between him and his Maker. That wall was making him hard, Paul realized, and he was afraid that he would lose himself in his pain altogether.

As he arrived at the homestead, Paul tied Raider to a hitching post at the back of the house. He would stable him later after the day's work was done.

"Esther!" he called out, entering the house through the kitchen door, and then bit his lip. He was so distracted from the events of the morning he had forgotten his wife didn't, or couldn't, respond to spoken words. He needed to find her. He was already in the kitchen, fearfully looking in the direction of the stove, but Esther wasn't there. He looked in the living room and the dining room and then stepped out onto the porch. He listened for any sounds, but heard none, not even the rustle of pages or the swish of a broom.

Panic building up within him, Paul sprinted up the stairs and went straight to Esther's room. The door was ajar, and she was nowhere in sight. He looked in his room, but she wasn't there either. Had she fled? Had she run away somewhere because she couldn't endure living like a prisoner anymore? And then he saw the ladder hanging from the trapdoor in the corridor ceiling.

Paul looked up, his mouth working furiously, beset by a surge of different emotions. "Why are you there?" he shouted, secure in the knowledge that he could roar out loud and she wouldn't react. "Why do you always go where you aren't supposed to?"

He mounted the ladder with his heart hammering against his ribs and his body trembling with suppressed anger. Emerging through the trapdoor, Paul saw Esther seated in the middle of a pile of books. She appeared to be lost in one of them, with an expression of great peace and contentment on her face. At first glance, Paul felt mingled pain and rage. Those were Angie's books, which he had hidden away in the attic because the mere sight of them caused him to weep uncontrollably. Angie had been an avid reader, and her books were her treasures. This was not Esther's place. How had she even come upon the attic?

He began to hyperventilate, and all at once, as Esther became aware of his presence; she turned to face him. Through the diffused light from the single small window, Paul saw Esther glance up at him with joy. But then, perceiving that he was far from pleased, she rose to her knees and gave him a look that expressed her contrition while pleading with him not to banish her from that spot. Paul was at war with his emotions as he looked at his wife clutching a book and silently beseeching him to allow her the privilege to enjoy something she appeared to love. Paul had to ask himself what Angie would want—both for him and for Esther. Angie would want peace between them. She would also want somebody to appreciate the books she had loved so much. As Esther continued to gaze anxiously at Paul, his features relaxed, and though he couldn't summon a smile, he managed a nod of assent.

Esther sank back onto the floor again and drew the book she was holding against her heart. Then she gestured to the books surrounding her and asked Paul, in mime, to whom they belonged. Paul shrugged. He didn't want to reply. He just wasn't ready to explain his past to Esther. To talk about Angie would be to open up a deeply personal part of himself, and he didn't feel like the time was right to do that. He and Esther still barely knew each other.

He nodded reassuringly at Esther, concealing his displeasure beneath a smile. He would not reveal to her that he was upset at her exploring the attic without his permission and would leave her to enjoy the few pleasures life gave her. Moments later she followed, carrying a book along with her. She held it out to him. It was *The Canterbury Tales* by Geoffrey Chaucer. Paul seldom or never read. That was something Angie had done, and now Esther.

Esther nodded her approval of the book as she offered it to him to read, but he didn't want to hold anything that had belonged to Angie. He backed away, shaking his head, and Esther looked at him in confusion. He was upset with himself for his behavior. Those were just books. Yes, they had belonged to his late wife, but at the end of the day, they were just things, he reasoned.

That evening after supper, Esther picked up a lamp and gave him one of her intense looks. He knew that meant she was going to ask him something, and he nodded to indicate that she should go ahead and communicate whatever it was.

Esther held up the lamp and jerked her head upward. Then she set it down on the table and placed her hands together, side by side, turning them up slightly to look like a book.

She was trying to convey to him that she wanted to go up to the attic and spend time amongst the books. He nodded reluctantly because he realized he would miss her company. He had gotten used to watching her sitting by him, reading her Bible. It was strangely comforting that at least one of them was close to God. It reminded him there was a door open for him, and he hoped he hadn't strayed so far that he couldn't find his way back.

Esther smiled, and her whole face was illuminated. She folded her hands and bowed her head. This was her way of saying thank you. It was also her way of apologizing. But it was in the expression in her eyes that he distinguished between the two. A "thank you" was accompanied by a smile. A "sorry" came with a genuine look of contrition and tear-filled eyes. It struck Paul that Esther was too expressive to be cognitively slow. Perhaps her only disability was in her hearing, which led to her inability to speak. He kept going back to what he had learned about her accident, and the dots seemed to connect. An explosion could cause loss of hearing.

Esther left. Paul sat down at the dining table, and his eyes fell on the box of wooden toys lying there in the center. He opened it and took the toys out one by one, lining up the horse, the cow, three pigs, a hen with her chicks, and a duck with her young ones. There was a pony cart too and a barn. He had hand-carved each one for the child Angie had carried. Their child. And now these toys remained a sad memory of what could never be. He put the toys away, remorseful at the way he had treated Esther when he had found her with them. They were husband and wife, for better or worse, and he needed to let her into his life a lot more. He left the table and climbed the stairs to his room. As he closed the door, he heard a sound in the attic above him, and he couldn't help wondering if there was a chance for him and Esther to find happiness together. Perhaps not immediately, but maybe with time?

He left his room and decided to go up to the attic.

"Esther," he said, emerging through the trapdoor and tapping on the wooden floor.

She looked up, and he understood that the vibrations of his actions had made had drawn her attention. Nevertheless, it felt good to say her name. It made their situation more real than it sometimes appeared to be.

He pressed his fingers together in a steeple and then put his hands together to the side of his head and closed his eyes. When he opened them, he saw Esther staring at him with her eyes bright and shining in the lamplight as he mimed for her to hurry. She steepled her fingers and nodded excitedly to him. Paul nodded. He had conveyed to her that she needed to go to sleep, as they had to go to church the next day. And she was excited. He held his hand out for the lantern, and she gave it to him, looking back at the pile of books to pick up the one she was reading. Then she climbed down the ladder after him, clutching *The Canterbury Tales*.

Yes, there was silence in the house, Paul mused, but he was now beginning to hear Esther's heart, and it filled him with a sense of wonder.

Chapter Thirteen

It was with a sense of urgency that Esther ran downstairs to get her chores done. Despite Paul telling her to go to sleep early, she hadn't been able to resist staying up for a while and reading *The Canterbury Tales* in the lamplight.

After she milked the cows, she went to the stables to clean out the stalls, hesitating by the one occupied by Typhoon, the one Sandy and Paul had warned her about. She held her lantern aloft and gazed at the majestic creature, and he whinnied in response. She knew he was making a sound because of the movement of his mouth.

Fearlessly she went into his stall and dragged a shovel through it, then moved on to Honeycomb's stall. She didn't touch either of the horses; she had no wish to incur Paul's displeasure on such a day as this, so she concentrated on filling the water troughs, raking enough hay into each of the stalls, and then, unable to resist it, returned to Typhoon and stroked his muzzle. Not to leave out Honeycomb, she stroked her muzzle too, feeling the warmth. She felt a surge of joy as she left, aware that she had made a connection with the horses and she was no longer afraid of them.

"What time did you wake up?" Paul mimed, pointing at the kitchen clock.

Esther held up four fingers, and Paul's eyebrows shot up. He smiled, and she blushed. She was happy he appeared pleased with her. She liked making him smile.

Esther saw Paul point to the dish of oatmeal and the coffee pot on the table, but she put a hand on her stomach to convey that she didn't feel like eating. Truth be told, she felt like she would choke from the excitement of going out with her husband.

"I insist you eat something," Paul mimed, his expression stern.

Esther heaved a sigh and sat down at the table, unable to eat more than a few spoonfuls of oatmeal and take a few sips of coffee. That done, she quickly washed the dishes and then hurried to her room to get ready.

Back in her bedroom, she took her yellow church dress out of the closet. It was plain and simple, but she was glad her first outing with her husband let her wear such a celebratory color. She had cleaned her shoes the previous night, and she slipped them on now. Then she brushed her hair, braided it, and pinned it up. She saw the door open a crack and raced forward to open it more.

Paul stood there, holding something out to her. It was a cloak, and it appeared to be brand new. Esther gazed up at Paul. The cloak was thick and warm, and it was a rich shade of brown that matched her hair. She folded her hands and smiled her gratitude into his eyes, noting his face seemed slightly flushed and his eyes grew misty as they sought hers. When he reached out and tucked a strand of her hair behind her ears, she caught her breath. Her heart was racing. Her eyes hesitantly sought his as his hand lingered by her ear and then slowly stroked her cheek.

"You are very kind to me," Esther said without words, pointing to Paul's heart and then to herself and hoping he would understand. She wanted him to know just how much she appreciated his goodness.

"You are very kind to me too," he replied, and Esther felt her heart overflow with an unfamiliar emotion. She felt warm and safe as she looked up into her husband's face, noting his strong jaw, expressive eyes, and determined chin. She wished she could draw him. Perhaps when the time was right, she would go into town and purchase some drawing materials and attempt sketching. She used to be good at it at one time, but she had stopped asking her parents for money to buy materials to draw with and stopped sketching altogether. But now, all she wanted was to draw the man standing before her—her rescuer, her husband. She dropped her gaze and could feel blood suffuse her cheeks. She had obviously been staring so hard at Paul that he was giving her a quizzical look.

"Are you ready?" Paul mimed sometime later.

Esther nodded vigorously and followed him down the stairs, stroking her new cloak. As they got onto the buckboard, Esther saw it was hitched to Honeycomb, and she patted the horse before she climbed on. And as they set off and the wind blew against her skin, Esther said a prayer of thanks to God for her cloak and her shoes, recalling how she had once knelt on the forest floor and prayed for them.

It was a half past nine in the morning when they reached the church. Esther looked around her eagerly, recalling that this was the first time she had been anywhere but the ranch since she was married. Paul got off and helped her out, and she waited while he tied the horse to the hitching rail. She looked at the people walking up to the shining white church building and smiled eagerly at them, her smile fading in confusion as they looked away and refused to acknowledge her. One lady crossed herself and moved to the other side of the pathway as if Esther was evil. Tears sprang to her eyes, and she realized that Paul had also noticed how people were treating her because he took her hand and gave it a reassuring squeeze as they walked inside. He didn't let her hand go, and she blinked back her tears, stronger now for having her hand in his.

As she and Paul took their seats in a pew in the center, Esther noticed people who were already seated there moved away, and those who walked in later refused to sit next to them. Even if she was an outcast, it was unfair they regarded Paul as one too. Esther felt torn inside. Was she dragging Paul down? She deserved to be treated like an outcast, because she was. She was different from the others, but Paul wasn't. He deserved so much better. Was she punishing him just by being there? Should she run out of the church now and keep running so that Paul had a chance at a better life with somebody more worthy of such a wonderful husband? She looked uncertainly at the object of her tumultuous thoughts, and he nodded to her as if telling her he didn't care at all about how the people were acting. It was alright with him.

Sandy and his wife walked in with their two children, and Esther was grateful when they slid into the pew next to them. At least they had company. And then Esther saw her parents. They were already seated in one of the front pews and turned to look at her and Paul coldly. Esther smiled at them, but they didn't respond. She crumpled up inside, and her lips puckered. She bit down hard on them. She wasn't going to cry and embarrass Paul any further. But she wanted some acknowledgement from her parents. Seeing them there, she realized she missed them. She turned to Paul again, and he shook his head and shrugged. She kept staring at the back of her parents' heads, and then, on an impulse, she got up and hurried over to them. She could sense Paul reaching out to hold her back, but she moved so quickly that he couldn't do anything to stop her.

"Mama! Papa!" Esther called out to them in her mind while her smile, the pleading look on her face, and her outstretched arms communicated to them that she was pleased to see them. Arnold glared at her, and Bernice waved her back to her seat. This was no place for emotional reunions, her mother's expression conveyed. Esther backed away, feeling lost and alone in the aisle, as she turned around and retraced her steps back to their pew. For the rest of the service, she tried not to notice how people stared at her or how they whispered to each other and the malicious smiles that accompanied the judgmental looks cast her way.

All at once, Esther remembered what her parents had thought of her after she was assaulted in the woods. They had hinted it was all her fault and that she had encouraged her attacker's advances. She felt herself crumble up inside even more, and she looked down at the Bible clutched in her hands. She opened it and saw, through the mists of her unshed tears, the words from Matthew 5:11. "Blessed are you when others revile you and persecute you and utter all kinds of evil against you falsely...."

Esther blinked back her tears and looked at the pastor as he commenced the service. She squared her shoulders and resolved not to look either right or left at any of the people in the pews, including her own parents, but straight in front at the stained-glass window with the scene of the crucifixion, the cross and candles on the altar, and the yellow bells that spilled off the pulpit.

This was all that mattered, Esther realized. She had come to church to encounter God and to give Him thanks and praise. She hadn't come expecting to see her parents or even expecting to gain greater acceptance by the townsfolk. She glanced to her side to look at Paul. He was staring straight ahead of him, his Bible unopened in his hands, and she hoped he would be able to convey to her the contents of the sermon when they went home. But she could sense from the way he clenched and unclenched his hands and the tenseness of his jaw that he was less than comfortable and that he was also, for some reason, quite angry.

Esther was glad when the service was over, and they walked out with Sandy and his family. It felt comforting to have them acknowledge her when even her parents hurried out of the church without so much as a farewell. The pastor stopped Paul as they were leaving and drew him aside to talk with him, beckoning to Esther to follow. Esther stared intently at his lips and the expressions that came and went on his face, and she gauged he was giving Paul some advice. Whether Paul was receiving it well or not was unclear right then.

"What did he say?" Esther queried with her hands as they left the church.

"Those people today," Paul said, "they behaved badly."

Esther looked down at her hands, her fingers so tightly interlaced that her knuckles were going white even as she stared at them.

"It's because of me, isn't it?" she wordlessly asked, pointing to herself and inclining her head. "They treated you badly because of me?" she added, pointing to him, hitting her palm with her fist, and then pointing to herself. At that moment, she wished she could bring herself to write a note to Paul as she wrote to her diary, but long years of staying locked within herself made that impossible. She was a laggard; he wouldn't believe a note from her. She was confined to a life of silence where actions were the only way she would express herself.

They were near the buckboard now, and Paul faced her briefly and shook his head.

"Not your fault," he seemed to say, using words.

"I'm sorry," Esther apologized, joining her hands together in a gesture of contrition as they seated themselves in the buckboard and drove away.

Paul stopped the buckboard when they were just out of view of the church and looked at her full in the face.

"Esther," he said, "please stop doing that. Stop apologizing. This isn't your fault. Nothing is your fault."

Esther felt the tears prick her eyes as she read the words off Paul's lips. She was getting better at interpreting the shapes his lips took when he spoke, though sometimes she missed some because she got lost in staring at his lips and thinking of how perfectly formed they were. She had held her tears in during the service, and she didn't want to cry now. She didn't want her husband to think he had married a weak woman.

"I am sorry I am like this," she mimed, pointing to her head.

Paul looked closely at her. "You are not wrong in your head," he said firmly. Then he repeated the words and mimed them at the same time.

"I think, Esther, that maybe, after the explosion, . . . you can't hear? The pastor thinks so too."

Esther gaped at Paul. He was saying words and miming, but she was confused. She could see what he was saying, but she needed to think about it. However, she was ready to just sit there and stare at him, at his sensual lips and strong hands and feel his reassuring presence.

It appeared that Paul was not going to continue on their journey home without ensuring that she understood everything he was saying, so Esther focused all her attention on him as he explained what he had said one word at a time. Esther concentrated on his lips, his expressions, and his hands. But most of all, she realized she was developing the ability to understand his heart.

Chapter Fourteen

It was an hour to lunch on a summer morning, and Paul and Esther were in the kitchen.

"The kindling goes in here," Paul explained, looking up at Esther as he hunkered down by the stove. "You don't want to overload it. Leave just enough room for the air to circulate and the fire to build to its required strength and not so much that it gets out of control."

He paused, realizing that he was going too fast, but he had indicated the space above the kindling he had just loaded into the firebox, and Esther was nodding. She got down beside him and put her hand inside the firebox to gauge how much she needed to fill it. She was so close that Paul could smell the sweet, fresh fragrance of her hair. All at once, he thought of how much he would like to set her hair free from her braid and watch it flow down her shoulders—almost as much as he wished to set Esther free from the confines of her silence.

As Esther got to her feet, Paul quickly moved away from his musings and concentrated on the job at hand. This was the first time Esther would be cooking, under his supervision, and she was eager to learn how to get it right.

"Now this is how you light the wood," he said, striking a match and holding the flame close to the kindling.

He saw Esther step back involuntarily, and an expression of fear crossed her face. Paul stood up and put his arm around her shoulders to reassure her, noticing their delicate curves.

"See, the wood hasn't caught the flame yet," he said as she turned to look up at him, her eyes on his lips. "Why don't you try this time."

He observed Esther's shoulders tense, but she nodded. Then she took the matches from his hand and struck one. As her hand hesitated by the firebox, Paul gave her shoulder a reassuring squeeze, and she took the flame closer to the wood.

"I'm right here," Paul said, aware she couldn't hear him but nevertheless saying the words out loud so she might feel them.

Moments later, Esther was gesturing in glee as the kindling crackled to life and the firebox began to heat up.

"Now you can cook," Paul said, spreading his arms wide, pointing to the stove top.

To his surprise, when he spread his arms, Esther walked into them and looked up at him, folding her hands in gratitude. He took her folded hands in both of his and looked at them. These were her instruments for communication. These and her beautiful, expressive brown eyes. He stepped back, overcome with emotion and wary of frightening her by any expression of his gradually increasing feelings for her. At first, he had felt merely protective, but now, he felt almost possessive of her.

As he watched Esther cook, Paul's thoughts went back to Angie. He needed to set those memories to rest and make new memories with Esther. It would be difficult to let go of the past. The pain of losing Angie and his child still had an edge, and he knew that if he moved on too quickly, he would get cut anew. But he no longer wanted to feel that Esther, with her disability, was his punishment for neglecting Luther or failing to save the lives of his wife and child.

After his first visit to church with Esther, Paul had felt conflicted. He had been ill at ease in the House of the Lord and felt like the prodigal son returning home. There had been several moments when he wished he could get up and run out the building, but he had to remain by Esther's side.

On that first visit to church with her, it was as if her presence had determined that he remain and listen to the sermon. And it had been about the prodigal son. Paul had felt like the good pastor may have spontaneously decided to speak on a parable Jesus used to describe God's grace and forgiveness toward any black sheep who may have strayed. He felt the message was for him, and that God was speaking to him through it. Yet he wasn't completely ready to forgive himself for Luther's transgressions or to absolve himself of Angie's death and the death of their first child. Esther had been persuasive about returning to church on the subsequent Sunday and thereafter, and though he wrestled with his feelings, he had to admit he was slowly allowing his heart to open to the experience of being in God's presence.

Sitting there while Esther found her way around the stove, Paul could sense she felt liberated. And he experienced an overwhelming desire to be set free from the shackles of his own past. He wanted to shrug off his old self and don the new. Esther turned around, saw his eyes were on her, and smiled, and Paul felt engulfed by a wave of peace. Maybe this was a sign the Lord was giving him that he could move forward and that he was deserving of some happiness.

He smiled as his eyes settled indulgently on his wife. She had been so happy amongst Angie's books. He hadn't yet opened up to her or told her about his past or about the owner of the books. And when she had begged to sleep up in the attic among the books, he thought, at first, that it was a strange request. But she made no demands at all, and he wanted to make her happy, so he not only said she could sleep in the attic, but he had also gone up there and helped her clean it up. It provided an opportunity to get rid of some of the things that had laid there for years and to turn it into quite a charming living space. He painted it for her and put in a bed, a small closet, bookshelves, and a dresser.

She had moved her books up there as well and arranged them on a bookshelf with all of Angie's books. Then she'd gone out to gather armfuls of yellow bells with which she festooned the attic. It became her favorite haunt, and she spent hours there in between chores and meals.

When Paul retired to bed each night, it was comforting to hear her footfalls above him and imagine the expression of wonder on her face as she turned the pages of a book.

Esther had been whittling away at his stubborn decision not to allow her near the stove, and he had relented and shown her that it was easy to stack the firebox and light the kindling when following the proper guidelines. She had blossomed since he had favored her with that act of kindness, and now she was even happier to be cooking a meal for him. He had to admit to himself that he was happy too to have a wife set a hot meal before him and take such delight in doing so.

"The food is ready," Esther signaled a while later, beaming with pride at the pot of beef stew on the table, next to a loaf of bread and ball of butter she had churned herself.

Paul sniffed at the air appreciatively and smiled his approval of the food as he took his place at the table. Esther served him and then sat down, waiting for him to taste what she had cooked. Paul obligingly took a spoonful of the stew and nodded at her. The beef and vegetables were tender, and there was just the right amount of salt. "This is very good!" he said slowly, feeling his pulse quicken as Esther stared at his lips and then gave him a beaming smile. He glanced guiltily out of the window, thinking of all that needed to get done around the ranch, yet here he was enjoying lunch with his wife.

He looked at Esther and saw she was eagerly watching him eat. He smiled at her again as their eyes met across the table and thought how much better he knew her since the wedding. The seasons had changed, and as spring gave way to summer, Paul felt a shift in his relationship with Esther. They were learning how to understand each other and were communicating more effectively.

He was so lost in his wife's eyes Paul didn't hear the first faint rumble of thunder. When his ears caught the second rumble, he jumped up from the table and rushed over to the window. Almost immediately there was a rapping on the kitchen door, and Sandy rushed into the kitchen, not waiting for someone to open the door.

"It's a thunderstorm, isn't it?" Paul asked, noticing the kitchen was now dark enough to require a lamp. He hurried to light one, but Sandy stopped him.

"Yes, I just wanted to alert you," Sandy replied, nodding to Esther, who pointed at the dish of stew and motioned for him to sit down and eat. He shook his head politely and pointed out the window.

"Let's not alarm her," Paul said. "She needn't worry about wildfires unless she has to."

But Esther had left the table and was standing by the window, looking out. Paul was uncertain how to react as she turned around and looked at him enquiringly. The skies were rapidly becoming more overcast, something they hadn't noticed before because they were so absorbed in the meal and in each other.

A violent flash of lightning forked through the clouds, and Paul looked anxiously at Esther and then outside. He was torn because he knew he would have to get to the corrals quickly and help the men. Summer storms in Springford, Montana, were often dry, but the lightning would sometimes cause wildfires, which could be dangerous.

"I'll join you in a minute, Sandy," Paul said. "Send one of the men to scout the periphery to ensure no wildfires have been set off by the lightning. Tell them to fill buckets of water from the creek—however many buckets they can find on the ranch. Just hurry! I'll explain the situation to Esther and then come out to help you all with the cattle." He paused. "Actually, I'll head to the stables first. The cattle will be fine in the corral. I'm concerned about the horses bolting."

"I've got some of the men herding the sheep out of the pasture and into the pen," Sandy said, holding his hat down on his head as he left the kitchen. "I'll get to the cattle and make sure they're alright."

"I have to go out to the stables," Paul said, turning to Esther and enunciating his words carefully while pointing to the section of sky visible through the kitchen window.

"I'm coming with you," Esther seemed to convey, pointing to herself and then to him.

Paul shook his head in reply, but Esther folded her hands pleadingly.

He didn't want to endanger her life in any way—she could get struck by lightning or trampled by a panicked horse or bull, amongst other things—so he began to shake his head again, but the next thunderclap made up his mind for him. He couldn't stay there arguing with Esther, and neither did he want to be separated from her at a time like this. So he took her hand, and they ran outside.

The breeze had gathered intensity and whistled through the trees while the sky above grew darker. Paul squinted up at the sky and then into the distance, his eyes combing the horizon nervously for signs of a wildfire. Esther's hand was in his, and it was clammy. His wife was nervous, but when he turned to look at her, she was smiling bravely up at him.

When they got to the stables, Paul let go of Esther's hand. The horses were stomping about in distress and needed to be calmed down. Opening the stalls was going to be tricky, he knew, because the more edgy amongst them would bolt at the next thunderclap.

"Easy, boy," Paul said, going into Raider's stall and stroking his muzzle. He turned around and saw Esther standing right behind him, looking uncertain. Paul was once again conflicted. He needed help. He could hear distressed whinnying and guessed that Honeycomb and Typhoon needed calming down. Esther gave Paul a questioning look, but before he could nod to her, she rushed toward Honeycomb's stall.

"Wait!" Paul shouted, frustrated that Esther wouldn't be able to hear. No sooner had he cried out than his eyes widened as Honeycomb darted out of her stall, almost knocking Esther down.

Paul swung the door of Raider's stall shut and simultaneously reached out to stop Honeycomb from bolting. Honeycomb, however, dodged Paul's hand and fled, even as a blinding flash of lightning rent the skies. Paul threw his hand over his eyes and turned to follow Honeycomb. He glanced around briefly to see where Esther was but realized that in the split second when he had covered his eyes, Esther had bolted along with Honeycomb.

"Esther!" Paul cried, ignoring the stomping and the whinnying of the horses and risking Typhoon breaking down his stall door and bolting. All he could think of was that Esther had disappeared after Honeycomb. He knew her well by now. She would blame herself for opening the stall door too quickly, thus allowing Honeycomb the opportunity to make a run for it. And she would try to repair the damage herself. Paul's heart pounded painfully against his ribs as he ran out, the violent breeze in his face, to see Honeycomb galloping away with Esther chasing after her.

"Esther!" he cried out again, wishing she could hear him. But there was another flash of lightning that forked down into a patch of dry grass several hundred feet from them.

"Esther!" Paul roared as the grass caught fire.

Honeycomb was startled by the fire and now turned and came racing back. Paul's cry froze in his throat as Esther ran into the horse's path and reached for Honeycomb's bridle.

"No!" Paul wanted to cry out, but the sound wouldn't come. He was staring, horrified, as Honeycomb reared up, but Esther stood her ground, and suddenly, to Paul's utter amazement, the horse planted her feet on the ground and let Esther stroke her muzzle. She was still visibly agitated, however; her nostrils were flared and her ears were flat back against her skull, and she was bucking and stomping about while Esther tried to pacify her.

Paul took off and ran toward Esther, throwing his arms about her, feeling her body tremble with fear and emotion. His own heart was racing. She clutched Honeycomb's bridle, refusing to let it go even when Paul tried to ease it out of her hand. It mattered little to him if the horse bolted. All he needed was for Esther to be safe.

With a sigh of relief, he saw his men approaching the fire with buckets of water. They had formed a line going up to the creek and were passing buckets back and forth.

"Thank God for the creek," Paul whispered, aware he had acknowledged his Maker for the first time in a long while.

Tom the ranch hand ran up and stood poised, ready to take the bridle from Esther when she let go.

"I'll take care of the horses, boss," he said. "You take the missus back inside."

Esther shook her head violently and pointed in the direction of the creek and then at the stables. But Paul was too disturbed to comprehend what she was trying to convey. Eventually he realized she wanted to help bring the fire under control before it reached the stables. He sent her and Tom off with Honeycomb and went to join his men who were fighting the fire. He didn't want her near the fire after what had happened in the kitchen. He didn't know if her trauma would rise up and didn't want to make this day any more stressful for her than it already was. But when he turned around, he saw that Esther had joined the efforts, a lone woman in the midst of a line of men, passing buckets back and forth to douse the fire. Her face was calm and determined, and his heart swelled with pride and affection.

"Thankfully it was a small one," Sandy said, coming up to Paul. Paul's eyes were on Esther. "She's quite something, isn't she?" he added.

Paul heard what his friend was saying but couldn't tear his eyes off Esther nor could he find his voice to respond to

Sandy's comment. But he knew, beyond the shadow of a doubt, that yes, Esther was really quite something..

Chapter Fifteen

Esther pushed open the door of the root cellar and walked out into the sunlight with a sense of excitement. She had carrots in the capacious pocket of her apron, and Paul was waiting for her at the stables. She was wearing the blue dress he had given her because it always made her feel cherished.

Paul turned around when she entered the stable and smiled at her. He was standing by Honeycomb, and he gestured for her to come closer. She went up to him, and he pointed to the pocket of her apron. Esther took out a carrot and held it up to Honeycomb. She was comfortable with the horse and was grateful Honeycomb had responded to her on the day of the storm. But it was Typhoon she wanted to ride. She knew, however, that Paul would only teach her how to ride Honeycomb, and she wouldn't protest or be difficult. She wanted to please him and not cause him any more anxiety than she already had. She looked forward to seeing him smile and loved the way his hazel-brown eyes twinkled when he was relaxed and happy.

Honeycomb accepted the carrot and munched on it happily, and then Paul moved to the next stall. Esther's heart beat faster. This was where Typhoon, the different horse, was. Since her first encounter with him, she had only silently communicated with him from outside his stall, occasionally stroking his muzzle but never going closer or even grooming him.

Paul looked down at her, and she gazed adoringly up at him. She knew she would do anything for this man, even give up her great desire to ride Typhoon or go closer to him, but she hoped he would let her ride him one day.

Paul didn't open Typhoon's stall but signaled for Esther to offer him a carrot as well. Esther took a carrot out of the pocket of her apron and offered it to Typhoon. She stroked his muzzle while he was munching on the carrot, and then Paul took her back to Honeycomb. Esther looked longingly back at Typhoon, and she saw the light of understanding in Paul's eyes.

"One day, maybe," he said, and she nodded. She said a silent prayer of thanks to God. She was getting even better at reading the movements of Paul's lips. She watched as he led Honeycomb out of the stable, beckoning to Esther to follow.

Later that day, Esther pulled out her diary and opened to a fresh page.

Dear diary,

I will never forget this day for all of my life. My beloved husband, Paul Orton, taught me how to ride. I do believe he was happy with the way I handled Honeycomb when she ran out of the stable on the day of the thunderstorm, and perhaps this was his way of rewarding me.

I think he was also happy when I helped with dousing the wildfire. He has been looking at me quite differently in the past days. As for me, I feel as Cinderella must have for Prince Charming. When he is close to me, I almost forget to breathe because I am so happy. Like today, after showing me how to mount a horse, he climbed up behind me and put his arms around my waist to demonstrate how to hold the reins.

I had to make every effort to concentrate on what he was showing me. Each time he leaned forward to put his hands over mine on the reins and show me how to relax and tauten them, I felt the vibrations of his chest against my back. I would know then that he was speaking, and I would have to turn around to decipher what he was saying from the movement of his lips. I noticed this glow in his eyes, like a wildfire, while it felt like there was a thunderstorm in my chest. I can catch most of the words now, but often I am distracted by his lips and his closeness. I am overwhelmed by the scent of him and by the warmth he exudes.

Paul is such a good teacher. He is so patient and kind. I am reminded of the passage from the Bible in 1 Corinthians 13:4, which says, "Love is patient and kind." If I had to name one person I know who matched that description of love, it would be Paul. He truly reflects the love of our Savior.

My experience of riding for the first time was exhilarating and so joyful, dear diary! It made me feel so free. There was such a surge of excitement as Honeycomb transitioned from a slow canter to a gallop. I felt like I was flying. And I felt Paul so relaxed behind me, his hands over mine on the reins. I could tell that he was happy to be riding too and teaching me.

I realized today I really do love horses. Before, I was too intimidated by them, but today I conquered my inhibitions. As I rode, I remembered the verse from Isaiah 40:31: "But they who wait for the Lord shall renew their strength; they shall mount up with wings like eagles; they shall run and not be weary; they shall walk and not faint."

Today I felt like I had mounted up with wings like an eagle. I flew over the landscape. Today I felt my strength renewed.

She was fond of sketching and often used it as a way to express herself. She had sketched Paul next to different notes she had made in her diary, but now she sketched a horse with a woman riding it.

As Esther put her diary away, slipping it between the pages of the *Encyclopedia Britannica*, she had an overwhelming desire to do something special to show her appreciation for her husband. She wanted to give him a glimpse into her past. He had married her without knowing anything much about her, and he must wonder about her just as she wondered about him. Today she would reveal to him some truths about her life.

Esther had thus far only used her ability to mime for basic communication. She had stopped using that particular gift in more theatrical presentations, but she felt she would like Paul to see one of her plays. Especially as it was going to be about her life. She wanted to connect with the man she was falling in love with on a deeper level. Yes, she was falling in love with Paul. Esther put her hand over her heart as she admitted this truth to herself. And she very much wanted him to feel the same way for her.

She prepared her play carefully. She would choose a good time for it. Most evenings after supper, she would escape up to the attic and read herself to sleep. That was her haven, a place Paul had done up especially for her. But that night, she would ask Paul if she could do a play for him. She looked up at the clock. Paul had told her he wouldn't be in for lunch because he had to take some cattle to the market. He would be back in time for an early supper, he had said.

Esther missed having Paul home for lunch, but she was also glad to have the time to prepare her play. It would take some work, and so she practiced before her dresser mirror. Then she went about her chores. The chickens had to be fed and the stables cleaned out. She took more carrots for the horses and stopped by Typhoon's stall to stroke his muzzle before going to Honeycomb and spending time thanking her silently for her ride that morning.

Then she went to weed and water the vegetables. Paul had shown her a stretch of land toward the rear of the homestead, and they had planted carrots, potatoes, beets, and even some green beans. She tended the plants with care and eagerly awaited the yield.

Soon it was time to prepare the evening meal, and Esther went back to the chicken coop to pick out a bird. *This evening has to be special in every way,* she thought, *beginning with a special supper.* She was glad her mama had taught her how to dress a bird, and thus the chicken was ready to cook in no time at all. She scooped some lard into a skillet and set it on the burner, pleased she had learned how to stack the firebox and use the cookstove. Using her instinct combined with whatever she had observed her mama do when she was helping her in the kitchen, she fried the chicken and boiled some potatoes to go with it.

By the time Paul returned, the food was on the table, the lamps were lit, and she had washed and changed into a fresh dress. It was her church dress, but she wanted to look nice for her husband, especially when she was performing the play she had prepared especially for him. She had also unplaited her hair and brushed it till it gleamed in the lamplight, then braided it up again and twisted it into a neat bun at the nape of her neck.

"What's all this?" Paul mimed, walking in and hanging up his hat. He looked tired but glad to be back.

"Something special," Esther replied, using actions and pointing to him to indicate this was for him.

Esther waited till he was seated at the table and then served him.

"This is very good!" Paul complimented her efforts, bringing his thumb and forefinger together and then clapping his hands.

Esther felt the blood rush to her cheeks, and she caught her breath. Even after a day's work with his hair tousled and his clothes crushed, Paul looked handsome. And to see him enjoying the meal she had cooked filled Esther with so much joy she could barely speak.

When the meal was over, she got up and stood directly in front of Paul.

"After we finish our evening chores, I have something I want to show you," she mimed, moving her hands like she was washing the dishes, then pointing to herself, spreading her arms wide, and pointing to Paul. For a moment he didn't appear to comprehend what she was trying to communicate, so she repeated it again.

"Oh," Esther saw Paul's lips respond. "Okay."

She was trembling with anticipation as she washed and dried the dishes while Paul went out to wash and check on the horses. When he came back, he looked tired, and Esther wondered whether she should postpone her surprise. But he was waiting expectantly in the living room while she cleaned the kitchen and wiped down the stove.

"I'm ready," Esther mimed, standing directly in front of Paul and pointing to his eyes and then to herself. "Watch me closely," she communicated. "This is my story."

Paul leaned forward as Esther began her play. She started with her childhood before the accident and then drew him into her life as it had been before she met him on that fateful day near the woods. She could feel beads of perspiration break out on her forehead as she reached deep into her very soul to show her husband the truth about the woman he had married: the joy she derived from nature and how she had been prone to wander off on her own to explore the woods; how she became a source of shame to her parents and had to be locked away when people came to visit; the humiliation she had endured; and how she died within herself just a little bit more each day until he had rescued her. She was almost like a ballerina pirouetting, standing on the tips of her toes to reach a bird on a tree or twirling to show the changes of the seasons from bad to good.

While she performed her play, she hoped it would be well received and that Paul was not merely humoring her. He appeared to be genuinely interested in what she was conveying, and Esther acted her heart out. When she twirled gently to a stop and looked anxiously at him, she was astonished to see Paul's eyes glistening as if with unshed tears. And then, taking her completely by surprise, Paul stood up and came over to her. He hesitated for the merest moment before he took her into his arms and embraced her.

Esther couldn't breathe for the joy she felt to be in her husband's arms. He held her close and was whispering against her hair. She could tell he was whispering, because his breath fanned her cheek. She felt his fingers in her hair and his face partly against her cheek and partly buried in her tresses. She could tell he was breathing heavily because of the rise and fall of his chest against hers, and she felt like she was losing consciousness. And then Paul drew back and looked into her eyes. She dared not blink for fear of shattering the moment, that blissful moment, when Paul leaned over and his lips, those sensual lips, caressed her forehead. Oh, he was so gentle. So gentle, and yet she sensed him reining in his emotions as his body tensed —just the way he had taught her to tauten the reins. But she wished he would slacken the reins and fly with her as they had that morning on horseback.

It felt like something was unleashed within her, and tears spilled from her eyes. They just rained down, and now Paul was brushing them away with his fingertips, and his lips were caressing her eyes and following the path of her tears. Before long, Esther didn't know whether she was crying tears of sorrow, relief, or pure, unbridled joy at being in the arms of the man she loved.

Chapter Sixteen

"You were right," Paul told Sandy. They were leaning against the corral fence, watching a group of ranch hands break in a horse the next morning. "Esther is definitely not cognitively slow. There may be other reasons why she is unable to communicate verbally, but she is a sensitive, intelligent, capable woman."

Sandy looked at Paul in surprise. "I'm glad you've discovered that. You seem more at peace now," he remarked.

"I am," Paul replied, feeling surprised at being able to make such a clear admission without even the shadow of a doubt. His eyes never left the horse as a ranch hand reviewed commands, even as he conversed with his friend. But his heart was back in the homestead with Esther.

He had pulled away from her reluctantly that night after her play. Her cheeks were flushed as they mounted the stairs together, and he had watched her climb the ladder and disappear through the trapdoor to her little haven. But he had lain awake long after, listening to her footfalls and to the sound of the bed creak when she lay down, then had imagined her gentle breathing and her long eyelashes lying against the softness of her cheeks.

"Paul," Sandy said, and Paul glanced up.

"Do you think that what the pastor said that time at church could be the reason why Esther can't communicate other than by actions?"

"Saul was blinded by a bright light on the road to Damascus," Paul murmured. "Esther could have been deafened by an explosion. It's possible. The idea has occurred to me before."

Sandy grinned. "I see you've returned to the Good Book," he remarked. "Esther is a positive influence on you."

Paul shook his head. He was still not completely right with God. "Esther wanted to know my name," he explained. "She showed me hers in the Bible. Then she asked me if my name was also in there, so I showed her."

Sandy's eyes narrowed. "How did she know where her name was? And how did she learn what your name is if she doesn't read?"

Paul shook his head and shrugged. "She has moved into the attic, where she found Angie's books. She has been immersed in them since the day she discovered them, and I have to say that I have often wondered if she just likes the feel of the books or if she actually reads them. With the Bible, maybe her mother or pastor showed her where her name was. But with the books . . . If I knew the stories well, I would ask her and then compare, but as you know, I'm not much of a person for reading."

"What does it matter," Sandy said, "as long as things are going well for you both?"

"Yes," Paul murmured, and returned his reflections to Esther.

"You are very far away right now," Sandy teased him. "If you don't watch out, that horse is going to throw a tantrum and run you over!"

Paul shook his head. His attention was wholly on the horse. He had broken in so many horses that it was second nature to him, and even though the horse still tested the reins and ignored a command every now and then, it was clear the ranch hands had everything under control at the moment. But there was a difference. After Angie died, he had just wanted to be out amongst the animals. Now, however, he yearned to get back to the homestead. He wanted to take whatever pain Esther had endured in her past and carry it for her. *How could her parents have put her through such acute pain?* he wondered. How much rejection had she suffered after her accident? How could anyone put such a sweet person like Esther through such trauma? He knew that he couldn't ever forget what she had revealed to him. Although he had only understood the general ideas, it was all etched on his heart.

"What convinced you?" Sandy asked, breaking into his thoughts. "I mean, that Esther isn't cognitively slow?"

"Just the way she has been opening up recently," Paul replied. "She is very expressive. Nobody who is cognitively slow can express themselves in such a creative manner without words."

***

The horse was now tired and trotting around the corral. Its breaking session was over for today. Paul entered the corral, and the ranch hand on the horse dismounted and led the horse to him. This was always the best part for Paul. It had taken three weeks of working each day with the horse, building up its confidence and helping it feel relaxed around people. This beautiful creature still had a will of its own yet recognized him as its master. This was the moment of understanding. Paul pulled an apple from his pocket and gave it to the horse, then stroked its forehead as it crunched away and murmured little nickers of pleasure.

Sandy had seemed pleased that Paul had referred to the Bible just then. But he still felt far away from his faith. He wished he could fully recognize and be surrendered to his Master. It seemed like he was going around and around like the horse in the corral, not acting out but not listening either, and that God was waiting for him to follow His lead completely. Going back to church had in many ways brought him peace, but it also brought his insecurities to the fore.

"I have to get back to the house, Sandy," Paul said, moving away from the horse. "I think I will give Esther another riding lesson today. She really enjoyed the last one."

"See you later, boss," Sandy said.

He left the horse in the care of the ranch hands and mounted Raider. As he trotted back to the house, Paul felt a sense of anticipation because he was about to see Esther, but simultaneously he also felt a familiar twinge of fear. This time it bordered on panic so that he had to rein in Raider and take a breath. He had never imagined he would fall for Esther, and it made him so afraid. What if God punished him for his negligence of Luther and also took Esther away from him? What then? Paul clutched at his chest. He knew that he would then be lost forever. He admired Esther's strength in remaining true to her faith despite the cruel hand life had dealt her, but he wasn't that strong. His faith still wavered.

As Raider trotted forward again, Paul was faced with another realization. He was apprehensive of how Esther would perceive him if she knew of his weakness. Thus far she looked up to him. He could tell she leaned on him because she thought of him as strong, and he couldn't bear if that changed and if she regarded him in any other light.

He cooled his face down at the tap before going inside, entering through the kitchen door, his eyes alighting on Esther's as she looked up from where she stood, peeling potatoes. She gave him a dazzling smile, and his heart turned over. Yes, he would never be able to return to his faith in the Lord if even Esther was taken away from him. He wanted to run to her and take her into his arms, but suddenly he was afraid.

"I thought we could go riding," he said, the words coming out with an effort because of the direction his thoughts had taken. He mimed tugging on the reins and saw Esther's face glow.

"Now?" she asked, her forefinger pointing down. It had taken Paul a while to understand some of her actions, but he had made the effort, and it was paying off.

"Yes," Paul replied. "Right now."

He grinned as Esther hastily tossed the potatoes into the pan of water she had waiting on the side and followed him out of the kitchen, wiping her hands on her apron as she did so.

"Today, you ride Honeycomb by yourself," Paul said when they entered the stables. "And I will ride Raider."

"Myself?" Esther beamed, pointing at herself, incredulous.

It cheered Paul's heart to see her like that. They rode out to the creek, Paul keeping Esther close, but she was even more comfortable and confident on Honeycomb that day. She would glance at him every once in a while with her eyebrows raised, as if asking if she was doing alright, and he would nod. Sometimes he would lean across and take Honeycomb's reins to help her steer the horse. Their hands would touch, their eyes would meet across the gap between the two horses, and Paul's heart soared with an indescribable fire she ignited inside of him.

They stopped at the creek. Paul remembered the wildfire and how fortunate it was they had this water so close. It was a beautiful day, with a pristine blue sky and the banks of the creek awash with the varied hues of wildflowers.

Esther pointed to the flowers and then slid off Honeycomb. He grabbed the reins and held them while his wife plucked the flowers, her eyes glowing with pleasure. He couldn't help remembering how far she had come from the girl he used to see wandering in town with similar bunches of flowers. His eyes grew misty as he watched her, reluctant to turn back and resume their chores before the day was done.

**

It was a day later when Paul had to take the money from selling the cattle to the bank. When he was homeward bound after the day's work, he found himself hurrying to get home. He washed outside the kitchen and then went inside, trying not to burst through the door in his eagerness to see Esther and ascertain she was safe.

"What happened?" Esther's hands and eyes queried as she looked up anxiously from the stove where she was cooking. He realized then that he had come in and was just standing there, feasting his eyes on her.

Paul shook his head. "I'm hungry," he replied, rubbing his belly and miming the stirring of a pot. "What are you cooking?"

Esther smiled and pulled out his chair, indicating he should seat himself. Then she served him his meal of beans and biscuits. She watched him eagerly as he ate, waiting for him to give his customary nod of approval, which he did. The food was tasty, and his own heart was warmed when her face lit up.

After he had finished his evening chores, he came back to see that Esther had finished doing the dishes and was on the porch with her Bible. He stood, watching her turn the pages of the Good Book, wondering all the while if she could actually read. Then she looked up and saw him. Her eyes shone, and she patted the chair next to her, inviting him to join her. He sat down, and she turned to him and gave him the Bible. It was open to 1 Samuel 25, a passage she had referred to before.

"Please read this," Esther said, folding her hands and then turning them palms up, together, like a book. Paul began to read and then turned to see Esther staring intently at his lips. As always, his heart began to race. She leaned forward, looking up into his face, and then mimed what he had just read. Then she motioned for him to read on, so he did, and each time he stopped, Esther mimed the story as it progressed. Paul set the Bible down on his lap and stared at the page. Esther's fingers brushed his arm, and he gave her his attention. She pointed to Abigail's name and then to herself. Then she pointed to David's name and then to him.

"They are like us," she seemed to say.

Paul's eyes suddenly opened to the text. He reread the passage, and it became abundantly clear to him that if Esther could follow him reading and mime what he had read, then not only could she read, but she could also discern what he was saying by looking at his lips. Esther was lip reading!

Paul took both her hands in his and stared intently at her.

He didn't have to say anything. It was as if Esther was aware he had finally made the connection, and she took a deep breath, releasing it slowly.

"You are my David," Esther mimed. "You saved me."

"No," Paul said, shaking his head. "You saved me, Esther."

He drew her into his arms and held her close, burying his face in the side of her neck so that she couldn't tell that tears, so long held back, were finding their way past his tightly shut eyes. He never wanted her to think of him as weak. He so wanted to be her David, the strong warrior king.

Esther stroked his hair, her fingers moving like the wings of a butterfly over the back of his neck. Perhaps she knew, with the intuition of a woman, that he so badly needed to be comforted. He had always had to be strong for Angie, then for Luther, and subsequently for her, but for that moment, he just wanted to stay there in his wife's arms and exhale just as she had a moment before.

When he straightened up, Esther opened the Bible again and leafed through it, turning to Acts 13:22. She gave him the passage, and Paul read, "I have found in David son of Jesse a man after my own heart."

"You are a man after God's heart," Esther mimed, pointing to him and to the heavens, then placing both her hands over her own heart.

Paul got to his feet. "It's time for bed," he said, abruptly terminating the conversation.

Esther was telling him something that he wasn't about to believe. A man after God's own heart was true to his faith. He was strong even in adversity, and like Job in the Bible, he would never cry out against God or criticize His will. So no, Paul concluded, he didn't fit the description Esther seemed eager to pin on him.

He wanted to do whatever was best for Esther, but he couldn't admit to being something he wasn't. That would be deceitful. Yet he didn't want Esther to think less of him, so he would continue to hide beneath the façade he had created.

Esther was looking at him anxiously, perhaps wondering if she had offended him in some way. Even as the thought crossed his mind, she folded her hands, mutely apologizing if she had spoken out of turn.

"No, it's not that," Paul replied, facing her so that she could read what he was saying. "It's not that at all." He mustered a smile. "I am just very tired. We broke in a new horse that I have been working with for the past three weeks."

But Esther wasn't looking at his lips. Instead, she was looking away, and her eyes were troubled.

They climbed the stairs together, but Paul felt that Esther had retreated into herself. He reached out and took her hand, giving it a little squeeze. Esther turned to him, searching his face. He tried to hold her gaze, but he couldn't, and so he turned away almost guiltily. Even as he did so, he reminded himself that Esther was astute and would soon figure out he was concealing something from her. It was almost as if the loss of one of her senses had intensified all the others.

"Sleep well," he said as they reached the ladder to the attic, and he let go of her hand.

Esther pointed to him and mimed the act of sleeping. Paul nodded, once again struck by her sweetness and wishing he could melt into it and forget himself completely.

Chapter Seventeen

Esther hung the washing out to dry and went to the vegetable garden to see if there were some carrots ready to pick. There was a certain inexplicable thrill about eating vegetables she had grown herself. But that morning, even the sight of the big, juicy carrots couldn't dispel the heaviness in Esther's heart. The pall of gloom had descended when Paul had suddenly ended the conversation at her suggestion that he was a man after God's heart. In her eyes, he was. But she sensed Paul wasn't entirely at peace with himself, or God, though he masked his feelings quite effectively.

Esther had stolen furtive looks at Paul during church services and seen the tenseness in his jaw as if he was fighting for composure. The townspeople had begun to either ignore her or act with cold politeness, so she knew he was not so angry at how they treated her anymore. There was something disturbing him, and Esther wished he would share it with her the way she had opened up about her past to him. She was his wife after all, and she wanted to be a source of support to him in whatever way she could be.

Each time in church when she had watched him clench and unclench his fists, Esther had felt like there was some deep-rooted anger Paul was struggling to overcome. Sometimes his eyes would glisten and he would bite down on his lower lip. One time, during a sermon, maybe something in the pastor's message pierced his heart. He had stared ahead of him stoically but then had suddenly left his seat and darted outside, returning almost immediately and looking anxiously at her. It had struck her then that he might have left the building altogether had she not been present. She had tried to question him about it on their way home, but he had been reticent.

She had been praying for him to open up his heart to God again and to know how much he was loved by the Lord. It was becoming quite apparent Paul didn't think God looked upon him with favor, perhaps because of some hardship he had endured. Esther hoped she would soon be able to help him return to the foot of the cross and lay down whatever burden he was carrying.

She filled her apron with carrots, and as she went to the kitchen to wash and chop them up for lunch, she suddenly remembered Paul had said he would be going into the market and would only be back for supper. That left her with more time on her hands than she wanted. She wished he would surprise her the way he had some days ago and take her riding.

She finished all her chores and then decided to go up to the attic and spend some time reading. To her delight, she had found another box of books. This was quite by chance, and she may have missed it, because it was hidden behind the bookshelf. Paul had cleared out most of the unnecessary furniture and possessions but appeared to have overlooked this particular box. It was small and contained no more than four books. Esther took out the first one. It was *Pilgrim's Progress* by John Bunyan. She had read it once and always wanted to read it again. Finding it now was like a divine gift, and she immediately got down on her knees and thanked God for it.

The next book she took out had no title but had a fine leather cover. Esther stroked the cover and turned it to examine the spine in case she had missed the name of the book printed there or who it was written by, but there was nothing. Now quite mystified, she opened the book and saw, written in a slanting hand the words, *The Diary of Angie Orton.* Esther snapped the book shut and slipped it back into the box. She gasped. This was somebody's diary. But then the name rang a bell, except she had seen it written as Angela in the family Bible downstairs.

Esther's hand shook as she reached for the diary again and guiltily lifted it out of the box. Suddenly it felt heavier, and her heart did too. Instinctively she knew she was going to make a discovery that might be distressing. Already her mind was working furiously, unravelling the mystery, but the words in the diary, page after page, confirmed her worst fears. She had always wondered how a man like Paul could have remained unmarried for so long, but now she knew he had in fact been married to someone called Angie.

Can I be more blessed? I am married to my most beloved Paul Orton. Oh, how overjoyed I am. And so much in love that I can scarcely speak whenever I look at my husband. Husband! How wonderful to finally call Paul my husband!

I am overjoyed. I am carrying my darling Paul's child. I couldn't be happier. I always wanted to give him a child, and now I am going to have one. He is so excited too.

Paul has been carving little wooden toys, often working late into the night. How I love to watch him. He has such strong hands, and I could stare at them forever as they whittle away at the wood, turning shapeless little logs into horses, carts, and sheep. Our baby is going to love these beautiful toys.

Paul has been working so hard at the ranch that I have barely seen him in the past few days. It's getting harder for me to move around the house now, and climbing stairs is the hardest of all. I have been spending a lot of time reading my beloved books. Last night I read Pilgrim's Progress to Paul as he was carving the toys for our child. He likes the story.

I feel just a little bit afraid. I haven't been feeling very strong recently, and Paul had the doctor visit. I have been asked to rest more. Since I can't climb the stairs any longer, Paul has put a bed in the living room. He can't seem to sleep these days, and I sometimes wake up and see him watching me. Sometimes he sits on a chair by my bed and holds my hand while I sleep.

Paul won't let me do any chores. He won't even let me cook and has been preparing all the meals. I have to say that he cooks very well. I wish I didn't feel so weak and lacking in energy. This is a difficult pregnancy to be sure, and I can't wait for our baby to be born.

I know I wasn't supposed to climb stairs, but I did, and I am paying for my mistake. I just wanted to check on the crib that Paul has made and get it ready with the sheets I have been embroidering. I suppose I misjudged the distance between one step and another, and I had a fall. I don't think I have injured myself, but Paul is beside himself with worry. He sent Sandy to fetch the doctor. By the grace of God, the baby seems to be doing just fine. But Paul keeps saying it is all his fault and that he should have been here, watching me. I told him he has to *attend to work on the ranch. He has been inspecting new heads of cattle, and that is important. But he still insists on taking the blame for my own folly in climbing the stairs when I was told not to.*

I feel a lot of pain. I think I am going into labor, but isn't this a little too early? I can barely write, but, I feel it is important to document my experience of giving birth. It's the biggest gift I can give my husband: a child, possibly a son and heir. He has already begun making plans to teach the little one to ride as soon as he is able to sit on a horse. I laugh when he talks like that, though I know he is serious. Paul will make a wonderful father.

The diary slipped out of Esther's trembling fingers and fell to the floor, where she sat on the rug Paul had brought up to the attic and spread out for her. She felt mortified. She had just taken all of his kindness and never once thought of what he must have been hiding beneath his sensitive smile and kind eyes. Obviously, he had been completely in love with this woman—Angie, *his wife.*

Esther's lips puckered, and she began to cry. Paul had suffered a tragedy far worse than any she had endured. From the fact that there was a diary lying forgotten in a box and no evidence of a loving wife or child, it was apparent Paul had suffered a bereavement so great that he couldn't even bring himself to talk about it. It was obvious from his wife's account of events that he even blamed himself for it. *Perhaps that's why he distances himself from church,* Esther realized.

She was sobbing uncontrollably now. He was a good man and didn't deserve so much sorrow. Suddenly the pieces of the puzzle fell into place, and Esther saw the reason for

Paul's outburst over the toys and his momentary displeasure over finding her amidst his wife's books. Yet how generous and tolerant of him to allow her access to the books, even going so far as to do up the attic for her. She had felt his tears when he had buried his face in her neck that time when he had held her close after she mimed the story of David and Abigail. Maybe he needed to talk about his pain so that he could let it go. She knew she had felt relieved after sharing her past with Paul.

Esther looked down at the blue dress she was wearing. It was her favorite and her best dress, apart from her church clothes. Paul had given it to her on the day of the fire. Could it have belonged to his late wife? It must have torn him up inside to even look at it, let alone give it to someone else. Esther felt great remorse at being oblivious of her husband's past until then. She would make up for it, she decided. She would help him deal with his pain, so long suppressed.

Esther put the diary back into the box and sat back on her heels, an idea forming in her mind. She knew exactly how she would help her husband come to terms with the tragedy he had faced.

That evening after supper, she signaled to him to come into the living room.

"What for?" Paul asked. He looked tired, like he hadn't been sleeping too well.

"I want to tell you a story," Esther replied in mime, pointing to herself and then to him, then spreading her arms wide.

She saw Paul's features soften. It seemed like he was happy when she did a play for him and was happier still when she shared her heart with him. She waited for him to seat himself and then began. With her unique silent eloquence, she told the story of a man who once had a wife and lost her. A man who had lost his one and only child before it was even given a chance at life. He was a kind man and a good man and didn't deserve such a fate. But this man needed to know that God was not punishing him. God was a loving father. And Jesus said, in John 16:33, "In the world you will have tribulation. But take heart; I have overcome the world."

Paul's face had darkened, and his eyes were narrowed.

"Who told you all this?" he asked, his hand gestures sharp and angry.

"I found a journal up in the attic," Esther mimed in reply. "And I'm so glad I did, because now I know more about you and can help you." She wasn't sure if Paul actually understand every word she was communicating, but she mimed them anyway.

"You pried into my personal life?" Paul asked.

Esther shook her head violently.

"You had no business to read that journal," Paul continued. "That diary is private and personal!"

He spoke rapidly, his face taking on the hues of anger, distress, and disappointment. Esther tried to interpret the words he was saying. She caught some, but not all. But one thing was apparent: Paul was enraged she had trespassed on his privacy. And she began to flounder tearfully, because with every word either of them attempted to communicate, an abyss was opening up between them. Esther felt like she was on one side, and Paul was on the other. Between them was a valley that was getting deeper by the minute.

Esther felt the floor vibrate forcefully as Paul stomped out of the room, leaving her alone and bereft. Her expressive hands fell to her sides, and her face drooped on her chest, and Esther wept for all Paul had suffered and everything she had endured. She had thought they had emerged from behind the shadow of death and darkness, but oh, how much deeper that shadow seemed now. Paul's anger was tangible even though he was no longer in the room. Esther's hands clenched into fists as she sobbed, dropping to her knees on the living room floor, wondering whether she would ever feel her husband hold her again.

She began to silently rail against her own folly. That had been selfish and insensitive of her, she realized. She questioned her motives, tying herself up into knots as she searched her heart for the reasons behind doing that play for Paul. She knew she had no sinister motive, just a burning desire to share with him that she knew of his silent suffering and was there for him. She knew, firsthand, what it was like to suffer in silence. She wanted to offer Paul an avenue of escape.

She knew what it was like to be unable express her innermost emotions, and she had wanted to release Paul from those bonds that were weighing him down. She wanted him to be able to open up to her, but obviously she had done something wrong. So she asked God's forgiveness and prayed Paul would forgive her in time.

Chapter Eighteen

Paul saddled Raider, intending to get a early start on the day, but he changed his mind and headed to the mountains where he had first encountered Typhoon as a young, wild mustang. He needed to find peace. The days after Esther had performed the play based on information she had gleaned from Angie's diary had been hard. Paul had avoided any communication with her and couldn't bear to look at her because of the expression in her eyes.

The chasm between them had widened, and it almost seemed like the occasions when they had connected and come closer to each other had never occurred at all. This made Paul even more guilty. While he was upset Esther had gained access to his secrets and had even picked up on the fact that he couldn't forgive himself, he was aware that the warm glances and unspoken messages that passed back and forth between them all seemed to have slipped beneath a pall of his own making.

Sandy had sensed his mood almost immediately. But Paul didn't want to reveal what had happened, because Sandy had great respect and fondness for Esther and would undoubtedly find a way to justify what she had done.

Hence, that morning, Paul's mouth was set in a grim line. He felt alone and bitter. He also felt the rage rising in his gut like a storm brewing that needed an outlet. Above, the first streaks of dawn were breaking through the night sky, but he was too bowed down by his emotions to even look up. *Yes,*

God is punishing me, he thought. That was why Esther had found the diary and read Angie's entries. Her play had opened up the wounds. Maybe God didn't want him to forget that he was responsible for Angie's and his child's deaths.

He had been working long hours at the ranch, justifying his time away by reminding himself that he was preparing to provide for his child in the best way possible. How ironic that all those hours away earning meant losing out on time with Angie and ultimately the loss of his family.

If only he had been home that day when Angie decided to go upstairs to lay the embroidered sheets in the crib, he would have stopped her. He would have insisted she stay in her bed, which he had brought down to the living room, while he took the sheets upstairs. He would have saved their child from being born ahead of time. Though only a few weeks early, the little one had not been strong enough to survive. Angie herself had succumbed soon after delivering the baby.

Paul drove his spurs into Raider's sides and was soon galloping with such speed that he felt he might be blown off the horse. He didn't care if the wind took him, or the mountains, or if God's hand itself picked him off his horse and threw him to the ground as he had done with Saul in the book of Acts. Paul looked up at the heavens, and a great sound erupted from his chest. Taking the trail that snaked up the mountain, he was forced to slow down, and he fell across Raider's back, his body convulsed by sobs. They tore out of him and rent the silence as she shouted out to God.

"Forgive me Lord," Paul cried, "Help me! I can't do this anymore. Just take me away from myself, because I can't do this by myself. I can't live like this any longer!"

Raider whinnied and came to a standstill, and Paul slid off and sat on the side of the trail amidst the towering pines, hunched over with his head in his arms, his hair curtaining the sides of his face, his shoulders heaving, and the air filled with the release of his long pent-up emotions. The image of a child being embraced by his father rose up before him, and Paul's sobs intensified, then slowly eased. He felt a warm blanket of peace settle over his shoulders. His body relaxed, and a sense of weightlessness came over him. He wasn't alone; he had never been alone. God had been waiting for him with open arms the whole time, ready to cradle him an listen to his woes, ready to relieve him of his burdens and his guilt. Time seemed suspended, and all thought took flight. Paul heard nothing, not even the sound of Raider cropping the grass or the whisper of the pines. He didn't know how, but he found himself face forward on the grassy verge of the trail, his limbs stretched out. When he eventually turned over, he saw that the sun was high in the sky.

Reluctant to leave, Paul knew he would have to return to the ranch. Though it would be difficult to face Esther and have a conversation with her, he knew he would have to. Something significant had taken place in his heart in the past few hours when he lost track of time. Paul was aware of feeling lighter, and suddenly he didn't hate himself or feel anger at God. He knew now it wasn't his fault Angie and their child had passed. Their passing had always been God's plan, and though he would forever miss them, it was time to accept the way things were. Like God, they would always be with him.

Paul's eyes softened when he thought of Esther. She had taught him so much. He saw her play in a new and different light. It brought him catharsis. He felt cleansed and healed. Above all, he felt forgiven, not only by God but by himself. But he had to go and extend that same forgiveness and understanding to his wife. He had seen the tortured look in her eyes day after day when he had distanced himself from her after the play, and now he needed to hold her close and tell her she was right in doing what she had done.

Raider was still standing there patiently waiting for him, and Paul mounted the horse and turned back for home. But something gently tugged him back. There was one thing left to do, and he turned Raider around, facing the upward mountain path. Strangely, though the path was steep, he didn't feel the gradient of the slope. Raider took it at a good pace, and then Paul guided him off the path and into a grove of trees.

He had buried them together, mother and son, amidst tears and recrimination, heartache and self-condemnation. He needed to give them their peace. He felt like he could finally lay to rest the memory of Angie and his child—his son. It had always pained him to acknowledge that he had lost a son, an heir. But now he could finally speak the name of his son. He slid off Raider and stood by the grave. It was a mound with a headstone on which he had etched Angie's and Stephen's names himself.

He filled his arms with lupine and forget-me-nots growing wild on the mountainside and covered the grave, then knelt down and said a prayer. "Stephen Orton, rest in peace, my beloved boy. Angie, I know you want me to move on, so I will. I have waited to fully know Esther as a wife, and I will follow the lead of the Lord in all things. Thank you, God, for never leaving me and for helping me to love again, and please don't let me hurt Esther any more than the world has already done. Amen." He placed his hands on the grave even as he looked up at the patches of sky he could glimpse through the trees. Then he stood and walked determinedly away, mounting Raider and flying down the path toward home.

As the homestead came into view, Paul slowed Raider down to a canter and then to a trot as he prayed for the right words and actions to convey to Esther that he was sorry for treating her the way he had.

When he didn't find her in the kitchen or on the porch, he felt the same sense of panic. What if she had left him and gone away? He ran from room to room, shouting out for her even though he knew she couldn't hear him. He suddenly saw her silhouetted in the living room doorway. As she stepped out of the light that poured into the room from outside, he saw that her brown hair was loose and flowing over her shoulders. She was wearing the blue dress he had given her and was looking at him anxiously.

"I was outside in the sun, drying my hair," she explained, pointing outdoors and indicating her damp hair.

Paul rushed forward, and Esther's eyes widened in momentary alarm. She began to fold her hands in a gesture of repentance, taking the blame for everything as she always did. But he quickly silenced her by taking her hands in both of his. She relaxed and gazed up at his lips.

"I'm so sorry," Paul burst out, his eyes bright with emotion. "I was wrong to treat you like that. It's not your fault. It's not mine either. I see that now. I was hurt because your play opened up a wound, but it was necessary. That wound needed to be exposed and cleansed." He paused as Esther searched his face.

"You look . . . different," she remarked in mime, withdrawing her hands from his so that she could convey what she had to say.

"I feel healed," Paul replied. "I went to the mountains and . . . prayed."

Esther's face lit up when he said that.

"He came to you, didn't He?" Esther asked, pointing upward and then using her sign for Jesus, which was to point to her palms where the nails had been driven in to pin Him to the cross.

Paul didn't think he would actually agree with what Esther was suggesting, but when he thought of how he had fallen forward on his face, remaining there for hours, and how he had seen the image of a child in its father's arms, then he had to nod.

"Yes," he said, a smile breaking out on his face. "Yes, I think He did!"

Esther had tears running down her cheeks. "This is joy," she responded, pointing to the tears and then to her heart. "I am filled with joy for you."

"I couldn't talk about my pain before, but now I can, because it's gone," Paul said. "I went to Angie and Stephen's grave, and I made peace with their passing. It was very hard to live without them. I couldn't forgive myself for not being there when Angie had that fall. I couldn't understand why I had to lose her and my firstborn son. So I was angry and hurt. When you enacted my story so beautifully, it wasn't you I was upset with. It was myself—and God."

"It's alright now," Esther mimed, placing one hand on his arm and the other on his chest. Paul reached up to place his hand over hers. His heart was pounding as her eyes sought his lips and remained there.

"Yes, it's more than alright, my dear Esther," Paul said. Swept up in the intimacy of the moment, he leaned in and kissed her upturned face. He brushed his lips across her forehead and then, hesitantly, trailed them down over the bridge of her tip-tilted nose. Then he drew his head back, looking into her eyes as if asking for permission. He could smell the fragrance of her freshly washed hair. She was his wife, and he wanted to show her how much he loved her. Paul's eyes grew misty. He loved her, and now he needed to tell her. Esther's eyes were drawing him in, and he looked into their depths. *Like honey, sweeter than a honeycomb,* he thought, placing his lips over them, one at a time.

"I love you, Esther," he whispered against the softness of her cheek. "I love you so much." He didn't want her to pull away to mime a reply. He knew exactly how she felt from what he read in her eyes, so he slid his hands around her waist and drew her closer, and his lips came down on hers.

Her lips were soft and tremulous, quivering under the impact of his. He could taste the salt of her tears as they spilled out from her eyes. He buried his fingers in her hair as she reached up and wrapped her arms around his neck, holding him in a way that was at once sweet, sensual, and protective. In that moment, Paul saw her completely as a woman, and she was his. He cherished her. He was proud of her. He wanted to give her something to seal that moment.

He took her hand, led her up the stairs, and opened the door to his room. She paused in the doorway, but he beckoned her inside. Then he opened Angie's closet and took out her Bible. He had clung to Angie's possessions, and now he felt the need to give them away, because that was what his late wife would have wanted.

"For me?" Esther's hands and eyes asked as Paul held the Bible out to her. She took it from him and bowed her head over the Book.

"It was Angie's," Paul said, "and now it's yours."

Esther's face glowed. She gazed up into his eyes, and Paul felt the urge to take her into his arms again, but he felt like the idea to give her Angie's Bible had come at an opportune moment. There were some things he didn't want to rush into with Esther. Yes, they were getting closer and they had just kissed. But this time was possibly what God wanted them to regard as their courtship. They had a whole lifetime before them, and he wanted to savor every moment with her.

"These are Angie's clothes," Paul said, gesturing toward the closet filled with dresses. Angie had come with an extensive trousseau. "Please wear them."

Esther smiled and folded her hands, but she shook her head.

"I will keep one or two, but you must give the rest to those who have no clothes," she mimed. At first, he didn't understand what she was saying, but then when the impact of her words hit him, he was even more convinced of what a priceless jewel Esther was. She who had so little could have enjoyed having so many clothes, but no, she wanted to give them away to those who had none. She was going to be content with whatever little she had and keep just two of Angie's dresses.

Paul couldn't believe how rich a blessing God had sent him in the form of his wife. He had chastised himself for being so caught up with earning money to provide for his family, with spending more hours at work and less with Angie during her pregnancy, and now God was opening up an avenue for him to share what he had with others. Beginning with Angie's clothes. There was so much more he wanted to do for those who had nothing. The thoughts rushed into his mind as if a dam had burst, and he wanted to share all his ideas with Esther. She gazed at him in delight as he began to talk about things they could do together for the community. Perhaps this had been the will of the Lord all along.

"Now that you have shown me what's in your heart," Esther declared, "it's my turn. I don't want any secrets between us." Paul could almost hear what she was conveying because of the clarity with which she mimed each word.

She took his hand and led him out of his room and up to the attic, climbing up first and then waiting for him to join her.

Paul wondered what she was going to reveal to him. When Esther took out the *Encyclopedia Britannica* from the bookshelf and handed it to him, he gave her a quizzical look.

Esther smiled and motioned to him to open the book. He felt something concealed there, and he drew it out from between the pages.

"What is this?" he asked.

Esther replied by leaning over and opening to the fly leaf, which had the title *My Journal.*

"Please take it and read it," Esther said through actions.

"This is personal," Paul replied.

"It's about me," Esther signed. "I want you to know about me. My thoughts. My heart."

Paul nodded and folded his hands in a gesture of thanks. He turned the pages over and saw that the words were often interspersed with drawings. There was one of a man. Paul paused and looked closely at it.

Esther was looked adoringly up at him, watching his lips.

"Is that me?" he asked.

Esther nodded.

"I don't think I'm that good looking," Paul remarked with a chuckle.

"Even more than good looking," Esther mimed in reply. "In your face I see your good heart."

Paul stared down at the image Esther had drawn of him. There were others he saw as he turned the pages. This was the part of the diary after he had found her outside the woods and after they had been married. What would he learn about her from the entries she had made before they were married, he wondered.

Chapter Nineteen

It was late summer. Esther led Typhoon out of his stall and gazed up at the horse's face. Paul had relented and trusted her with him. She had begun with grooming him regularly, and then, when she was confident riding Honeycomb, Paul had taken her out riding on Typhoon.

"He's so gentle," Esther had mimed when they got back from the ride, holding out the crook of her arm and stroking it with her right hand as in the depiction of a shepherd holding his sheep.

"You've changed him." Paul had laughed.

He had referred to her diary then and what he had learned about her from it.

"You have been through so much hardship," he had remarked. "I want to make you happy from now on."

"My life made me who I am," Esther had mimed in response. "And it brought me to you. So I am already very happy and blessed."

"I think you're changing me too, like you changed Typhoon." Paul had said.

That had been several weeks ago. And now Paul permitted her to take Typhoon out riding alone on the condition that she stay within the perimeter of the ranch. Esther smiled to herself. She would go and surprise her husband at the corral. When she reached it, however, she found Paul missing.

Sandy loped over to her as she scoured the corral for her husband, her hand shielding her eyes.

"Where's Paul?" Esther signed.

Sandy didn't answer immediately. Instead, he commented on how well Esther was doing with Typhoon.

"I was surprised when Paul let you ride him," he said, looking directly at her so that she could read what he was saying while he stroked Typhoon's muzzle.

"Me too," Esther responded. "So where is Paul?" she mimed again.

"He'll be along shortly," Sandy answered.

Esther sensed something was not quite right. "Is Paul okay?" she mimed, her hands expressing her anxiety.

"Yes," Sandy replied. "He just had to take care of an emergency, that's all."

As Esther read the word "emergency" off Sandy's lips, her instinct told her something was definitely wrong.

"I'd better get back to work," Sandy said, and without waiting for Esther to respond, he hurried away.

Esther turned Typhoon around, no longer eager to spend the morning riding. If there was something wrong, then she needed to be back home, waiting for her husband to return to help him in whatever way she could.

When she got back, however, there was no sign of Paul. She cooked lunch and then went up to the attic to pray. *Whatever it is,* she said from the depths of her heart, *may Paul have the strength to deal with it.* She was still on her knees when she felt the floor of the attic vibrate and knew that Paul was climbing up. She knew the vibration of his footfalls. She eagerly anticipated them every time, but today there was a heaviness about them even as he climbed the ladder and emerged through the trapdoor.

She was facing the trapdoor and looked straight at him. He said nothing but climbed up and sat down next to her on the rug.

Esther's right hand went up in a query, and she saw Paul heave a deep sigh. She could tell it wasn't a sigh of relief but one of distress because of the way his features tensed. He took her hands in his and looked into her eyes. Esther stared at him in silence. *How could I love him more than I already do?*, she thought. His hands tightened around hers. This was yet another sign that Paul was troubled.

"Tell me," Esther indicated with a single movement of her head. She had to draw her hands away from his in order to more emphatically indicate that he could tell her anything and it didn't matter.

Paul leaned forward and spoke.

"It's . . . Luther," he said.

Esther felt her blood run cold, but she kept her eyes on Paul's lips.

"He is here," Paul continued.

Esther's right hand flew to her heart, and her left hand gripped Paul's hands.

She shook her head and kept shaking it until Paul reached out and cupped her face with his hands, holding her steady and looking intently into her eyes.

"He is in trouble with a gang. They are after his life," Paul said.

Esther felt her body begin to tremble as images of that day outside the woods returned to haunt her.

She hit one hand against her palm, freeing her head from Paul's hands so that she could gesture forcefully, communicating through signs and motions, "He is dangerous. He is bad. It is not safe with him here. I cannot bear this."

She saw Paul's hands go up to his face and then to his head in a gesture of hopelessness, and she realized he was in a quandary. He couldn't make a decision, and he was obviously looking to her to make it for him.

"He wants to take refuge here . . . at the ranch," Paul said.

Esther couldn't believe what she was reading off Paul's lips. This was worse than anything she had feared.

"Don't you remember what he did to me?" she couldn't help miming.

Paul shook his head. "How could I ever forget?" he replied. "That's why I told him I would ask you. You are my wife now, and after what you endured at his hands, I couldn't impose the impossible on you."

A verse from the Bible came to Esther's mind. It was Matthew 19:26. "With man this is impossible, but with God all things are possible." But she didn't want to hear what God was telling her to do. She couldn't.

She was trembling and weeping now, overcome by fear and dismay. Just when things were so right between her and Paul, this shadow had to fall upon them. It was unfair.

"Luther said he was so angry he was sent away from the ranch that he joined a gang," Paul explained. "It's the McGuire gang, led by Frank McGuire. He was looking for a new family, he said, so he joined them. But things got bad, and now the gang wants his blood."

Esther felt overcome by sorrow mingled with fear. The mention of Luther's name only served to stir up the most frightening recollections of the day he had assaulted her.

"It's up to you, Esther, whether Luther goes or stays," Paul said, standing up. "You tell me what you decide." She continued to stare at him in mute fear. "I have to get back to the ranch," he added.

"I'm alone here," Esther signed. "What if . . . ?"

"I will never let anything happen to you," Paul said. "There are two ranch hands watching the house, one at the back and the other at the front."

"So you don't trust him either," Esther mimed.

"He is repentant and has begged my forgiveness," Paul replied. "But I am not ready to trust him yet, so I will take the necessary precautions to ensure your safety."

After Paul left the attic, Esther got to her knees and prayed again. She prayed for wisdom and strength. She was aware how much Paul had blamed himself for the way Luther had turned out, and she didn't want to add to his burden. A good wife would help her husband bring his lost brother back into the fold. But then she had the looming memory of how Luther had attacked her, and it was still fresh in her mind.

As always, when she needed an answer to a problem, she opened the Bible. And she felt God speak to her through the parable of the prodigal son. Esther read and reread the story, and each time she thought to herself that the prodigal son was not as bad as Luther was. She could forgive Luther, but she wasn't able to forget just how cruel he could be. She wrestled with her feelings and her memories until her legs were sore from kneeling, but she still couldn't find an answer to give Paul.

But then, instead of fixing her mind on Luther, she thought of Paul. Paul was kind and loving. He had accepted her for who she was, and now he needed her to accept Luther and fight for the salvation of his soul. His brother who was lost had now returned, like the prodigal son. Esther had to support Paul. She had to make sure Luther wasn't lost again, either physically or spiritually. She got to her feet and descended from the attic. To her surprise, Paul was seated at the kitchen table, waiting for her.

"I thought you had to get back to work," Esther's hands and eyes conveyed.

"It's almost lunchtime," Paul replied. "So I thought I'd eat with you and then get back."

"Where is Luther?" Esther mimed.

"Sandy is keeping an eye on him," Paul answered. "Let's eat."

"Bring him home," Esther mimed. "He is your blood."

Paul sprang out of his chair. "Are you sure?" he asked, the relief on his face palpable.

Esther nodded. "He is your brother," she replied, interlacing her fingers. "You won't forgive yourself if you send him away . . . and I won't forgive myself either."

"You are an angel," Paul said. "You are giving me the opportunity to help Luther get right with God."

No sooner had Esther said yes to having Luther back on the ranch than the doubts crept in. She had become accustomed to having Paul to herself. They had fallen into a pattern she didn't want disturbed. She longed for more intimate moments like the one they had shared on the day Paul had made peace with the loss of his first wife and child.

Soon after that, they had taken all but two of Angie's dresses down to the church and asked the pastor to give them to those in need. And then, the very next day, Paul had taken her to town and bought her a new dress. It was her first in a very long time, and she couldn't believe how lucky she was to have something so lovely. It was made of sea-green dyed linen, with a white collar and cuffs. Paul had said it showed off her honeyed locks to an advantage. Esther had blushed, thinking all of this was vanity, but it made her so happy that her husband noticed her hair. With Luther there, would Paul even have time for her? she wondered.

"Where's your brother?" Esther asked when Paul came back in the evening.

"He says he will stay at one of the bunkhouses with the ranch hands. He was afraid to face you."

Secretly, Esther was relieved Luther wouldn't be in the house with them, but then Paul gave her an uncertain look. "I told him to come and eat his meals with us even if he doesn't stay here. He has become really thin and looks sickly. Obviously he hasn't been eating very well, and—"

Esther nodded. "We will make sure he looks healthy again," she said stoically, though she remembered the last time she saw him—lurching drunkenly. She felt such revulsion even at the merest image of him.

"Are you alright?" Paul asked.

Esther nodded, lying to protect her husband's feelings. She owed him that much.

"I have insisted that Luther come over and apologize to you," Paul said, standing directly in front of her.

"When?" Esther signed.

"Tomorrow morning, when he comes for breakfast," Paul answered.

Esther felt the blood drain from her face. They were standing by the kitchen table, and she gripped the back of a chair for support. Things were moving too fast. She couldn't bear to look upon the face of her attacker and see that leer, that look of contempt on it. She still remembered the frightening experience of being groped and her dressed ripped. Seeing him might send her hurtling back to a time in her life she wished to forget.

"I'll be right beside you," Paul reassured her. "He has changed. You'll see. He left Aunt Tillie and Uncle Mack's house because he didn't want to put them in danger. But the McGuire gang doesn't know about us, and that's why he came home."

Esther drew in her breath. If the gang wanted to find Luther, they would, even if it took them some time to do so. She knew how dangerous gangs were from the newspapers she used to skim while helping at her parents' store.

"We will need more men around the house," she conveyed to Paul. Paul was distracted and didn't understand what she was trying to communicate, so she repeated herself. "Two men are not enough," she added.

That night, she turned down her lamp after she had climbed up into the attic and sat by the window, peering through the glass into the night. For the first time in a long while, she didn't feel safe.

The next morning, when she went out to do her chores, she found Paul already awake and the kitchen, smelling of coffee.

"We will do our chores together from now on," he said. "I can't risk leaving you alone this early in the day or late in the evening."

"Are you afraid the McGuire gang will come here?" Esther mimed anxiously.

"I just want you to feel safe and not worried that Luther will seek you out and harm you. Though that time he was very drunk and possibly had no idea what he was actually doing," Paul replied.

But Esther wasn't thinking of Luther. She was thinking of the larger danger that threatened their very existence.

When they returned after milking the cows, cleaning out the chicken coop, and gathering the eggs, Esther started on preparing breakfast.

"Perhaps, instead of oatmeal, we could have eggs and bacon," Paul suggested. It was apparent he wanted Luther to enjoy food he had been deprived of all the past months.

Her mind flew back to the story of the prodigal son getting a job minding pigs during a famine and wishing he could eat the pods the pigs were being fed for the hunger that gnawed at his wasted body. But then he rose up and returned to his father's house, and when he was yet far off, his father ran to meet him and embraced him as he apologized for all he had done. And then his father killed a fatted calf because his son, who was lost, was now found.

When Paul went to get the door, Esther froze. Paul opened it, and Esther dared not even look at the man who stood there. Before she had the opportunity to react in any way, Luther came forward, hesitantly, and stood before her with an attitude of penitence. At that moment, Esther felt mingled pity and revulsion for the man before her. Luther looked emaciated and old. Paul came swiftly to her side and took her hand.

"I'm sorry," Luther said. "I was not in my right senses. I am deeply repentant and ashamed of my behavior."

But Esther averted her gaze, unable to look at his lips because they only reminded her of that day by the woods. She missed the rest of what he was so earnestly saying, but Paul turned her to face him and repeated what Luther had just said.

"Can you find it in your heart to forgive him?" Paul said.

Esther had thought she could be strong for Paul, but she was quickly running out of courage.

"Tell him to ask the Lord's forgiveness," Esther mimed to Paul. "Not mine."

She saw the look of disappointment in Paul's eyes. Obviously he had hoped she would rush to forgive Luther and forget the humiliation she had suffered at his hands.

"Please, Esther," Paul said.

"Breakfast is served," Esther mutely announced, spreading her arms wide. She herself had lost her appetite and could eat no more than a piece of bread, but she couldn't help notice Luther wolfing down the bacon and eggs. It was quite apparent he hadn't had a meal like that for breakfast in a very long while. But while she felt compassion for what he had been through, she couldn't help but think he had brought it upon himself.

Esther caught Paul's eyes on her again. He obviously wanted her to be more welcoming, and she was disappointing him because she was unable to.

"Luther will be working with us on the ranch," Paul remarked, holding Esther's gaze.

Esther inclined her head slightly and nodded but didn't mime. She felt paralyzed inside.

Chapter Twenty

"Luther has been working on the ranch with us, and he is doing a good job," Paul remarked as he and Esther sat out on the porch after supper. They sat a few feet apart, and he felt it indicated the yawning chasm that had opened up between them when Luther had arrived. He knew he was asking a lot of his wife when he expected her to welcome Luther and to forgive him. But she couldn't even look at him.

"I'm so sorry," Esther said with her eyes and hands. "I feel like I have let you down."

Paul didn't have a response. He had to admit he was disappointed in her reaction to Luther's presence, but he didn't want to say it out loud. He knew he needed to be sensitive to the trauma she had suffered. He had read about it in her diary, and his blood had run cold at the account of her assault. But he felt it was time she rose above it and considered all the good that had come out of it.

It occurred to him that he hadn't known how terrified she had been or how cruelly his brother had behaved and that he was asking a lot of her now. But Paul felt like God had given him a second chance with his brother. He needed to take it and use the opportunity to make up for all the time he had neglected to help Luther evolve into a man who was responsible and good. But he required his wife's unmitigated support to fulfill his obligation to Luther.

He felt Esther's hand on his arm. She had left her seat and walked over to him, where he sat aloof and withdrawn.

"I want to help you," Esther mimed earnestly, clutching one hand with the other, a sign she employed to indicate her desire to support him. "I just don't know how. I feel in my heart that Luther hasn't changed. I can't look at his face, so I can't communicate with him. I know it feels like I am ignoring him, but when I look at him, I go back to that day outside the woods, and I am that same frightened child again."

Paul got up and stood before her. "You are no longer that person, Esther. You are a strong woman now. And I need you to be that strong woman for me. Please." He folded his hands in supplication. "God has given me a second chance with my brother. If I don't use it, then Luther will be forever lost, and I will be responsible. Truth be told, Esther, I can't do this without you. I need your help."

Even as he spoke, Paul was silently praying God would give Esther the strength she required for the task ahead. This wasn't going to be an easy road, he could tell, but he knew if they weathered that storm together, they would come out stronger as a couple. If, however, they fought the battle on opposite sides, they might forever lose what they had, and the thought terrified him, because he couldn't bear to live without Esther.

"Think of how our Heavenly Father forgives us and how He asks us to do likewise," Paul said. "This is a time to forgive, Esther. Otherwise this situation is going to hang heavily upon us, and already it's causing a rift between us."

He saw Esther start when he said the word "rift." It was obviously hurting her as much as it was keeping him up at night. He couldn't help remembering the closeness they had shared before Luther returned to the ranch. It was almost as if it had never happened and Esther and he were back to where they were before they had begun to understand each other.

"Please ask Luther to come here tomorrow," Esther mimed. "There is a play I want to perform for him."

"What is it about?" Paul asked anxiously, hoping it wasn't going to be based on what Esther had endured at Luther's hands.

"It's about forgiveness," Esther responded.

Paul's love for his wife bloomed. No matter the hardship, she always tried her best. He wanted to reach out and kiss her forehead, but the rift between them was still there. "I will ask him to come," Paul said. "But please find it in your heart to really and truly forgive him."

Esther nodded and stood up. "I'm going to bed," she signed. "Good night, Paul."

Paul longed to reach out and take her hand, to hold her close and tell her that it was going to be okay. But he had to admit to himself that he wasn't entirely sure things would be alright. Getting Luther on the right track was one part of his responsibility. The other was to keep his home, ranch, and Esther safe.

Paul was insightful enough to know that the McGuire gang must be getting closer to discovering where Luther had run. He had taken to sleeping with a pistol by his side and had the ranch hands take turns keeping watch through the night. He got up from his chair and went inside, closing and locking the door before he went up to bed.

As he lay down, checking to see that his pistol was within easy reach, he felt like he was beset by danger on every side.

***

"Luther is here," Paul told Esther after tapping her on the shoulder to capture her attention. She was cooking and kept stirring the pot on the stove while she fixed her eyes on her husband in order to discern what he was saying. Then she turned to Luther and nodded.

"Let's eat," she mimed, signaling to Paul and Luther to be seated.

Paul looked at her expectantly, hoping this would be the moment she looked at his brother and extended her forgiveness. He watched her closely as she laid the food on the table and then, to Paul's amazement and relief, Esther picked up a plate and served Luther first.

Luther sprang up from his chair and, folding his hands, bowed to Esther. Paul saw her eyes glisten with unshed tears and her features tense as she fought for composure. It was apparent Esther was struggling but nevertheless desired to please Paul by forgiving Luther.

When the meal was over, Esther did the dishes and wiped down the stove. Luther went out to sit on the porch.

"May I help you?" Paul asked. Esther's eyes went to his lips, and Paul felt overcome by emotion, recalling the day when their lips had met in an expression of all they were beginning to feel for each other. It seemed like their lives had been suspended by the very person who was responsible for their marriage.

"No, thank you," Esther mimed. "You don't need to help me. Please rest on the porch, and I will join you shortly."

Paul joined Luther out on the porch and, for a short while, they reminisced about their childhood.

"Remember the catapults we used to make?" Luther remarked.

Paul nodded. "I do. Those were good times."

"But we never did get any of those birds that we used the catapults on, did we?" Luther laughed.

"I recall we hit one and broke its wing, although I don't think we really aimed to kill them. Just scare them a bit. We just wanted to play," Paul replied.

"That didn't stop Pa from tanning our hides us and taking the catapults away." Luther sighed.

"He said we should never harm one of God's innocent creatures unless it was necessary. He didn't believe we never meant any harm."

"And we were so guilty that we took care of the bird until it healed and was able to fly. That was so long ago, but it seems as if I haven't learned anything. That bird . . . ," Luther said, staring at the scenery before them. "I know you may not believe me, Paul, but I never intended to hurt Esther. I never intended for any of this to happen."

"I suppose these things happen when we let our guard down and think we don't need God in our lives," Paul remarked. "That's a mistake we all make. The thing is, we will invariably slip and fall without Him."

When Paul mentioned God, Luther's mouth twisted, and there was a moment of silence. Then he spoke, looking reflective. "Look, Paul," he began, "I am really sorry to have imposed on you like this. And above everything, I am very sorry for what happened with Esther."

"You've already apologized, Luther," Paul said, "and Esther is a godly woman. She will forgive you. The fact is, you are my brother, and I want to help you start over. While I know now that only you can take responsibility for your actions, it is still mine to help you. And you know how I feel about what you did to my wife, but I know the Lord wants me to forgive you."

"I'm also sorry about getting involved with the McGuire gang," Luther continued. "They are not good people. I thought they would be my new family, but in time it I realized they were just using me to get their dirty work done. However, nobody leaves the gang and then lives to tell the tale, as Frank McGuire would often say, so I am doubly regretful for having become involved with them in the first place. I suppose I will be running from them for the rest of my life."

"Well, you're home safe," Paul replied, though he felt a stab of apprehension at what Luther had just revealed. "Though that's quite a strong threat Frank McGuire threw at you. Hopefully he won't find you."

"I promise I didn't want to place you in any kind of danger. I didn't tell them about the ranch or about you," Luther declared emphatically. "That's one of the reasons I fled Uncle Mack and Aunt Tillie's house—because I didn't want them involved."

"I know," Paul said. "We hope we can soon put this uncertainty behind us."

Luther shook his head from side to side. "I haven't been a good person, and God knows I don't deserve Esther's forgiveness. I was cruel toward her, but please, Paul, convey to her that I am indeed sorry," he pleaded.

"I will," Paul reassured him. "Though you will have to give her some time to come to terms with the fact that you are back here. It's been difficult for her to even look at you, as you have no doubt noticed. The only thing she thinks of when she sees you is—"

"Please, Paul," Luther begged, "don't speak of it. I am deeply ashamed of my actions and can't think what went wrong with me."

Paul heard the porch door open just then and turned around to see Esther standing there with her Bible. She motioned to him and Luther to sit down. Then she placed her Bible in Paul's hands, and he saw it was opened to Luke 15. Esther leaned across and ran her forefinger down the chapter and indicated to Paul that he should read from verses 11-32.

"Please read verse by verse," she mimed. "And please tell your brother to follow this play carefully."

Paul turned to Luther. "Esther has something she would like to convey to you. It's a passage from the Bible."

"Oh," Luther replied, his eyes darting everywhere except on Esther and the Good Book. "But you know I'm not much of a Bible person, Paul."

"Luther," Paul said firmly. "Perhaps you should begin to be one." He tapped the Bible. "I'm going to read now, but you keep your eyes on Esther."

He saw Luther turn to Esther, and he observed that Esther kept her eyes on Luther as she began her play. As he began to read, however, she watched his lips, and he was yet again struck by how vividly Esther could depict a scene and tell a story through her hands and the movement of her eyes. His eyes went from the lines of the passage up to his wife's lovely face as she enacted the story. And he realized how much it must cost Esther to set aside her fears and trauma and stand in front of her attacker, relating to him a story of God's forgiveness.

When the narrative centered around the prodigal son sitting amongst the pigs, looking hungrily at their food and thinking of his father's house, Esther went down on her knees, miming the intense longing of the son for his father. Paul himself felt a rush of emotion, and when he glanced at Luther, he saw tears slipping down his cheeks.

As Paul read Luke 15:18, "'I will arise and go to my father, and I will say to him, "Father, I have sinned against heaven and before you," "" a sob broke from deep within his brother's chest. He dropped his head into his arms, weeping. Esther didn't stop her play, and as Paul reached Luke 15:20, "'But when he was still a long way off, his father saw him and felt compassion and ran and embraced and kissed him,'" Luther crumpled up into a heap on the floor, and his sobs were loud and agonized.

Paul's eyes grew misty as his heart empathized with Luther's anguish. He looked at Esther. She had joined her hands together in prayer and was looking upward. Then she went forward, knelt down by Luther, and placed her hand on his shoulder. Paul couldn't believe what he was seeing. But then he knew that Esther had been asking for a forgiving heart like her Heavenly Father's. Paul slid to the floor beside them and held his brother, and he heard him speak words in between sobs that he never thought he would ever utter in repentance.

"Father, I have sinned," Luther said, sobbing. "I am not worthy of your forgiveness, but I beg you for it. Please give me a second chance."

"He has given you a second chance, Luther," Paul said. "That's why you're home."

Esther had taken the Bible from Paul's hands and opened to another passage, which she signaled to him to read to Luther. It was from John 8:11. "'Neither do I condemn you; go, and from now on sin no more.'"

Luther wailed. "I'm so sorry! Thank you—I'm sorry, thank you, thank you...."

Sometime later, after Luther had calmed down and left for the bunkhouses on the far corner of the ranch, Paul turned to Esther. "Thank you for what you did," he said. Then he took her hand. "I would like to ask Luther to stay in the house with us. For his safety," he added. "But I will wait for you to give me the word, and only then will I ask him."

"You are a good brother to him," Esther signed. "But please could we wait for just a few days before he comes to stay?"

"Of course," Paul replied. He was aware the only spare room was the one Esther had used when they were first married. Neither was there a door to the attic where Esther now slept. He realized then she had still not been able to get over her fear of his brother even though she had forgiven him.

"One step at a time," he said, meaning it for both Esther as well as himself.

Chapter Twenty-One

"It's not good news, is it?" Esther signed as Paul burst into the kitchen. She had been longing for him to come running to her and take her in his arms, but it seemed like that wasn't about to happen. Esther often wondered if she had just dreamed of the day when Paul had kissed her. Since Luther's return, the brothers had been enjoying each other's company, and she almost felt like she had no place in their lives apart from keeping house and cooking.

Paul nodded. "Yes," he said. "It's very bad news, I'm afraid. In fact, it's a telegram from Aunt Tillie."

Esther stared mutely up at him, her mind going to every possibility that might lead to Paul's aunt sending him a telegram.

"Uncle Mack was assaulted by the McGuire gang," Paul said.

Esther's hand flew to her mouth, and she shook her head in shock. Her worst fears were coming true. The McGuire gang had found Paul's uncle and aunt, and now it was only a matter of time before they landed at the ranch, demanding Luther's life or taking theirs.

"Why did they attack Uncle Mack?" Esther signed. Her heart was like a block of ice in her chest as she asked the question, and when Paul answered, the feeling of panic intensified.

"That's the frightening part," Paul replied. "They beat him so badly that Aunt Tillie thought he would surely die. She had only one way of preventing them from killing Uncle Mack, and that was to give them the information they asked for."

Esther's hand flew to her mouth again, and her eyes were stretched so wide that they hurt.

"Aunt Tillie said she was sorry. She fears the McGuire gang could be on their way over here," Paul added, turning away from her to pace up and down.

"Then you must bring Luther into the house and hide him here," Esther mimed, moving to stand right in front of Paul. "And we must be prepared to protect ourselves." She was silent for a moment, then queried, "Why is this gang after Luther? Did Aunt Tillie say?"

"No," Paul replied.

Esther turned this over in her mind. There didn't seem to be too much time left for them to run for cover, so to speak. So they would have to stand strong and face the enemy when they arrived and attacked.

"Are you afraid?" Paul asked anxiously.

Esther surprised herself by shaking her head. "We are together," she replied, her actions emphatic, "so I'm not afraid." She looked intently at him. "Have you told Luther?"

Paul sighed and shook his head. "He is just beginning to believe in God again and had such a moment reconnecting with the Father that I didn't have the heart to tell him his worst fears are about to be realized."

"He needs to know," Esther signed urgently. "It's important."

"Of course," Paul replied. "I will tell him when I see him next, which should be soon."

"I hope your Uncle Mack is alright," Esther signed anxiously.

"There's no way of knowing, unfortunately," Paul replied. He turned to go out the kitchen door. "I'll fetch Luther and tell him he needs to move in here immediately," he added.

***

"So you want me to move in here?" Luther asked as he sat down to supper with Paul and Esther. "This is sudden and surprising."

"We were just waiting for things to fall into place and for Esther to feel comfortable," Paul explained, distractedly carving into a piece of roast beef.

Esther gave Paul a significant look, silently urging him not to delay and to get to the point quickly.

"Actually," Paul said, clearing his throat, "there's something that happened a little while ago."

"What is it?" Luther asked nervously, setting his knife and fork down and leaning forward.

"I had a telegram from Uncle Mack and Aunt Tillie," Paul replied.

Luther looked away, then back at Paul. "Look," he said, "I've been meaning to come clean about that too, especially after the other night when Esther's play made such an impact on me."

"Come clean about what, Luther?" Paul asked, and Esther could discern from his expression that his tolerance was wearing thin. Her eyes darted from Paul's lips to Luther's, anxious not to miss any part of the conversation.

"I took some money from Aunty Tillie's closet," Luther declared, shamefaced. "They were bound to find out sooner or later, but I didn't mean to rob them blind. I just needed enough to—"

"Enough to *what*?" Paul asked coldly. "Enough to buy yourself a bottle of whiskey at any and every saloon you passed on your way here? And thereby leave a clear trail for the McGuire gang to follow?"

Esther's food lodged itself in her throat, and she choked. She got up and moved away from the table to fetch herself some water but positioned herself so that she could still watch their lips.

"Paul," Luther said, "I took the money when I joined the McGuire gang. I needed to have something with me to get away in case things didn't work out as I wanted them to."

"Tell me you didn't visit any saloons on your way here," Paul said quietly, his face white. Esther's spirits plummeted.

This was even worse than she thought. "What is your answer, Luther?" Paul asked, quite obviously overwhelmed with indignation and swiftly running out of patience with his brother.

Esther saw Luther's eyes falter. He was unable to hold his brother's piercing gaze. She shook her head in dismay.

"You were still pursuing your old ways just before coming here, weren't you, Luther?" Paul asked coldly.

Luther said nothing, and Esther shifted uncomfortably. She wondered if she should step into the fray and plead with him to favor them with the truth because they would have to act fast and prepare for an attack by the McGuire gang.

"Paul, I'm sorry," Luther replied. "I was scared and distraught. I only took a few dollars from Aunt Tillie's closet, and yes . . . I used some of it for drink. But also for food. And I didn't get inebriated the way I used to. I wouldn't make that mistake when I was alone out there with nobody to get me out of the lockup. I lay low and didn't give anybody my name in any of the saloons I visited. I didn't stay long. I ate, drank a little, and left."

"This is not the time for blame," Esther mimed earnestly as Paul opened his mouth to speak. "We need to find a way around this situation. We must not waste a moment more in raking up the past."

As Esther looked over her shoulder, miming the motions of raking, she perceived that Luther was asking Paul what she was attempting to communicate.

"Focus on the present and the future, and don't keep raking up the past," Paul said. "Esther is right. We need to stand together against this enemy and make sure we don't lose." He then explained the contents of the telegram.

Luther rose from the table and faced Paul squarely. "Thank you, my brother," he said. "But I cannot allow you to fight this battle with me. This is my fight and mine alone. I got myself into this mess by my selfish, willful nature, and I need to get myself out of it."

"We will stand with you," Paul said firmly. "And we can go to Sheriff Basley and ask him to help us."

Esther moved to stand by Paul, nodding her head vigorously. No matter what Luther had done, she knew in her heart he also deserved a second chance.

Luther shook his head. "I've done enough to endanger your lives, Paul," he replied. "I can't do that anymore. Nor can I expect you to keep fighting my battles for me. That wouldn't be right on my part." He shrugged. "Besides, I haven't exactly been a model citizen, and Sheriff Basley might not be willing to help me." He heaved a deep sigh. "If the McGuire gang finds the ranch, then I will go out and face them alone," he declared.

Esther looked from Paul to his brother. Paul was silent. She knew him. It would destroy him if anything happened to Luther, but at that moment it seemed like he had run out of things to say. He looked exhausted.

"I have prepared the room for you to sleep in," she mimed to Luther. Luther didn't follow everything she had attempted to convey, so Paul interrupted.

"Esther says your room is ready upstairs," he said. "Let's get to bed early. There is much to think of and plan."

"I have to fetch my things from the bunkhouse. Not that there's a lot. Just a saddlebag with a change of clothes," Luther replied.

"We can fetch it tomorrow," Paul said. "Just go up to bed. I'll keep watch for the first part of the night, and then you can take over."

Luther shrugged and went up to bed. Esther climbed up to the attic, and Paul went to his room. Esther was particularly alert, starting at every vibration. She turned her lantern down, placed it on the dresser, and positioned herself by the window, fully dressed. Then she wiped the glass and peered through it. She couldn't see much except the trees and the night sky. In her hand, she clutched a bell. She had found it on the sideboard in the kitchen and asked Paul if she could keep it. She looked at it now. It was a simple metal bell, perhaps the kind to tie around a cow's neck, but to her, it was a weapon. She got up and rummaged in a dresser drawer and found a ribbon to string the bell on to, then knotted it and placed the bell on her lap.

She nodded off after a while, her head against the windowpane, and woke up with a start. Her keen senses discerned something was not in place. She quickly slid the ribbon over her head, and the bell dangled against her chest like a large pendant. She turned up her lantern and climbed down from the attic, holding the lantern aloft. She knocked on Paul's bedroom door.

"Something's not right," Esther signed, holding up the lantern and using one hand to communicate.

"Are you unwell?" Paul asked, misunderstanding. Then he spied the bell around her neck. "An alarm bell," he said. "That's good, under the circumstances."

"I'm alright." Esther responded to Paul's question with a single gesture. She pointed at Luther's bedroom, the room that used to be hers when she and Paul were first married.

"He must be fast asleep," Paul said, and Esther raised her lantern to read the words off his lips.

"Look inside," Esther mimed. But Paul retraced his steps into his own room, unwilling to wake his brother up.

Esther decided to take matters into her own hands and knocked on the door. When Luther didn't answer, she pushed the door open. And, as she held her lantern aloft, she saw the room was empty.

Looking over her shoulder, Paul raked his fingers through his hair. Then he rushed back into his room and picked up his pistol. Esther's eyebrows rose in alarm when she saw it.

"Don't worry," Paul said, reassuring her. "I don't use it unnecessarily. This is for protection."

He laid a hand on her shoulder, and she looked at him. "You stay here and keep safe," he said. "I'll go out and try to find him."

"My place is by your side," Esther communicated in her firm, precise way.

There was a brief moment as Paul thought. "Alright. The more people looking, the better chances we have of finding him. But stay close," he said, and she nodded, then followed him out the door, her bell swaying against her chest.

"There's no time to saddle the horses," Paul said, facing Esther in the light of her lantern. "Hurry."

They ran along, Paul a few feet ahead of Esther. Esther held on to the bell to prevent it from jingling and prayed silently and steadily. She knew they had no idea where to even begin to look for Luther. It was obvious he had fled, not wishing to put them at any further risk, as he had said. Paul looked back at her, obviously eager to move faster. She held her lantern up to her face and signed for him to go on. She would go to the stables and see if anything was amiss. She held the lantern out for him, but he gestured at the sky, indicating there was sufficient starlight to help him find his way. Then he ran toward the bunkhouses.

She dashed to the stables, intending to saddle one of the horses and go out to help Paul. Running from Raider's stall to Honeycomb's, she aimed for Typhoon. She stopped, gasping. Typhoon's stall was empty; he was gone. Esther felt an overwhelming surge of anger. Luther had taken Typhoon to help him escape just as he had taken money from Aunt Tillie to help him on his way. He was used to taking anything he wanted to further his own interests. She was so affected by his actions, her chest felt constricted. She leaned back against the stable wall and took deep breaths in an effort to calm herself. Otherwise, she thought she might just pass out.

Esther stumbled out of the stables into the night air. Typhoon was gone, and she felt bereft. She ran back inside for Honeycomb. She would go after Luther herself and bring Typhoon back. He was Paul's favorite horse and hers too, and she would do her best to find him. She saddled Honeycomb in the lantern light, extinguished the flame, and left the lantern outside. Then she climbed onto Honeycomb and galloped away.

"Lord," she prayed silently, "I don't know which way to go, but you know where Luther is and where he has taken Typhoon. Please show me which direction I should take and where I should go."

A wild rabbit bobbed onto her path, and Esther wondered if it was a sign. She could just about tell it was there from the silhouette of its ears against the backdrop of starlit grass. Esther veered away from it and galloped on as she continued to pray to God to lead her to Typhoon and thus to Luther.

More rabbits appeared in the undergrowth, and Esther veered away from them. It was strange how they didn't flee at the pounding of her horse's hooves, but she didn't have time to think about it too closely. She turned Honeycomb around and galloped back the way she assumed she had come, but soon she realized she was lost. Thankfully she knew she was still on the ranch, although perhaps going around in circles, trying to feel useful and obviously not succeeding in doing anything except ride wildly this way and that.

And then Honeycomb slowed down all of a sudden and began to balk. As Esther tried to calm her down, a horse streaked past them. It had to be Typhoon, though in the darkness, it was hard to tell. The horse flew past them some distance away, and Esther was aware that if it was Typhoon, then he had probably thrown Luther off, in which case Luther would be lying somewhere on the path up ahead.

If she found him, she would be alone with him. Fear crept around the edges of her mind, and Esther hesitated, locked in an internal debate about whether she ought to keep searching for Luther or try to find her way back to the stables and get help. Immediately she prayed for strength and courage, then saw the all-but-forgotten bell dangling against her chest. She reached for it and rang it wildly. *This could work in two ways,* Esther thought. She could be attracting trespassers, or she might actually summon help from the ranch hands. Paul had told her they would be stationed all around the perimeter of the ranch, but it seemed like there was nobody in sight.

She rode farther, ringing her bell and hoping she would find someone to guide her back, because she wasn't certain Honeycomb could take her home. Honeycomb balked again, and then reared up. Esther clung on for all she was worth, hoping the horse wouldn't throw her, and then she saw a figure lying across the path. It seemed to be beckoning to her. Esther calmed Honeycomb down and slid off, acting with greater courage than she actually felt. And then she recognized him. It was Luther. He was gesturing to his leg, and Esther realized he must have been hurt when Typhoon threw him off. She signaled to him to try to get up, and then, though she was trembling with fear as memories of her assault rose up to taunt her, she reached out and gave Luther her hand.

She steadied herself as Luther took her offer and pulled himself painfully up to his feet. Esther pointed to Honeycomb and asked if he could get himself up on the horse. But even as he tried to climb up, Esther was beset by a wave of suspicion. *What if he takes off on Honeycomb?* she thought. She would be left there all alone. She chastised herself for her suspicion and remembered the story of the Good Samaritan in the Bible. God would not let her down when she was trying to help someone in need. She would have to trust Him even if she didn't trust Luther.

Climbing on first, she waited for Luther to get on behind her. He did so painfully and may have even cried out, but she couldn't hear. Then she turned Honeycomb around and galloped forward, hoping she was going in the right direction. Once again she saw wild rabbits hop onto her path and veered away from them. They were possibly just romping in the grass, but Esther suspected they were signs from God, guiding her toward home on that dark night. He was with her; her fear ebbed as the lights of the homestead twinkled into view.

Chapter Twenty-Two

Paul was incredulous. "You brought Luther back by yourself?" he asked Esther when they were all back on the homestead.

"She did," Luther replied on Esther's behalf.

"Esther," Paul began, "I told you I wanted you safe, and yet you went off on your own?"

"Paul," Luther interrupted. "Please don't chastise Esther. She was kind to me. And I'm back here because of her."

"You're here because Typhoon threw you off his back," Paul retorted. "Really, Luther, what were you thinking?"

"I wanted to release you from the responsibility of getting me out of this latest scrape of mine," Luther replied.

"So you stole my horse?" Paul queried. "A horse, I may add, that is also very dear to my wife's heart. She would have been devastated had you managed to get away with Typhoon."

"I would have brought him back when things settled," Luther replied. "I was just taking him to get away safely."

"Like you took money from Aunt Tillie," Paul shot back. "This has got to stop here and now, Luther. This time you had Esther to rescue you. You should count yourself very fortunate."

"I was"—Luther hissed as he accidentally jostled his injured leg, clenching his teeth—"just trying to help myself."

Esther was silent, ministering to Luther, who was lying on the couch in the living room. Paul watched her bind his brother's leg with surprising expertise and tapped her on the shoulder to thank her.

"We need to call in a doctor," Esther signed, turning to him.

"It might attract undue attention," Paul replied. "Does the leg appear to be broken?"

Esther put her hand up to her forehead. This was something she did when she wasn't quite sure how to respond to a query.

"Are you saying it might be broken, but you aren't quite sure if it actually is?" Paul prompted.

Esther nodded. "We need a doctor," she mimed, now with a greater sense of urgency.

"We'll have to wait until we can talk to Sheriff Basley first and ask him for help," Paul replied. "In the meantime, it looks like you've done a good job with Luther's leg."

Paul was overwhelmed by Esther's response to Luther running away. She could very well have let him escape, because that would ensure she never had to encounter him again. But instead, she had gone out into the night, found him, brought him back home, and tended to his wound. He learned more and more about her every day, but more than that, he learned about God just by watching Esther. She showed compassion, patience and forgiveness, overcoming all her fears by her faith. She often quoted, in mime, Philippians 4:13: "I can do all things through Him, who strengthens me." Watching her tend to the man who had assaulted her showed Paul how true that scripture was.

When he had seen her riding back to the homestead with Luther behind her, the bell around her neck heralding their arrival, he hadn't known whether to be angry or filled with admiration. He himself had scoured the bunkhouses for his brother, sent the ranch hands to look for him, and then returned to the stables, expecting to find Esther there. When he saw the empty stalls, he knew what she had done and had almost gone sick with worry. That night, Esther had proved she was a true helpmate. And Paul was humbled by her efforts to do what she knew to be right under the circumstances.

"I'm going up to bed now," Esther mimed to Paul after she had drawn a table up close to the couch and put a jug of water and a glass on it for Luther.

"I'll sleep down here too," Paul said. "In case Luther needs anything."

Esther nodded and turned to leave the room. Paul followed her.

"Esther," he said, moving to stand right in front of her. She was holding a lantern, and her face was bathed in an ethereal glow. "You are an angel," Paul whispered.

Esther watched his lips, then shook her head. Paul knew she was always reluctant to accept praise of any kind.

He took the lantern from her hand and led her up the stairs.

"Could I come up to the attic with you for just a minute?" Paul asked when they reached his room, turning around and holding the lantern up to his face so Esther could read his lips. "There's something I need to say."

Esther nodded.

"I just want to say thank you," Paul said after they had climbed up to the attic and sat down, Paul on a chair and Esther on the edge of her bed, where she could clearly watch his lips. "What you did—bringing Luther back—was courageous and heroic. You are a true woman of God."

Esther pointed to herself and then upward. She seemed to like being called a woman of God. She smiled.

"Thank you," Paul repeated.

"I did it for the Lord—and for you," Esther replied. "Please don't thank me."

Paul looked around and found Esther's Bible lying on her bedside table. He picked it up and opened it to Deuteronomy 31:6. "Be strong and courageous. Do not fear or be in dread of them, for it is the Lord your God who goes with you. He will not leave you or forsake you."

Pointing to the verse, he laid the Bible in Esther's hands and waited while she read it. Then he motioned for her to look at his lips. "I thought I knew what strength was. My father taught me it was to push my emotions aside and only rely on myself. Today you taught me that your faith makes you strong. Your love and trust for God is why Luther is here. And today I want to ask forgiveness of the Lord for ever doubting His ability to take care of me."

Esther's eyes shone in the lamplight, and she leaned forward eagerly as he continued to speak. "We need Him now more than ever, and I can see that though I didn't, or couldn't, believe it, He was always with me, helping me through the hard times."

Esther nodded vigorously, encouraging him to go on. "I want to recommit my life completely to trusting and having faith in the Lord," Paul declared, and Esther took a deep breath and then released it. Paul saw how happy she was and how it seemed to reassure her when he said those words. He took her hands in his. "May we pray together?" he asked.

Esther nodded happily, and Paul closed his eyes but held his head in such a way that she could read what he was saying.

"Our loving Heavenly Father," Paul prayed. "I have not trusted you enough, but I return now and humbly ask your forgiveness for not relying on your promises. I was far from you, but you were never far from me. I have realized, more and more each day, that your love has always reached out and drawn me back to you. Father God, we face a powerful adversary, but we claim your promise that you will never leave us nor forsake us. Therefore, we stand together in faith and courage upon the strong foundation of your promises to fight this enemy, who we know you will vanquish for us. We say this prayer in the mighty name of Jesus. Amen!"

***

Paul helped Luther get off the buckboard and then gave Esther a hand. Luther was still hobbling about painfully, but seeing a doctor didn't seem to be an option for reasons of anonymity. Luther pulled his hat down low over his forehead and walked into Sheriff Basley's office after Paul.

Sheriff Basley was sitting at his desk, peering at some papers. "You again?" he remarked, putting the papers down. "What have you done this time?"

Paul flushed, indignant. "Actually, Luther needs your help, Sheriff Basley," he said.

"I'm in trouble," Luther said. "I have done something wrong, and I deserve what I am going through, but I need help because I'm running for my life."

"Whoa!" Sheriff Basley said, raising his hand to get Luther to pause. "Slow down and tell me what you're here for."

"After Luther was sent away to my aunt and uncle in South Dakota, he apparently got involved with a gang. The McGuire gang, to be precise," Paul said.

"Frank McGuire is a dangerous man," Sheriff Basley declared. "Very dangerous, in fact. How did you get mixed up with him and manage to return? Nobody ever leaves that gang and lives to tell the tale."

"That's what we're here for," Paul declared. "Sheriff Basley, Luther's life is under threat. The McGuire gang are after him. They actually went to my aunt and uncle's home and beat up my Uncle Mack so badly that my aunt, to save her husband, gave the gang the information they wanted."

"Which was?" Sheriff Basley asked, confused.

"They wanted to know where Luther was," Paul replied. "And my aunt told them about the ranch. Then she sent me a telegram to alert me that the gang may just show up here."

Sheriff Basley sat back on his chair and scratched his chin. "What do you want me to do?" he asked.

"Please, Sheriff, could you request the men of the town to stand with us and fight the McGuire gang and prevent them from taking Luther's life?" Paul asked.

"I can't promise anything," Sheriff Basley replied. "You see, you might have found it in your heart to forgive your brother, and the Lord knows that your wife is a saint for even allowing him into your home, but the folks of this town . . . well, they don't forgive and forget that easy."

"I admit that I have messed up, and messed up bad," Luther replied. "But all I ask is one more chance to make things right and to prove to you Luther Orton isn't a lost cause."

"A lost sheep, more likely," Sheriff Basley remarked wryly. "But we all know the Lord goes after those lost sheep and brings them back to the fold. So, Luther, though I still haven't forgotten all the trouble you have given this brother of yours, I am willing to give you one more chance to change your ways and make things right."

"Thank you, Sheriff Basley," Paul said, exhaling.

"I won't disappoint you, Sheriff," Luther declared.

"Well, you folks go on home, and I will assemble the townsfolk and see what their views are," Sheriff Basley said, standing up.

Paul doffed his hat to the sheriff, and Luther followed suit. Esther dipped her head. She had been quiet through the entire conversation, her eyes watching the sheriff's lips closely.

"I'll come around to the ranch, Paul," the sheriff said as they trooped out of his office. "Let you know what the people say. No point arousing suspicion."

"Of course," Paul said, nodding in assent.

"We need a doctor," Esther signed to the sheriff.

Sheriff Basley crinkled his brows, confused at Esther's direct address, so Paul hastened to explain what she had requested.

"Esther feels Luther's leg needs medical attention," Paul said. "He is in considerable pain."

"By golly, she knows what's going on?" Sheriff Basley said.

"My wife is intelligent and is perfectly capable of communicating," Paul said, keeping his voice calm. "You just have to learn how to listen to her."

"Keep your hat on, son. I wasn't expecting it, is all." Sheriff Basley smiled and nodded at Esther, then turned back to the men. "A doctor, eh?"

"Obviously I don't want too many people to see me," Luther added.
"I'll bring a medic along with me when I come to visit, then," Sheriff Basley said, looking directly at Esther, curiosity in his eyes.

But when he visited the ranch the next day, Sheriff Basley didn't come bearing good news. Esther showed him to the living room, where he sat down heavily in a chair. Luther was already on the couch, and Esther and Paul stood nearby; he was too anxious to sit.

"I met with several men from town," Sheriff Basley said, "but they are reluctant to get involved with a fight they say isn't theirs."

"I was afraid of this," Paul remarked.

"They feel Luther has brought this misfortune upon himself, owing to his wayward living, and that he must therefore bear the consequences and pay for his sins himself."

Paul felt his spirits sag. This was a blow to them. He didn't know how they were going to take on a notorious gang on their own.

"I'm sorry," Sheriff Basley said. "I did try to convince them to give Luther a second chance, but they were up in arms against him."

"What about the doctor?" Esther signed. "If he has to fight, he needs to be in fit shape to do so."

Sheriff Basley gave Esther an apologetic look, then turned to Paul, who translated for her.

"I'm sorry about this too. Even a medic holds a grudge. As you know, we have only one doctor in town, and he is away at the moment. Doesn't get back for another day or two. I approached his assistant, who seems to remember an occasion when Luther picked a quarrel with him and coerced him to give him money, then beat him up. He's refused to help."

Luther hung his head, and Esther looked distressed.

"Something must be done for Luther's leg," she signed to Paul.

"Is there nobody else who can treat my brother?" Paul asked.

Sheriff Basley smiled. "Well, there is one: me!"

"You?" Paul queried incredulously.

"I'm no medic," Sheriff Basley said, "but I have set a bone or two in my time. My pa taught me."

"Was he a doctor?" Paul asked.

"Of sorts," the sheriff replied. "Now show me that leg, Luther."

After a brief examination where he gently felt Luther's leg, he said, "I don't feel a definite break, so it might just be severely sprained. Maybe only cracked a bone. After all, he has been walking on it, correct? But just to be sure, I'll need some alcohol, a shaft of wood to use as a splint, and some clean linen to bind the leg with."

"You stay with Luther," Esther signed to Paul. "I'll fetch the things."

"Paul," Luther said, "I think it was meant to be this way, and I need to face the gang by myself."

"I'm not going to let you do this alone, Luther," Paul replied.

"Neither will I allow you to fight this battle on your own," Esther signed as she returned with the things Sheriff Basley had asked for.

"Look, I've known you boys for a long time now," Sheriff Basley said as he got to work on Luther's leg, "and I wouldn't forgive myself if I didn't do whatever I could to protect you. So here's what I think. I think we can fight the gang if we have Sandy and all the ranch hands standing with us. And hopefully Luther's leg will have healed by then so he can do whatever he can to help us along too."

"You think we can get the gang to back down?" Paul queried.

"I think so," Sheriff Basley replied. "I'll simply tell them I won't ride them down if they turn around and leave Montana. Besides, a messy shootout wouldn't be in their best interests."

Luther sighed. "If we won't do this my way, then I might as well throw in my lot with your plan. The chances are slim, but you're right," Luther said. "We can do this. From what I know of Frank McGuire, he may be callous and cold blooded, but he can also be made to see reason."

"Please stay and have a meal with us," Esther signed to the Sheriff, and Paul conveyed her request.

"I would be happy to," Sheriff Basley replied. "But I need to be on my way. And you, Paul, need to meet with your men and tell them what to prepare for."

Paul nodded. "Thank you, Sheriff," he said. "I appreciate your help."

After Sheriff Basley rode away, Paul set off to see Sandy and his ranch hands. He found them all gathered at the horse corral and explained the situation.

"We can do this," Sandy said. "We took on a wildfire together, and we can take on a gang."

"Not the same thing at all, Sandy," Paul said wryly. "But I appreciate your optimism. Is everyone willing to fight for us?"

"You can count on me, Paul," Sandy reassured him. The other ranch hands nodded, and a murmur of assent rippled through the men.

"For a start, we are going to need some of you to get busy with cleaning all the weapons we can muster," Paul said. "Guns, axes, knives, pitchforks—anything and everything. And then we need to plan our strategy."

"Shoot to kill is what I propose as strategy," Sandy declared. Several of the men chuckled darkly.

Paul shook his head. "Reaching a compromise would be far better. We need to do whatever it takes to ensure we are not going to be engaged in an ongoing battle with the McGuire gang. It will be ideal if we can talk them out of fighting for Luther, forgiving him, and going on their way."

"Easier said than done," Sandy replied. "But I see your point. You don't want to expend all your resources in the next few years fighting meaningless wars."

Chapter Twenty-Three

Esther watched Paul and Luther talk. They were sitting together at the kitchen table, discussing strategy, and she was reminded, once again, of David and Abigail. She stood by the stove, cooking their lunch, turning around every once in a while to see what each of them was saying. They were obviously getting more anxious, enough to leave work on the ranch and sit at the table mapping out a plan like generals in an army.

"Oh, my Lord," she prayed in her heart. "Please give Paul the abilities and success of the mighty warrior king David. He faces a Goliath in the form of a notorious gang, and the ones with us are few in number. I know Paul, my Lord, and you know him even better. He will ride out at the head of his men, and he will be the most vulnerable to attack. But we rely on your strength within each one of us and especially within Paul at this time. May he prevail against the enemy."

Almost immediately the verse from 2 Chronicles 20:15 came to her mind: "Do not be dismayed, and do not be afraid of this great horde, for the battle is not yours but God's."

Esther reached for her Bible, which was never far away, on the sideboard. She opened to the passage that had just given her strength and comfort and placed it before Paul.

"Thank you, Lord," Paul said, looking heavenward. "And thank you, Esther," he said, looking at her. Then she saw, from his lips, that he was repeating the verse to Luther. She felt a thrill of joy. For Paul to be quoting Scripture and trusting in God was a big step. Her prayers were being answered, as she knew they would be. She glanced at Luther, not surprised to see he was still a little reserved when it came to placing his faith completely in the Word. She smiled to herself. She had been praying for his attitude to change and for a transformation in his life just as there had been in Paul's. And she had faith God would answer her prayers.

Already, after her play about the prodigal son, Luther had softened considerably. He had admitted his faults and seen the error of his ways. Even now, as he listened intently to what Paul was saying as they made plans for the battle, Esther could see his outlook was completely different from what it used to be. Esther was confident he would also come around.

She had begun to set the table for their lunch when

Paul got up and went to the door. Someone must have knocked. Moments later, Sheriff Basley came into the room, red-faced and breathing a bit heavily. Despite the fall chill in the air, he had beads of perspiration on his brow. Esther looked at him, alarmed.

"What happened?" Paul asked, pulling out a chair and asking the sheriff to sit down.

"The gang," Sheriff Basley gasped, motioning for Esther to please give him a drink of water.

Esther's heart raced as she filled a glass from the tap and set it down before the sheriff. Whatever his news was, it clearly wasn't good.

"I have information from a reliable source that the McGuire gang is headed this way," Sheriff Basley said, his voice low.

Esther watched his lips closely, and she felt a momentary surge of fear. "'The battle is not yours but God's,'" she repeated silently. As the verse played over and over in her mind, it stilled her heart, and her breathing evened. She squared her shoulders as the sheriff continued to speak.

"You need to get your men together," he said. "And be prepared for an attack at any point."

"Why wait until they attack us?" Paul queried. "Perhaps we should ride out to meet them and propose terms of peace, not war."

Sheriff Basley gave Paul an uncertain look, but he nodded. "I suppose it's better to show that we're ready, vigilant, and capable of defending ourselves rather than giving the impression we are unprepared," he said.

Paul got up. "Let's go and talk to our men," he said.

Esther wiped her hands on her apron. The food was ready, and she set the pots on the counter, where they would keep warm.

"I'll serve lunch when we return," she said, moving to stand in front of Paul so he could interpret her.

"Esther, you don't need to come with us," Paul began but she gave him an appealing look.

"I'll feel better knowing what is being planned," she explained to Paul in mime.

"What seems to be the problem?" Sheriff Basley asked Paul.

"Esther says she would like to come along with us to talk to the men," Paul replied.

"No harm done," Sheriff Basley remarked. "We never know when we may need the intuition and wisdom of a godly woman."

"You've never uttered a truer word, Sheriff," Paul replied. "Let's fetch the horses."

"At least my leg is better," Luther remarked, "and I can ride again."

"For the encounter, Luther, you will ride on Honeycomb," Paul said. "She's fast enough for cattle drives, but she's gentle, so she won't irritate your leg overmuch."

"Of course," Luther said. "I'm glad about that. Honeycomb seems accustomed to different people riding her."

"Unlike Typhoon, who is choosy," Paul remarked, "and only tolerates Esther or me."

Esther read the words off Paul's lips and smiled to herself. She really loved riding Typhoon.

"I wish I'd known that before attempting to make off on him," Luther remarked wryly.

They reached the stables, and Paul led Raider out of his stall.

Esther led Typhoon out, and Luther hastily limped out of the stable, leading Honeycomb.

"How's your leg feeling?" Paul asked. "I hope it's strong enough for you to ride."

"I'll manage," Luther said. "Once I'm in the saddle, I'll be fine."

"Follow us, Esther," Paul said, and she wished he didn't seem so offhand. It was apparent he wasn't entirely comfortable with her being around when they were discussing the battle and laying plans, but she was tenacious, if anything. She would keep insisting she be around when they discussed anything to do with the battle.

She watched Paul and Luther keenly. The brothers seemed closer and more comfortable around each other. Paul had helped Luther while he was in pain and hobbling around, and Luther, it would seem, finally realized that he had a family. But Esther was sad about one thing. Paul appeared to have forgotten her and the feelings he had professed to have for her before Luther stormed into their lives again. She was now on the periphery of his world, while Luther was a part of the center. Paul was doing whatever he could to save his brother's life, and his interactions with her were therefore limited. She insisted on family prayers, and Paul obliged her. Luther, too, would sit in, and the brothers would take turns reading from the Bible and praying. Even on these occasions, Esther couldn't help but feel like the outsider because of her inability to hear and speak.

She sighed now, thinking of herself as being on the periphery of Paul's life. She began to take a closer look at the word and think of its different meanings. So, she reasoned, she was on the periphery, the border one had to cross to get to the center, the first line of defense that protected everything inside. She knew she was going off on a tangent, one few would comprehend, but to her, it didn't matter. She needed a reason to keep going despite Paul's casual treatment of her, and this was it. She was on his periphery. She was the guardian who would build the fence and keep them all safe. She would be that for him. It didn't matter that he didn't have too much time for her. All that mattered was that she could be there for him.

Paul and Luther had come to a halt and were talking to Sandy. Esther rode up to join them, staying just behind and was therefore unable to tell what was going on. But then she saw the men come up, all of them on horseback. They looked like an army, but so much smaller in number, maybe thirty at best, and she joined them where they lined up in front of Paul, Luther, and Sheriff Basley. Now she could read what was being discussed.

The men doffed their hats to her and cast approving glances at Typhoon. Paul had told her they had a newfound admiration for her after she had started riding him. The admiration she inspired in them began when, during the wildfire, she had fought the flames alongside them. She smiled at them all, but within her heart there was apprehension when she saw how few they were. Then she chastised herself for forgetting the battle was God's and not theirs. The story of Gideon in the book of Judges flashed into her mind and reassured her. God had sent Gideon against a powerful enemy with a small number of men to show how the might of men was nothing compared to the strength of God.

Esther played the story over in her mind as the men ranged themselves around Paul, Luther, and the sheriff. Then Paul began to speak, and Esther's eyes were riveted to his lips.

"The McGuire gang is closer now," Paul said, "and we have no time to waste. We need to get prepared to take them on. First we will approach them in peace and recommend a compromise, asking that they turn around, or the sheriff will ride them down. However, if they choose to fight, then we must be ready for a battle, however difficult."

"Where are the rest of the men?" Sheriff Basley asked, and Esther felt great compassion for Paul as she interpreted the question.

"These are all the men," Paul replied.

"Are you certain?" the sheriff queried.

"I know how many men we have working on the ranch, Sheriff," Paul said. "And these are all of them."

Esther saw Sheriff Basley shake his head in dismay. "We need more people to stand with us."

"But we don't have the time to muster any more people," Sandy said. Esther's eyes were darting from one person to the other, reading their lips, and the more she perceived of the situation, the more she felt required to do something. She was the guardian, the protector of the periphery. She had to do her bit to improve the chances of their men against the McGuire gang.

"When do we ride out?" Sandy asked.

Paul looked at Sheriff Basley. "Sheriff Basley has information that the gang is approaching. He will tell us when we need to move forward," he replied.

"I didn't want to alarm you all unduly, but the gang is fast approaching the ranch," Sheriff Basley said.

"Could you be more specific, Sheriff?" Paul said.

"By my reckoning, we should ride out tomorrow," the sheriff replied. He leaned closer to Paul, and Esther was glad she could read lips. "You have a few hours to get more men," he added.

"We will gather right here in this spot tomorrow after sunup," Paul said. "Clean and prepare your weapons, and above all, devote some time to pray for this situation."

"And guard the perimeter," Sheriff Basley said. "Make sure there are men patrolling the fence so that there are no vulnerable points where the gang could break in. We are dealing with unscrupulous people who have no qualms about killing. They are outlaws, and we need to be aware of that. Paul here wants to negotiate with them, but I advise that while he is negotiating, the rest of us need to be ready to strike back if they attack."

Esther read the words "perimeter" and "fence" off Sheriff Basley's lips. She knew it was absurd to think of herself as such, but even now, she felt like she had been relegated to the outer circle, disregarded because she was a woman—and a mute one, at that. The sheriff had also referred to vulnerable points in the perimeter. She mentally intoned the verse, "I can do all things through Christ, who strengthens

269

me,'" and felt stronger each time she repeated it. The more she repeated it, the greater the conviction within her that she was not meant to stand aside and do nothing while Paul led their small group of men out to the battle. She felt like God was showing her a way she could actually help out.

As they rode back to the homestead, Esther felt, yet again, isolated from the men's conversation. Once they were home, she served the men their lunch and then stood by and watched them eat while reading the words they said off their lips. She needed every bit of information she could garner. So far, she had discerned that Paul was certain of his ability to convince Frank McGuire of the sense of a peaceful resolution to the problem. She could also tell the sheriff appeared more positive about their situation than he actually felt. She watched him look from Paul to Luther, and in his eyes Esther saw apprehension and uncertainty. And then there was Luther. He was overwhelmed by guilt and was trying to convince both his brother and the sheriff that they would be able to prevail against the gang.

Esther cleared the plates off the table and washed up. Nobody had asked her to join them at the meal nor had Paul even stopped to ask her if she had eaten or was going to. So she served herself some food and took it outside under the yew trees. It was quiet there, and she could hear herself think. There was much to think about, and Esther prepared a list of prayer points. Then she looked down at her plate—the beans congealed and the potatoes cold—and realized she hadn't taken in even a morsel. At first, she considered tossing the food away, and then she firmly told herself she needed to keep her strength up for whatever it was that lay ahead.

And then it happened. As she ate the cold beans and potatoes, Esther was reminded of similar meals taken alone in another place. In a moment, she was transported back home to her lonely room, her plate of food slammed down on the dresser for her to eat by herself. Bernice's face rose up before her and Arnold's too. Esther kept chewing on the cold, congealed food, and the more of it that went down, the greater her conviction of what she needed to do.

Certain nobody would notice her absence, Esther harnessed Typhoon and headed for her parents' store. She felt at peace as she rode along the dusty track, dressed in one of the two dresses of Angie's she had agreed to keep for herself, the red one with layers of burgundy ruffles along the hem of the skirt and basque and two rows of little rose-shaped burgundy buttons lining the front. She felt strong and confident and was filled with resolve.

Esther saw her parents' eyes widen when they saw her through the window, spotting her while she tied Typhoon to the hitching post outside their store. In fact, they looked almost fearful.

"What is it?" Arnold queried once Esther was inside. Esther stared at his lips, reading the words off them with greater ease than ever.

"Has Paul Orton sent you away?" Bernice said, seeming alarmed.

Esther shook her head. She pointed to a notebook and pencil on one of the shelves and indicated she would like to have one.

"What, can that husband of yours not buy you a notebook and pencil?" Bernice asked, her face holding echoes of pity.

Esther chose to give her mother a dazzling smile instead of taking offense. She indicated she wanted just one sheet of paper and a pencil, and when Bernice handed it to her, looking bemused, Esther wrote on it:

"I need help please. Our safety is being threatened by a notorious gang."

"My goodness, you're writing!" Bernice exclaimed, while Arnold picked up the sheet of paper Esther had written on and perused it with a look of utmost incredulity on his face.

"Yes, I can write," Esther wrote on the paper when Arnold handed it back to her.

"You understood what your mama just said?" Arnold queried, his eyes even wider with amazement.

"I did," Esther wrote. "I can read lips. I have taught myself over the past years."

"You're . . . different," Bernice remarked, peering into Esther's face.

Esther smiled. "No," she wrote. "I'm the same person I was when I lived in your home and helped out here at the store. But now you are seeing me with different eyes. But that's not important right now. There is trouble coming."

Bernice and Arnold looked at each other. "Then we'll talk more about you later. What exactly is going on with this gang you mentioned?" Arnold asked.

"Luther Orton joined them, but then he left, so they are coming after him," Esther wrote, aware her parents were looking from her to the paper and back again in awe and wonder. "The men in the village refused to help when Sheriff Basley approached them, so I'm here to ask if you can please convince them to come to our aid."

"Did Paul Orton send you to ask us for help?" Arnold asked.

Esther shook her head. "Nobody knows that I'm here," she replied in writing. *Not even Paul,* she thought with a pang in her heart.

Chapter Twenty-Four

Paul looked up as Esther came into the kitchen, carrying a pail of milk in one hand and a basket of eggs in the other, the early-morning sun shining on her back and casting her in a warm glow.

"Good morning," he greeted her.

Esther nodded to him and set the pail down. Then she carried the eggs to the kitchen counter.

Paul regretted that he hadn't been more attentive to her in the past weeks since Luther's return and the looming visit of the McGuire gang. Esther had been reserved at times, and she seemed intent on making her presence felt in a positive way. He got up and went to stand right in front of her.

"I have to leave in a little while," he said.

"You must eat something," she replied.

Paul shook his head. "I don't have a desire for food. But I would like to pray with you."

"All will be well," Esther mimed as they sat down at the kitchen table. "Good always overcomes evil."

Paul took her hands in both of his as he bowed his head to pray. He said a special prayer for her, that she would be safe while he went out to take on the McGuire gang. A chill fell over his heart as a stray thought momentarily paralyzed him with fear. What if he fell before the might of the gang? What if he left Esther the way Angie had left him?

As if reading his mind, Esther withdrew her hands from his and reached for the Bible by her elbow. Opening it, she slid it across to him, pointing to Isaiah 54:17. "No weapon fashioned against you shall succeed...."

Paul took a deep breath when he read the passage.

"Stay in the house," he said, taking her hand in his again and looking intently into her eyes. "Bolt the doors, and don't go outside. We can't leave any men to guard the house today because we need them all."

Esther nodded. "I'll be here praying for your safety and that of all the men," she signed.

"You're a good woman," Paul remarked, wishing to say something positive since so many days had passed when he didn't seem to have any time at all for her.

"You are a blessing," Esther replied. "To me and to everyone who is riding out with you today."

Paul responded with a self-deprecatory shrug. He didn't feel at all deserving of such words of praise, particularly from the woman he had neglected to pay attention to for so long.

"I'm ready to go," Luther said, walking in, and Paul got up, casting one final look at Esther. "'No weapon fashioned against me shall succeed,'" he said, rewarded when Esther flashed him one of her beautiful smiles. He would take that with him into the battle. It would be the only armor he needed: the grace of God and the reassuring smile of his beautiful wife.

But as Paul, the ranch hands, Luther, and Sheriff Basley met their adversaries some distance from the ranch on a flat, grassy prairie, he wasn't so sure. Then he wished he had more men, better weapons, and even armor. Out there in the open field, with a gang that was at least a hundred and fifty men strong, Paul felt exposed and vulnerable. Their men numbered about forty, and most of them were young lads with no experience at all of rough fighting.

The McGuire gang looked intimidating, with their bandanas covering half their faces and pistols glinting in their hands.

"Each man has two weapons," Sandy, who was at Paul's right, remarked. "How do we respond to them if they open fire?"

"That's why we need to have a conversation," Paul replied. "No point in charging them or leaving them to charge us."

"Don't make any moves," Sheriff Basley said. "I'll go ahead and talk to them."

"Luther and I will flank you on either side," Paul replied.

"Alright, but don't shoot your mouth off," Sheriff Basley cautioned them. "Just let me deal with these criminals."

"Frank McGuire!" Sheriff Basley called out as they rode toward the gang. Paul and Luther stopped midway between the groups while Basley continued for another hundred feet.

"I'm Basley, sheriff of this town. Now I'm going to tell you real nicely that this town does not welcome the likes of you."

"We don't want your hospitality," one of the men shouted back. The man was to the left of the group, hidden behind the front line.

"And who might you be?" Sheriff Basley asked.

"The one and only Frank McGuire," the man said, coming forward. Paul was surprised to note he wasn't anything like they all had been imagining.

Frank McGuire was of medium height and build and wasn't particularly impressive, considering he was the leader. He wore dirty jeans, a faded button-up calico shirt, a brown leather jacket, and scuffed cowboy boots. A washed-out bandana was tied over his nose and mouth, and a ten-gallon hat sat atop his dull brown hair.

"Ah, I can see that I've taken you by surprise." He guffawed. He adjusted his hat on his head and pulled down the bandana to reveal his face. It was tan and a little wrinkled and spoke of years out in harsh environments. His eyes, however, were clear and sharp, sure to pick up on any sudden movement. "Give us Luther and we will be on our way," he said.

"Luther is a member of this community, and I fully intend to respect his position here," Sheriff Basley shot back. "I will give him my protection as a resident of our town. So I'm sorry, but I can't and won't hand him over to you."

"You're making a big mistake, Sheriff . . . whatever your name is," Frank McGuire sneered.

"It's Basley," Sheriff Basley replied. "And the person who has made the mistake is you, Frank McGuire, because I won't allow anyone to come here to our town and intimidate us. I don't care how big and powerful your gang is. You need to know that I don't take orders from anybody. So here's what's going to happen. If you cooperate and turn back, you won't be hunted down, and we will put this matter behind us. On the other hand, if you remain here and create a nuisance, I will be forced to ride you down, catch you, and lock you up."

Paul and Luther exchanged looks. Was this approach going to work, or was it going to result in a volley of bullets coming at them?

"Y'all would go so far to protect one man?" Frank scoffed, then seemed to think for a moment. "Fine. Keep him. That coward isn't worth the bullets or the blood."

Frank McGuire tipped his hat, pulled his bandana back up, and turned his horse around, signaling to his men to follow suit.

"It worked," Paul murmured, surprised, as Sheriff Basley began to ride back toward them.

A murmur went up through Paul's men, and he turned to look at Luther. Together, the brothers took a deep breath and exhaled. No sooner had they done so then a shot rang out and someone cried in pain. Paul looked around and saw Sheriff Basley slumped over his horse.

"They're circling us!" Sandy cried.

"Get to the sheriff and take him home, someone!" Paul shouted, seeing through the corner of his eye that the gang members were advancing on them. Over a hundred men on horses were approaching from the west, riding fast and guns in the air. The sound of hooves hitting the earth grew louder and faster.

Shots rang out from both sides, his men returning the fire they received from the McGuire gang. There were more yelps of pain as some bullets found their marks, but Paul couldn't tell which side uttered them. A horse screamed.

"Shoot to kill!" Paul ordered. "This is war!" With a whoop, he charged at Frank McGuire's men, aware that he might die in combat because they were considerably outnumbered and ill equipped for an adversary of this size.

Paul was concentrating so hard on taking down his opponents, he didn't immediately hear the shots ringing out from behind them.

"Paul! Look!" Sandy shouted, even as Paul noticed McGuire's men open-mouthed and thrown into confusion.

Paul allowed himself a moment to investigate the phenomenon Sandy was gesturing toward, and now his jaw dropped. Charging at their enemy was a posse double the size of the gang, nearly three hundred men carrying guns and blades and even bottles in some cases, most on horseback and the rest running on foot. And leading them was Esther's father, Arnold. Paul looked up to heaven and said a prayer of gratitude. Then with a cry of triumph, he opened fire. Around him men dropped from their horses and Paul was hoped they were all members of the McGuire gang. When they ran out of ammunition, they wrestled or knocked each other off their horses and engaged in combat on the ground, brandishing knives, pipes, or bare fists. The battle raged on, and More of the McGuire men fell. When few remained standing, Frank McGuire dropped his guns and held up his hand. He bled freely from a few cuts and scrapes, and his left arm seemed dislocated. A bruise was already forming where someone had punched him on the cheek.

"Enough!" he roared. "We surrender!" The gang members who could turned and ran, but the ones in the thick of the crowd had nowhere to go. They too dropped their weapons, disappointment, resentment, and surprise on their faces.

"Round them up and take them in!" Paul instructed two of his men. "Sheriff Basley's deputy will deal with them at the station."

Around him, Paul heard roars of victory from the men who had come with Arnold, and he went to thank them. Some of them were helping drag their prisoners away to be appropriately dealt with. Others were examining their wounds. Horses stamped and neighed. The winners and the losers both mingled, and the air was thick with both victory and defeat. Paul felt saddened standing there, contemplating the futility of it all. If only everyone would love as God loved them. If only everyone would spread peace and harmony instead of attempting to steal, kill, and destroy. And then the explanation came to Paul from the Bible, John 10:10, where Jesus says, "The thief comes only to steal, kill, and destroy. I came that they may have life and have it abundantly."

Evidence of the Lord's work in lives that had been lost was clear to Paul when Sandy and Luther came to him.

"Paul," Sandy said, "I'm going to take Sheriff Basley and the other wounded to the medic."

"I'm going with Sandy," Luther said.

Paul looked at his brother. Something had changed in him.

Then he saw Arnold Larson riding up to him, a little worse for wear but not seriously injured, and he tipped his hat.

"Paul Orton," Arnold greeted him as he slid off his horse, "you're probably wondering how I got to be here with all the men from our town."

Paul nodded. "I am," he replied. He gestured to Luther and Sandy. "We all are."

Arnold smiled. "It was Esther," he said. "She came to see us at the store, and we were amazed by the fact that she rode over on her own and can now write and read lips."

"By all accounts, Esther was always able to read and write. And she taught herself how to read lips," Paul said, feeling a rush of pride in his wife's abilities.

"But when did she come to you?"

"Yesterday," Arnold answered. "She has evolved into such a confident woman."

"Indeed she has," Paul said, nodding in agreement. He was still trying to process the fact that Esther had gone to her father for help and that Arnold hadn't hesitated but had arrived on the scene without demur.

"Believe me, even if all these men hadn't agreed to ride here with me and fight a battle that wasn't theirs directly, I would still have come and offered my services," Arnold declared emphatically.

"I am still overwhelmed by Esther's gesture," Paul said.

"We have not been good parents to her, and we have not treated her with the care and respect that she deserves," Arnold confessed. "But I hope she can find it in her heart to forgive us."

"Your daughter is the most loving, forgiving person I know," Paul replied. "She has already forgiven you, of that I am certain."

Paul turned to look at Luther. "You're safe, brother," he said. "And we have Esther to thank."

But Luther was looking at the fallen and wounded lying around them.

"I've asked the men to fetch as many buckboards as we can get so that we can take these men to the doctor. All of them, even the gang members. The women are readying their homes for the overflow, and the deceased are being taken to the pastor."

"Even the gang members? Isn't that dangerous?"

"Everybody deserves a second chance. You and Esther taught me that," Luther said with a grim smile. "We'll set up tents for them out here, though. Have to be able to keep an eye on them."

"You are a good man at heart, Luther," Paul murmured.

"If I were, this whole act wouldn't have played out like this today, Paul," Luther replied. "People have lost their lives because I was foolish and joined the gang and then left it. I am bearing the consequences of my actions, but they—"

"They joined the gang too, Luther," Paul replied. "They put their faith in a person and a practice that ultimately had consequences. They were as misguided as you were, so the Lord will be merciful to them just as he has been to you."

Arnold had been listening intently to Paul as he spoke. "You speak with such wisdom for one so young," he said.

Paul shrugged. "No, sir, I am not a wise man at all. But I know someone who is very wise, and I have learned so much from her."

"Who is this person?" Arnold asked.

"Your daughter," Paul replied. "Esther."

"You learn wisdom from her?" Arnold asked, incredulous. "We only learned yesterday that she can read and write. But for her to be so wise . . . that means she was never truly—"

"Cognitively slow?" Paul murmured. "Yes, that's a mistake everyone has made. But I praise the Lord that my foreman Sandy encouraged me to listen to my instincts, which were crying out that far from Esther being challenged, she was blessed. Your daughter's faith and trust in God is the reason we won this impossible battle today."

Paul saw that Arnold was standing there before him, weeping. He put his hand on his shoulder. "Come back to the house with us and spend a moment with your daughter," he said.

"My daughter. What do I say to her? Oh, I don't want her to see me like this," Arnold replied, dabbing a handkerchief to his eyes. "But if you don't mind, I will come by another day and bring Esther's mother with me."

"Of course," Paul said. "You are welcome to visit us any time."

***

"Luther Orton, will you swear on the Good Book that you will speak the whole truth and nothing but the truth?" the circuit judge asked him.

Paul and Esther sat together in the courthouse to witness the trial of the McGuire gang. The courthouse was packed; everybody wanted to see justice for the damages the gang had caused the town. Frank McGuire sat looking angry but defeated, casting bitter looks at Luther. His left arm was in a sling.

Luther looked straight at the judge. "I swear to tell the truth and nothing but the truth," he replied, with his hand, unfaltering, on the Bible.

Paul prayed silently. His brother's life hung in the balance. He may have changed paths now and was doing what was right in the sight of the Lord, but he was being tried for the mistakes of his past. He clutched Esther's Bible in his hands, loath to let go of the promises contained inside it. He opened it, seeking an answer, and the pages fell open at 2 Corinthians 5:17. "If any man is in Christ, he is a new creation. The old has passed away. Behold, the new has come."

Paul held the verse open for Esther to read, and she looked into his eyes and smiled. He knew then, as Paul the apostle had written in Romans 8:38-39, that nothing could separate them from the love of God. His tense muscles relaxed, and he leaned back in his seat with gratitude in his heart.

"After I left my home and went to live with my uncle and aunt in South Dakota, I ran into the McGuire gang," Luther explained.

"How did this encounter take place?" the prosecutor asked him.

Luther looked apprehensive, but his answer was clear and precise. "In the local saloon," he said.

"And did Frank McGuire approach you, or did you approach him?" the prosecutor queried.

Luther was clearly uncomfortable. His lips and eyebrows twitched as he fought for composure, but then he appeared to gain control of his emotions and spoke plainly. "I approached him. I was lonely and wanted a purpose in my life.

Unfortunately, I was misled to think that being part of a notorious gang would fulfill that desire."

"So *you* asked Frank McGuire if you could join him?" the prosecutor asked.

"Yes, I did," Luther replied.

"And you joined the gang willingly, and was not, at any time, coerced into becoming a part of this gang, am I right?" the prosecutor queried.

"That is correct," Luther answered. A few members of the audience gasped.

Paul began to pray harder that Luther would not veer away from the truth. He remembered Jesus saying, in John 8:32, "that the truth will set you free."

"So you rode with Frank McGuire and his men on all their destructive missions, did you not?" the prosecutor asked.

"I did," Luther replied.

"Did you participate in all the crimes they committed?" the prosecutor asked.

Paul saw Luther pass his tongue over his lips and prayed for God to grant him grace and strength.

"Yes," Luther replied. "I did."

"And could you outline some of the crimes the gang committed?" the prosecutor asked.

"Holding up coaches and wagons and divesting people of their valuables at gunpoint and making sudden visits to people's homes to steal provisions," Luther answered. He wiped his forehead nervously.

"We have been given to understand that you left the gang quite suddenly. Could you tell us why?" the prosecutor asked.

"Yes," Luther replied. He glanced uncertainly at Frank, who glowered at him. "I joined the gang to feel like part of a family," Luther continued. "It didn't feel right to rob defenseless women and take food from families who were poor and in need themselves, but I knew that I needed to get away when Frank McGuire planned and executed a bank heist. However, the plan failed, and we were about to be caught. While being pursued by the bank authorities, one of the gang members shot and killed a man."

Paul heard a ripple go through the gallery of spectators.

"What did you do then?" the prosecutor asked.

"I had to leave. So I went to Frank McGuire and told him I was going," Luther answered.

"And how did he respond?" the prosecutor asked.

"He said nobody leaves the McGuire gang and lives to tell the tale. So I hung on a few more days and then fled in the dead of night," Luther said.

"And Frank McGuire came after you recently, did he not?" the prosecutor asked.

"Yes, he did." Luther nodded.

"Why was that?" the prosecutor asked.

"He always said that anyone leaving the gang must die, or he would be a danger to the rest of them," Luther replied. "I knew where their hideout was and where they hid some of their loot."

Paul looked around at the spectators. There was shock on their faces.

"That will be all," the prosecutor said, and Luther left his seat in the witness stand.

Chapter Twenty-Five

Esther felt Paul's hand grip hers as the judge made his ruling. She craned her head so she could read his lips. But she missed words, so Paul turned to her. From his expression, she could tell it was a good verdict.

"Frank McGuire and his men are going to jail for a good long time," Paul said.

"And Luther?" Esther signed anxiously.

"The truth set him free," Paul said, ecstatic. "He told his story with honesty, and he was not a part of the killing of that unfortunate bank clerk. But he has to check in with the sheriff on a regular basis to ensure that he stays out of trouble."

Esther joined her hands and looked upward, weeping tears of joy. As she swept her tears away, she marveled that she was rejoicing in Luther's acquittal. It occurred to her with powerful intensity that heaven was also in a state of jubilation because, as Jesus said in Luke 15:7, "There will be more rejoicing in heaven over one sinner who repents than over ninety-nine righteous persons who do not need to repent.'"

As they walked out of the courthouse, Arnold and Bernice caught up with her. Esther turned to look at them. What could they have to say to her?

"You came today?" she signed to them, then paused to watch their lips as they replied.

"We had to," Bernice said. "We knew it was important to you."

Esther cocked her head in confusion. Were there tears in her mother's eyes?

"Papa," Esther mimed. "Thank you for helping to defeat the gang."

"Thank you for coming to us, my child," Arnold said. Now his eyes were glassy too. "You gave us the opportunity to make up for the way we've treated you. We are truly sorry for misunderstanding you for all these years."

"We are so proud of you, Esther," Bernice said.

They were . . . proud of her? She had done something right? Her request hadn't been a burden?

Something in Esther's heart snapped, and she felt all the hurt and shame of her childhood flow away.

"I forgive you," she signed.

Arnold and Bernice could not hold back their tears any longer. Hastily they wiped them away.

"We want to get to know you. The real you," Bernice said. "Would that be alright?"

Esther couldn't stop smiling, and she threw her arms around her parents. They were warm and solid, just as she remembered from when she was little.

She pulled back. "Please come to visit us soon," she signed. "I want to cook a meal for you." She laughed at the surprise on their faces, filled with joy at the thought of her parents eating her cooking.

She saw Paul standing by, waiting patiently for her. She also noticed that look in his eyes that she had missed for so long. It was soft, like a caress, and it warmed her heart.

"Come, Esther," he said. "Let's go and give Sheriff Basley the good news."

Esther nodded vigorously. Then she turned back to her parents, embracing each of them in turn.

They left the courthouse, hand in hand.

"Where's Luther?" Esther asked.

"He told me he wanted to have a word with Frank McGuire and his men before they were taken away. He wanted to tell them about Jesus and that there is salvation in Him."

Esther couldn't contain her joy. She couldn't help but leap into the air when Paul told her what Luther was doing.

"He took Sandy with him," Paul continued. Esther had stopped and was watching Paul's lips eagerly.

"And Sandy had an extra Bible, which he has taken along to give to them," Paul declared, his eyes glowing.

"I am overjoyed," Esther signed. "My heart is full!"

"Mine too," Paul replied. "And it's all due to you."

"No," Esther said. "It's all due to Him!"

The mood was light as Paul and Esther rode the buckboard to visit Sheriff Basley at the doctor's clinic, where he had been since he was shot. Luckily, the bullet had gone cleanly through his shoulder, and he was expected to make a full recovery.

Around them, the leaves on the trees were changing color. Esther pointed to them. "There is change in the air," she remarked, using the action of her hand turning over to convey her thoughts. "Like in Luther's life."

"And in yours with your parents," Paul replied.

Esther nodded happily. After that, they rode in silence, but she could feel Paul draw nearer once again. Even though he didn't move while he was driving the buckboard, Esther still felt him close. She turned to feast her eyes on him, and he looked at her at the same moment. She caught her breath in her throat. Paul was no longer the broken man bowed beneath his grief and responsibilities. He radiated inner peace; it leaked through his every pore. His smile reached his eyes now, and he seemed to love life and God with the same devotion she did. Looking into her husband's eyes always made her pulse race. And even when he turned his eyes on the road ahead, she knew his gaze was still upon her, and hers upon him.

When they reached the doctor's clinic, Paul helped Esther down from the buckboard and then took her hand before they walked inside.

The clinic was a single room, with the doctor's desk on the east side and two beds on the west side. One had the privacy curtain drawn; Sherigff Basley was awake and sitting up in the other.

"Well, well, well, look who's here!" Sheriff Basley greeted them cheerfully.

Esther's face broke into a smile.

"Howdy, Sheriff," Paul responded. "I expected you to still be passed out from all that loss of blood."

Sheriff Basley guffawed. "Paul, with this fine doctor taking care of me and my body making all the blood I need in addition to the prayers of all you good people, I am doing so much better! This doctor is leagues better than the one we had before," he declared.

Esther realized the doctor was right there, tucked behind a desk. He was a diminutive man whose capabilities were obviously not defined by his size. He stood up now and came toward   them.
"How is our sheriff doing, Doctor?" Paul asked.

"As he said, he is much better," the doctor replied. "I'm Doctor Martin, by the way." He glanced at the sheriff. "In fact, though the wound was deep, he will make a full recovery and can soon go home to his wife and family."

"He is a true hero," Esther declared, using her hands to speak.

To her surprise, the doctor understood her. "You think he's a hero?" he said, inclining his head so that she could read his lips. "If so, then I agree."

"How do you know what my wife just said?" Paul asked curiously, voicing Esther's thoughts.

"For one thing, I'm a doctor, so I am used to helping people who can't speak." Doctor Martin laughed. "For another, I have a sister who has overcome a similar challenge by learning sign language."

"There's an official way to learn how to communicate in actions?" Paul queried, once again putting Esther's unspoken question into words.

"Yes," Doctor Martin replied. "It's in Connecticut. We used to live there for a spell. In fact, my sister still lives there and now teaches in the school."

"What school is that?" Esther mimed, eager to know what he was referring to.

"It's called, quite simply, The American School for the Deaf," Doctor Martin replied.

"And people who go there learn how to speak through signs?" Esther asked.

Doctor Martin nodded. "Yes, they most certainly do. It's a year-long course, but it teaches people with hearing problems how to overcome their feelings of inadequacy in a world where everyone around them can hear. It helps them build up the confidence to operate as those who hear despite not having that ability. The students learn sign language, but they also learn how to see themselves differently."

"My wife learned that all on her own," Paul said.

"She is doing an amazing job," Doctor Martin said, looking directly at Esther. "You should be very proud of her." He turned to Paul. "But in order to truly refine what she has learned, a school of this kind might be the answer."

"Are you recommending that I send Esther away to learn how to communicate when she already can?" Paul asked.

"I am only recommending something I have seen yield great benefits," Doctor Martin replied. "Besides, if she learns the techniques, she could even pass those skills on to others and be a blessing to the community."

Esther had tuned out of the conversation. She could tell that Paul was disturbed by it, so she wandered back to Sheriff Basley's bedside.

"Please thank your pa on my behalf for his timely arrival on the scene," the sheriff said to Esther.

"I will," Esther signed in reply, smiling and nodding.

"It's a good idea, you know," the sheriff said.

"What is?" Esther queried, raising her eyebrows and tilting her head to the side.

"Doctor Martin was talking about that school in Connecticut. It sounds like it could be very good," he replied.

Esther nodded. An idea was taking shape in her mind, but she didn't want to distress Paul on a day when he was so happy with the outcome of the trial.

"It's so good to see the sheriff looking well," Esther mimed as they climbed into the buckboard. But Paul replied absently. He seemed preoccupied.

"Are you troubled about something?" Esther signed, watching Paul's lips anxiously.

He shook his head, but Esther was aware of the change in the atmosphere. There had been a lightness when they set out to see Sheriff Basley, and now she could feel the weight of Paul's thoughts.

She decided to do something about it.

"I am not interested in going to that school," Esther mimed, tapping Paul's arm to get his attention. He took his eyes off the path momentarily and turned to her.

"Why do you say that?" he asked.

"I thought maybe you were distressed because I asked about it," Esther replied.

"You taught yourself things because you were denied going to school," Paul remarked. "That shows how keen you were to learn. You read with such a hunger for knowledge, yet all your life you were denied the gift of learning."

Esther stared at his lips, bereft of words. She wasn't quite sure where this was leading.

"Because of your great desire to express yourself and the way you have already taught yourself . . . Oh, Esther, nobody more than you deserves to be given that gift of an education appropriate for your needs," Paul said.

"Actually, I am quite content with my life as it is," Esther mimed. "I don't need anything more than this."

"Remember when you encouraged me to give all Angie's clothes away to those in need?" Paul continued.

Esther wrinkled her nose, trying to figure out a connection to their conversation.

"I remember," she signed.

"That was the day I learned to look beyond the ranch and realized there are bigger needs out there," Paul said. He had his eyes on the path, so Esther had to lean in and look up at him to read what he was saying. "You have a lot to give to the world, Esther," he continued.

Esther didn't respond. She didn't want to interrupt Paul's flow of thought. Obviously there was something he was desperately trying to work out.

They were near the ranch, and Paul had gone silent after telling her that she had a lot to give the world. His internal struggle was tangible to Esther, and she felt for him.

As they rounded a corner and the homestead came into view, Esther's eyes were drawn to the fence. Each day, ranch hands were assigned to patrol the periphery and see if the fence was strong. They would regularly reinforce it to keep predatory animals away, and almost every day repairs were carried out along the periphery. The fence was not a central part of the ranch, but the ranch wouldn't be safe without it. In fact, she thought, the ranch would seem odd without the fence.

Esther was aware that sometimes her thoughts took a strange turn. She had tried reining them in, but ever since she had felt as if she was on the periphery of things, she had considered her role as that of one who repairs the fence, assigned to safeguard what was within. She had a role, and she had to fulfill it. So she couldn't ever think of being anywhere but at the ranch with Paul.

As they reached the homestead, she saw that all the ranch hands had come to greet them after Luther's acquittal. Luther and Sandy were there too.

Esther got down from the buckboard, and she and Paul were surrounded. But everyone was looking at her. She read their lips, one by one. They said her name and thanked her for fetching help when they had been outnumbered on the day of the battle. She looked up at Paul. He was gazing at her, and she could see pride glowing in his eyes. At that moment, Esther had a feeling of such deep fulfilment that was both unprecedented and unparalleled.

She felt Paul's eyes on her and turned to him again. His eyes were misty, as if he was experiencing some bittersweet emotion . She mimed, communicating to the ranch hands her gratitude to God for spurring her on and ask her parents for help. In her heart, she thanked God again for giving her the strength to go to her mama and papa for help. She didn't know anybody else she could have gone to, and in doing so she had enabled them to see her in a different light.

Esther entered the doors of the homestead as if she was doing so as a different person. And she was. She had been transformed by the experience of reaching beyond herself to embrace her purpose in life. So long had she lived within her walls of silence, existing on the edges of everyone's lives. So deeply did she now understand that it didn't matter where God had placed you. All that counted was that you fully knew your significance in the Creator's divine plan.

It was late afternoon. The trial had taken most of the morning, and their visit to the sheriff had taken the rest. Esther began to cook lunch with a renewed sense of purpose, searing a cut of beef in a pan and then transferring it into a pot, steeped in water. It would take at least an hour, simmering with the vegetables she chopped and added to the soup. She stirred the pot and set a lid on it, leaving it on the stove to cook. Then she went up to the attic to fetch her diary and her pencil and settled on the floor by the window, where the light filtered through the glass and fell onto the page.

Dear diary,

A few days ago, I grew up. The experience was so overwhelming that I haven't been able to write about it. But I can do so now. Before the men fought the McGuire gang, I fought a battle of my own, beating back the demons of my past to overcome barriers and find my way back into my parents' arms and hearts. God is good. He led me to them. I could feel Him urging me to go to them, because that was His plan all along.

Today something else of significance took place. We went to visit Sheriff Basley at Doctor Martin's clinic. We learned from the doctor about a special school for the deaf. It is all the way in Connecticut. But when I heard about it, something stirred inside of me, especially when Doctor Martin revealed to us that his sister went there. And that she teaches there now. Perhaps, if I could learn what they teach, I could, like Doctor Martin's sister, teach too. Except I would do so here in Springford, Montana, so that people like me can find a way to be understood and not judged wrongly for a faculty that they do not possess.

But Paul seemed conflicted when he perceived my interest in this school, and I am aware that I have a role to play here as his wife. So while I write about this school, I place my desire to go there in the hands of the Lord.

Chapter Twenty-Six

Paul stirred in his bed and then sat up with a start, automatically reaching for his pistol underneath his bed. Then, with a sense of overwhelming relief, he remembered that the McGuire gang was behind bars and Sheriff Basley was back in his own home with a completely healed gunshot wound.

Paul heard sounds from the attic above and smiled. Esther was obviously awake, probably saying her prayers or reading her Bible. He got up and sat on the edge of his bed. For a couple of weeks now, he had been holding on to a secret, and he needed to reveal it to Esther soon. He dropped his head into his hands. Yes, it was a struggle indeed. Would he tell her, or would he not? Would he make a decision that could change her life once and for all? He got up from his bed and began to pace, looking up at his ceiling and imagining his wife's face when he told her . . . if he told her.

He pulled on his clothes and went out, eager to start the day. But as he walked out of his room, he came face-to-face with Esther.

"Good morning," Esther signed with a smile. She wore a heavy cloak over her linen dress to keep out the fall chill, and her cheeks were a rosy red from the cold.

"Good morning to you too," Paul replied, thinking how lucky he was to have a woman like her in his life.

"You're looking at me in a strange way," Esther remarked, accompanying her hand gestures with a chuckle.

It amazed Paul that she could laugh and chuckle but not speak. Her laugh, he mused, high and clear and rich, was like a ripple that surged through her body. She laughed from the core of her being.

Paul shook his head. Esther was intuitive, and he wouldn't be able to put off sharing his secret for much longer. "I'm looking at you and thinking that I'm so lucky to wake up to see you every morning," he said.

"As I am to see you," Esther signed.

He followed her out to the dairy shed and watched her milk the cows. She did her chores with such dedication to each task and was so efficient at all of them. She turned around to see him standing there and looked at him anxiously.

"What's going on, Paul?" she mimed later when he went into the kitchen to have breakfast with her. Luther had moved to one of the bunkhouses and was talking of building himself a small cottage on the property. Things were falling into place, Paul mused, but some things were yet to be dealt with.

"I need to talk with you," Paul replied finally, aware that once the words were out, he couldn't retract them. Nor could he make something up, because Esther was perceptive and would know something didn't seem quite right.

"When?" she signed, stirring the porridge in the pot.

"Now?" Paul replied.

Esther left the pot and came to the table.

"I'm concerned, Paul," she conveyed, pointing to her head and then to her heart. "Is everything alright?"

"Of course," Paul said, motioning for her to sit down at the table.

Esther took the pot of porridge off the stove and then sat down, facing Paul.

"Stay right here," he said. "I'm just going up to my room to fetch something I must show you."

Paul's feet were heavy as he went up the stairs, and his hands almost felt unwilling to pick up the large envelope he had placed in his dresser drawer.

This would change life as he had come to know it, but it would transform Esther's future and the way she perceived it. He had agonized over the sacrifice he would have to make, but he had to do it if he truly loved her.

Paul paused. That was what he needed to tell her first before he gave her the envelope.

He found Esther sitting just as he had left her but with her face reflecting the anxiety she was experiencing. She looked up when he entered and raised her eyebrows.

Paul set the envelope on the table and then sat down, aware Esther was quite alarmed. He took her hands in his to reassure her all was well.

"Esther," he said, "before I say anything, I want to thank God for you. All things have worked together for our good. No matter what the enemy tried to do to cause us pain, God took it and transformed it into a blessing. How far we have come since that day when I first met you."

Esther nodded; she couldn't use her hands, as he was clutching them firmly. But he didn't need her to respond just yet.

"I used to think that God had abandoned me or was punishing me until you came into my life and changed my perspective," Paul continued. "You are truly like Abigail, because just as she made David a better man and healed his heart, so too have you made me a better man and healed my heart. I used to think I would be better off dead, but you came along and gave me the renewed will to live."

Paul paused for breath and looked deep into Esther's eyes as she gazed at his lips. "I know that recently I may have appeared neglectful and preoccupied, but the fact is, Esther, I can do nothing but think of you, and I want nothing more than to make sure you are happy and fulfilled."

He squeezed Esther's hands, and she nodded again, mutely reading what he was saying, but she still had anxiety in her eyes. He released her hands so that she could communicate with them and then said, "I am deeply in love with you, my dear beautiful Esther."

Esther's eyes were limpid as she gazed at him. She exhaled as if weight had been lifted. She smiled and signed with one hand against her heart, and he knew that she was saying she loved him too.

He leaned in, his lips encompassing hers, and this time his kiss was deep and passionate. He got up and pulled her to her feet and drew her close against him, holding her as if he never wanted to let her go. They kissed again, this time with greater intensity, but then reluctantly, Paul pulled away and looked down into Esther's face, flushed with emotion yet joyful.

"This is what you wanted to tell me?" she asked.

Paul shook his head and picked up the envelope. "Sit down, my dear," he said.

Esther sank back into her chair, and Paul handed her the envelope.

"What is this?" Esther signed, looking anxious once again.

"The future you so richly deserve," Paul replied.

Esther's hands shook as they opened the envelope and pulled out the document it contained.

"You may read it," Paul said as she looked questioningly at him.

Dear Mrs. Paul Orton,

It gives us great pleasure to accept you into our one-year program to learn sign language and communication skills at The American School for the Deaf.

Enclosed herewith are the course guidelines and instructions to aid you in your preparation for this very unique program we offer.

"Well?" Paul prompted as Esther's eyes went over and over the lines of the letter, and her expression went from incredulity to pleasure to sorrow and then to joy.

"I don't know what to say," Esther mimed, shaking her hands and pointing to her lips. Then she stood up and paced, still holding the letter in her hands.

When she stopped before him, Paul took her face between his hands and looked down into her eyes. His heart was heavy with sorrow from having to part from her soon, but from within the depths of that pain, he felt a flutter of joy. He also felt a wave of gratitude, because ever since he had fallen in love with her, he wanted to give Esther something special. Now he was doing what he so longed to do. He was giving her wings to fly.

She reached up and traced the outline of his lips with her forefinger, and Paul was overcome with such great longing to hold on to her forever that it hurt. But as the Bible said in Acts 20:35, "it is more blessed to give than to receive." He had received so much from Esther, and it was time to give her something significant.

"It will only be one year, Esther, and then you will be back in my arms and I will never have to let you go again," Paul whispered against her lips. He had to pull away and repeat the words so that she could read what he had said. He stroked her cheek. "You have such a big heart. I know you will come back and do something amazing with all you will learn at school."

"Paul," Esther signed. "I love you so much. Thank you for this generous gift. Nobody thought I deserved to go to school except you." She began to cry. "I can hardly believe I can still enjoy the opportunity to do what I couldn't when I was younger."

"It brings me immense joy to do this for you, Esther," Paul said.

Esther clung to him, pulling back to mime, "I can't bear being way from you for twelve whole months, but I promise to write to you as often as I can."

"I will be right here, Esther, waiting for you to return," Paul replied.

"Has this made you sad?" she signed.

Paul shrugged. "I'm happy to send you there, but I'm sad to let you go," he replied.

"I'm happy to go there but so sad to be parted from you," Esther signed, speaking with the eloquence of her hands.

As he continued to hold her, he wondered how things would have been had Luther not gotten involved with the McGuire gang and left them; had they not come after him; had a battle not ensued in which Sheriff Basley was injured; and had they not gone to visit him at Doctor Martin's clinic and learned of this school for the deaf. Paul played the possibilities over and over, but he always arrived at one conclusion: God had truly worked all things together for their good. And he was glad the circumstances had led to Esther being accepted into a program at The American School for the Deaf.

In the days that followed, Paul and Esther went to town and bought a suitcase, some new clothes to put into it, writing materials, and other supplies outlined in the instructions that accompanied the letter from the school. And, to remind her of home, Esther packed the toy horse.

"I must go and visit my parents," Esther said, a few days before she was due to leave.

"Then I will take you there," Paul replied.

As they rode the buckboard there, Paul couldn't help remembering that day, so many months ago, when he had taken Esther to her house after Luther had assaulted her. He recalled the insensitivity her parents had received her with , and the ease in which they had let her go and be married to a man she didn't even know. But God, ever a good father, was looking down upon them with kindness, so that today as they returned to Esther's home, it was as if they were two different people.

He looked at Esther, who had become such a mature, confident woman in a matter of a few months. And himself, a man who no longer looked at what he didn't have but at what he could give away. He was, in a way, giving Esther away, because he knew a woman like her would not take lightly what she received. She would use it to do something for others like herself, and he would be by her side every step of the way. She hadn't said anything to Paul, but he just felt, with prophetic intuition, that Esther would not want to hold any knowledge she gained to herself. If she had two coats, she would give one away. If she was given learning, she was bound to share it.

"Will your parents be at the shop or at home?" Paul asked.

"Home," Esther replied.

When they reached the house, Paul helped her off the buckboard and then led the horse to the hitching pole. Then he took Esther's hand and walked with her up to the front door.

She knocked on it, and Bernice answered. For a moment, mother and daughter stood there, staring at each other, and Paul wondered if Esther's parents had reverted to their old selves again. Then, to his surprise and pleasure, Bernice leaned forward and threw her arms around her daughter.

Paul heard the sound of heavy footsteps, and Arnold appeared.

"Esther!" he exclaimed. "Paul! What brings you both around? All's well, I hope?"

"Esther wanted to come and visit you," Paul explained. "She has something to tell you."

"What is it?" Bernice queried, looking concerned.

"Come and sit down," Arnold said, leading them into the living room.

Paul saw Esther cast her eyes around her erstwhile home and wondered at all the emotions she must be struggling with. This was the place where she had suffered pain, humiliation, and rejection, but it was also her former home, the place where her parents lived.

"What is the news that you have for us, Esther?" Bernice asked as they all sat down in the living room.

Esther began to mime, and then stopped. She looked appealingly at Paul, and he took over.

"We have come to give you the good news that Esther has been accepted into a one-year program at The American School for the Deaf in Connecticut," he declared.

Bernice and Arnold stared at him in shock, and Paul had to remind himself that these were the people who had denied Esther an education because they didn't think her worthy of it. He quickly swallowed the indignation he felt at their attitude and told himself they didn't know any better.

"Forgive us," Arnold said, "but we don't know very much about the world of learning."

At least he is honest, Paul thought.

"What can Esther learn at this stage of her life?" Bernice asked. "Shouldn't she be at home, bearing your children?"

It took Paul a moment to recover from that remark, and he had to remind himself that Arnold and Bernice were simple folk who had given birth to an extraordinary child. He did, however, sneak a glance at Esther; she was blushing.

"There is a lot Esther will learn at this school," Paul replied patiently. "And she will blossom there, of that I am certain.

She will learn how to communicate in sign language and operate in the world just like someone who can hear and speak."

He could see that Esther was following the conversation carefully from the way her eyes went from one pair of lips to the other. He also discerned from her demeanor that it didn't matter to her what her parents thought. She had merely come to say goodbye and tell them where she was going to be for the next year.

"She has our blessings," Arnold said eventually, and Bernice nodded in agreement. Then she fetched them some refreshments.

"May I see my old room?" Esther signed.

Bernice nodded and took her up the steps. Paul wished he had gone with her, since she took a while to return. He would have to ask her what it was like to reconnect with her past, however briefly.

While Esther and Bernice were away, Paul looked at Arnold.

"Esther is going to be just fine," he reassured him. "This program comes highly recommended. You'll see, when she returns, just how much it will do for her confidence, her self-esteem, and above all, her future."

Arnold shrugged. "I'm not worried in the least, Paul Orton," he said. "You have been the best man for her. You have seen what we didn't see and done what we should have done for this remarkable girl."

"It's been my privilege," Paul replied.

Epilogue

One year later...

Esther stepped out of the stagecoach, picked up her suitcase, and looked around. It felt good to be back in Springford, Montana. It had been fall when she left, and it was fall when she returned, and there was the same biting chill in the air and the same riot of colorful leaves on every tree that dotted the landscape. She missed her wildflowers, but the autumn landscape was every bit as beautiful as spring's. She sent a quick prayer of thanks to God for welcoming her back with such wonderous creation.

She scanned the faces of people passing back and forth, looking for Paul, her pulse racing at the merest echo of his name. How hard it had been to live apart from him, but how much she had learned at the school. She began to walk, thinking she would hire a pony cart to get home in case Paul had not received her letter and seen which stagecoach he was to receive.

But then, all of a sudden, there he was, hurrying toward her with a huge smile on his face and looking more handsome than ever.

"Esther!" he cried.

"Paul!" she signed, spelling out his name. He stopped short and looked at her. She laughed. She was signing differently— more authentically—and now she would have to teach him what she had learned. She threw back her head and laughed again as he swept her up into his arms and held her as if he would never let her go.

"It was the best experience I have ever had," Esther signed excitedly, using her old motions, unable to take her eyes off her husband as he took her suitcase from her and led the way to the buckboard.

"Your letters were so descriptive, I felt as if I was there," Paul remarked.

"I even felt like I could taste the rice pudding you were served every Saturday and the beef stew that was invariably the special dish for Sundays."

"Paul, I have more news," Esther said. "This year, I learned, was just the beginning of the rest of my life."

Paul took her hand. "I knew, one year ago, that you would feel that way," he declared. "And though I wasn't ready to share you with the world, I knew the Lord wanted me to." He slipped his arm around her. "Tell me what I know you're going to tell me."

"I want to start a school for the deaf here in Springford," Esther signed eagerly.

Paul stopped and turned to her. "I knew this day would come, my dear." He smiled. "Do you know God only gives the best to those whom he knows will share what they are given?"

Esther smiled. "How do you know so much?" she signed.

"I had to do a lot of reading this past year," Paul replied with a grin, "in order to be able to match the capabilities and intelligence of my amazing wife."

Esther laughed. "You are the most capable and intelligent person I know," she signed.

"You know what?" Paul said with a mischievously boyish smile, "I think I am. Because I anticipated my wife's decision and have prepared for it by investing in some land in town . . . and building on it a smallbut adequate facility for those who would benefit from what you have to offer."

Esther stopped and stared at her husband. "Paul, how did you know?" she signed. "I know my wife," Paul replied. "And I also listened to the voice of the Lord as He spoke to my heart."

"You actually *built* a place?" Esther queried.

Paul nodded. "Not just me," he said. "But Sandy, Luther, Sheriff Basley, the ranch hands, and your father as well. We all put in time and effort to get the building ready for your return."

"And what if I didn't come back with the desire to start a school?" Esther asked.

"That was never a possibility," Paul replied. "I know you too well."

***

Six months later...

"Hurry," Paul urged Esther, "everybody is waiting!"

Esther came forward and smiled up at him.

"I'm going to make the announcement now," Paul said.

He stepped onto the dais and stood there, picking out all the well-known faces in the crowd of people who had gathered to witness such a momentous event. There was Luther and Sandy, all the ranch hands, Sheriff Basley and Doctor Martin. Uncle Mack and Aunt Tillie had come in all the way from South Dakota. And there was Esther's new friend, Vera, a fellow student from The American School for the Deaf who had moved to Springford, Montana, to help Esther with her new venture.

"Friends," Paul said, "it gives me the greatest joy to present to you Esther Orton, my dear wife!"

As Esther approached the dais, a ripple went through the crowd. She was clearly pregnant. The bump of her stomach was unmistakable and threw her off balance as she walked. Paul stepped quickly off the dais and, together with Vera, helped Esther onto the stage.

"Shall we pray," Esther signed, and the assembled company bowed their heads when Paul interpreted what she had said. And as she prayed, he continued to repeat in words what Esther was praying in sign language.

"Our loving heavenly father," Esther prayed, "who did give your only son Jesus to give us new life, we dedicate this facility to you and to all of your children who will have a new life as they benefit from what we are to teach here. Amen."

Then she locked eyes with Paul and began to sign her speech.

"I used to be called the laggard," Esther began, "and many who have the same challenge that I do will be called many names. But the fact is, within our silence, God opens different doors and enriches us with an imagination. I dreamed dreams and read books hungrily, knowing there was more out there than I was aware of. God has created us uniquely, and those like me, who cannot hear, are in no way impaired. We are just different. So today I ask that you embrace this difference and support through your prayers, acceptance, and understanding all those who will come to this school to learn how to communicate through the walls of their silence."

Paul took over. "Friends," he said, "my wife Esther and her friend Vera will open the doors of The Springford School for the Deaf, offering residential programs to teach sign language. We anticipate that children and adults from all across Montana and other parts of the country will come seeking an education here. We ask for your blessings and good wishes for these two brave and enterprising women who have dedicated their lives to helping those without the ability to hear."

A cheer went up. Paul took Esther's hand and, leaning in, kissed her on the forehead. Then he handed her a pair of scissors and led her to the door of the new building his hands and those of his friends had lovingly built during the months Esther was away.

And, as Esther cut the ribbon, it was almost as if she was forever severing the barrier between those who could hear and those who couldn't.

***

Back at the ranch, a feast awaited them. Trestle tables, laden with food, had been set out under the trees vibrant with the colors of spring. Everyone who lived and worked on the ranch and all of Paul and Esther's friends from town were present. So were Bernice and Arnold and Mack and Tillie.

As Esther looked at the sea of happy faces, she could scarcely believe the celebration was for her. Her hands frequently strayed to her belly, growing with the young one inside. Paul came over and sat down beside her, gazing lovingly into her eyes. He placed his hand over hers on her belly.

"Did I just feel a kick?" he asked.

Esther couldn't help but stare at his lips with longing, and it was as if he'd read her thoughts, because he bent down to kiss her.

A cheer went up from around the table, and Esther blushed. Then Luther stood up.

"I would like to thank God for my sister-in-law, Esther," he said, signing what he was saying. "She is a woman of immeasurable forgiveness and love, and I am blessed to know her."

Esther smiled up at him, grateful she could look upon him and feel nothing but joy in the fact that he who had been lost was now found.

The house hadn't changed much. Angie's books were still on the shelves in the living room, though they were a bit dusty. The box of toys still sat on a table nearby. After the meal, when all the guests had left and the sky was scattered with stars, Paul took Esther's hand and led her up the stairs. She paused by the ladder that led up to the attic, remembering the day she had discovered it. Then she followed Paul into his room—now their room—and watched as he set the lantern on the table and turned down the wick.

Then he turned around and spread his arms wide, and she walked into them, feeling a sense of coming home and never having to leave.

THE END

Also, by Chloe Carley

Thank you for reading "**A Persistent Bride to Show Him God's Way**"!

I hope you enjoyed it! If you did, here are some of my other books!

Best sellers of mine:

#1 A Feisty Gracious Bride For the Rancher
#2 The Cowboy's Redeeming Love
#3 A Sheriff to Save Her
#4 Chenoa's Tale to Freedom

Get my "Colorado Reborn" series with more than 1,000 Reviews!

#1 His Stubborn Sweet Bride
#2 A Debutante for the Rancher
#3 A Cowboy to Save Esmeralda
#4 The Frontier Gambler's Lady
#5 The Rebellious Bride's Broken Heart
#6 His Mysterious Silent Bride

Also, if you liked this book, you can also check out my full Amazon Book Catalogue at:
https://go.chloecarley.com/bc-authorpage

Thank you for allowing me to keep doing what I love! ❤

CPSIA information can be obtained
at www.ICGtesting.com
Printed in the USA
BVHW041934170821
614633BV00020B/334